MYSTERIES OF
TRASH & TREASURE

The Secret Letters

ALSO BY MARGARET PETERSON HADDIX

THE SCHOOL FOR WHATNOTS

REMARKABLES

THE GREYSTONE SECRETS SERIES
THE STRANGERS
THE DECEIVERS
THE MESSENGERS

CHILDREN OF EXILE SERIES
CHILDREN OF EXILE
CHILDREN OF REFUGE
CHILDREN OF JUBILEE

UNDER THEIR SKIN SERIES
UNDER THEIR SKIN
IN OVER THEIR HEADS

THE MISSING SERIES
FOUND
SENT
SABOTAGED
TORN
CAUGHT
RISKED
REVEALED
REDEEMED

THE SHADOW CHILDREN SERIES
AMONG THE HIDDEN
AMONG THE IMPOSTORS
AMONG THE BETRAYED
AMONG THE BARONS
AMONG THE BRAVE
AMONG THE ENEMY
AMONG THE FREE

THE PALACE CHRONICLES
JUST ELLA
PALACE OF MIRRORS
PALACE OF LIES

THE GIRL WITH 500 MIDDLE NAMES

BECAUSE OF ANYA

SAY WHAT?

DEXTER THE TOUGH

RUNNING OUT OF TIME

FULL RIDE

GAME CHANGER

THE ALWAYS WAR

CLAIM TO FAME

UPRISING

DOUBLE IDENTITY

THE HOUSE ON THE GULF

ESCAPE FROM MEMORY

TAKEOFFS AND LANDINGS

TURNABOUT

LEAVING FISHERS

DON'T YOU DARE READ THIS, MRS. DUNPHREY

THE SUMMER OF BROKEN THINGS

THE 39 CLUES BOOK TEN: INTO THE GAUNTLET

MARGARET PETERSON HADDIX

MYSTERIES OF TRASH & TREASURE

The Secret Letters

KATHERINE TEGEN BOOKS
An Imprint of HarperCollins Publishers

Katherine Tegen Books is an imprint of HarperCollins Publishers.

Mysteries of Trash and Treasure: The Secret Letters

Library of Congress Control Number: 2022932437
ISBN 978-0-06-283852-0

Typography by Molly Fehr
22 23 24 25 26   PC/LSCH   10 9 8 7 6 5 4 3 2 1

First Edition

For my mother

The Beginning

If Colin hadn't found the first shoebox, nothing important would have happened that summer.

He and Nevaeh never would have met.

They never would have found the *other* shoebox.

They never would have made a secret pact behind their parents' backs.

They never would have solved a single mystery.

They never would have . . . well, it doesn't matter what else wouldn't have happened, does it? Nothing else would have happened.

But Colin did find the shoebox, hidden under the floor-board in a stranger's attic.

And that changed everything.

Colin's Summer, Day One

"Colin! Up and at 'em!"

Colin only bothered to open one eye, and that only to half-mast. His mother hovered over him, her grin much too wide and excited for six a.m.

It was the first day of summer. The. Very. First. Day.

"Mo-om," Colin moaned. Even that took more energy than he wanted to use. "Seriously. I'm old enough to stay home by myself this year."

"If you're old enough for that," she countered, "you're old enough to work."

Mom was already snapping his blinds open. Now she was in his closet, pulling a shirt off a hanger. Now she snatched a pair of shorts from his dresser drawer. Now she had his whole outfit for the day arrayed on his chair. Colin would have actually had to roll over to see, but he was pretty sure she'd also fished his sneakers out from under the bed and lined them up beneath the chair, perfectly parallel and perfectly aimed for the door.

And she'd done all that before he'd had a chance to blink.

That's how Mom was: a tiny dynamo. She *always* moved as fast as a hummingbird. Her favorite words were "lickety-split" and "pronto." (Recently she'd been studying French by podcast and begun saying "Vite!" a lot, too.)

Colin's favorite words were "wait" and "Let me think about that for a minute. . . ."

Colin still didn't move.

"Colin, remember . . . ," Mom said.

That was all it took. Because Colin did remember. He remembered how Mom had kept her head bowed, not even looking him in the eye the night she'd told him they couldn't afford the day camp program he'd gone to the past several summers. He remembered how many times he'd heard her take a call from a client and say in her bright, cheery Professional Voice, "Let me step into another room, to protect your privacy. . . ." And then not gotten far enough away before saying in a smaller, deflated tone that Colin could still overhear, "So you won't be needing my services, after all?"

He remembered that times were hard and small businesses were in trouble and that this summer Mom just couldn't hire all the workers it would take to stay afloat.

He remembered—though she hadn't quite said it in so many words—that she needed his help.

Colin forced himself to sit up. He tried to stretch his mouth into an imitation of Mom's wide smile.

"I am so ready to move boxes!" he cried. "And clean houses! And do whatever else you want me to do! I live to work!"

Mom . . . giggled.

"Okay, laying it on a little thick there," she said, ruffling his thick, dark, curly hair that was almost exactly like hers, only shorter. "But you get an A for effort. I *knew* it'd be fun having more time together this summer."

Colin did not say, *Yeah, that's every twelve-year-old kid's fantasy, to spend more time working for his mom.*

He was too busy staring in horror at the red shirt she'd picked out for him to wear.

"A collar?" he asked. "You want me to move boxes in ninety-degree heat *wearing a shirt with a collar?*"

Mom smoothed a wrinkle Colin hadn't noticed in the shirt.

"Image, remember?" she said. "Ninety-nine percent of the reason someone would hire me instead of you-know-who is my company's image. Nobody would believe a four-foot-eleven female is going to be best at moving boxes, if that's all it's about."

Mom drew herself up to her full height—which Colin was pretty sure was only four foot ten and a half, but he wasn't going to argue. He'd been taller than her since he was nine.

He couldn't even remember how old he'd been the first time someone had said, "Wow. Looks like your little boy got his height from his dad," and his mom said, "Yep," in a way that made it clear there would be no follow-up questions.

Mom didn't talk about Dad.

Neither did Colin.

He'd learned not to talk too much about Mom's business, either. Way back in second grade, he'd given a speech in front of the whole class about her. He'd been so proud. He'd practiced again and again just saying the name of her company: Possession Curation. (In second grade, he'd still had a little trouble saying *s*'s properly.) He'd memorized her company motto—"You Deserve Only the Best"—and explained how helping people get rid of things that were old and broken and useless made it so their houses were cleaner, and they had more room, and they could enjoy having nice things instead.

And then the meanest kid in the class, a boy named Hunter, spoke up without even raising his hand. "He means his mom is a garbageman! Colin's mom picks up trash! She's a *woman* garbageman!"

While the other kids laughed, the teacher tried to explain that, first of all, the actual term was "garbage collector," and secondly, "There's nothing wrong with being a garbageman—er, collector—and certainly not anything wrong with a woman doing that. And, anyhow, that wasn't exactly what Colin was saying, was it, Colin?"

Hunter had called Colin "Garbage Boy" the rest of the school year, anyhow. But that wasn't even what hurt.

No, what hurt was when the nicest kid in the class, a girl named Shivani, raised her hand right after that. Colin could see by the earnest look on her face that she wanted to help. Her voice was so kind when she said, "Do you mean your mom is like that guy on TV? The Junk King?"

Colin had started shaking, and he'd actually shouted back at Shivani, "No! My mom is not like the Junk King! She's nothing like him at all!"

And then he'd run and hidden in the bathroom. Because how could he have shouted at someone like Shivani?

And how could anyone think Mom was like the Junk King?

"Earth to Colin," Mom said now. "Where'd you go, just then?"

"Just thinking," Colin said.

"Think and move at the same time," Mom said. She handed him his shirt and shorts. "Breakfast's in five minutes. I want to be out the door in twenty. We've got a lot to do today!"

Colin was not good at thinking and moving at the same time.

He wasn't particularly good at doing anything. He was best at just . . . being.

This was going to be the worst summer of his life.

2

Nevaeh's Summer, Day One

Nevaeh tucked the cereal box under her arm, plucked a spoon from the silverware drawer, and, without looking, reached into the cupboard for a bowl. Her hand met empty air and then, a bare shelf. She glanced toward the sink and yanked open the door of the dishwasher. More emptiness.

"Dad!" she hollered. "Did you sell our dishes again?"

"Found a better set," he called back from his narrow office at the other end of the hall. "Look in the boxes on the dining room table. Not the ones with the sticky note about sending them out for eBay, but—"

"Never mind," Nevaeh said. "I'll have toast."

"Roddy's using the toaster for his latest experiment, remember?" Nevaeh's older sister, Prilla, said behind her, where she was leaning into the refrigerator. "Something about trying to make it solar powered . . ."

"Bread, then!" Nevaeh said. "I'll have dry, boring, tasteless bread. . . ."

"Oh, no—not today, little sister," Prilla said, emerging from the refrigerator with an open jumbo-sized container of yogurt with exactly one serving left. She eased the cereal box away from Nevaeh, shook granola onto the yogurt, and spun back toward the fridge, muttering, "Let's see, the perfect topper . . . yes!" A moment later, she presented Nevaeh with the plastic yogurt container as if it were a crystal goblet. Prilla bowed, truly hamming it up. "A yogurt parfait, complete with whipped cream and a maraschino cherry on top. Fit for the youngest Junk Princess on her big day!"

Yeah, fit for a Junk Princess because it's in a plastic container, and I'm going to eat it with a spoon that Dad literally found at a junkyard, Nevaeh thought.

But how could she complain, when Prilla was being so nice?

"Thanks," Nevaeh muttered, taking a big bite that was mostly whipped cream.

"And while you eat," Prilla said, steering Nevaeh toward a chair at the kitchen table, "I'll French-braid your hair so it's out of your way. Unless you want to pull a Roddy."

"Not my style," Nevaeh said.

Roddy, who was Prilla's twin, shaved his head at the start of every summer. Their other two brothers, Axel and Dalton, went the man-bun route.

All the Greeveys (except Roddy, now) had the same thick, dark blond hair. Also: the same too-wide mouths; the same too-big noses; the same pale, prone-to-freckling skin; and the same constantly surprised-looking brown eyes. The first day of kindergarten, Nevaeh's teacher had done a double take, gasped, and then said, "There's no way you could pretend not to be a Greevey, is there?"

Nevaeh didn't want to pretend she wasn't a Greevey. She wasn't ashamed that Dad was the Junk King of Groveview, Ohio. She could easily ignore it when stupid kids at school made fun of the slogan he always used in his TV commercials: "Got junk you don't want anymore? I'll take it. I LOOOVE junk!"

She just didn't want to have anything to do with junk herself.

Usually Nevaeh liked it when Prilla braided her hair, but not today. Today, it felt like Prilla was pulling every strand too tightly.

Still, Nevaeh didn't let herself squirm away.

"You know this is a big deal for Dad, having all five of us work for him this summer," Prilla said. "You know he loves that little ceremony he made up with the scepter and all—'You are twelve now, old enough to join the family business, old enough to claim your royal title. . . .'"

"I *know*," Nevaeh said, a little too sharply.

She hadn't even been born yet the summer Axel turned twelve, but Dad liked reminding her that she'd been there for his ceremony, at least as a fetus. She'd been three when Dalton turned twelve, and seven when it was Prilla's and Roddy's turn. She could remember jumping up and down and cheering for the twins as if they really had inherited a throne.

Of course, back then she'd also half believed that the scepter Dad had welded together out of spare car parts truly was precious gold, and the "jewels" at the top were real diamonds and rubies, not see-through little toy balls from a gumball machine.

"Mom's home," Prilla said, glancing out the kitchen window at the car speeding in a cloud of dust down their gravel driveway. Prilla finished the braid and expertly wrapped a rubber band around the end. "You ready for this?"

No, Nevaeh thought.

"Sure," she said.

Everyone else came crowding into the kitchen: Mom, back early from her overnight shift as an X-ray tech at the hospital. Axel and his fiancée. Dalton and his current girlfriend, who probably wouldn't remain his girlfriend but would likely be invited to holiday dinners at the Greeveys' for the rest of her life, because that was how the Greeveys rolled. Roddy with his newly shaved head, which gleamed almost as much as the toaster he was carrying.

And then Dad swept down the hallway. He carried both the scepter made out of car parts and a shimmery crown made out of . . . were those old compact discs?

"Hear ye, hear ye," Dad announced. "On this joyous day, Nevaeh Lenore Greevey comes into her inheritance. Nevaeh Lenore, do you accept all the rights and responsibilities of being a Junk Princess?"

Never, Nevaeh thought.

But she looked around at all the people who looked like her. Tucked among them, Axel's fiancée and Dalton's girlfriend both looked like they wanted to laugh, but in a kind way.

This was Nevaeh's true inheritance: all these people loving her.

This was what it meant to be the Junk Princess.

"I do," Nevaeh said.

Dad placed the compact-disc crown on her head, and it fit as if it'd been waiting for her her entire life.

This is going to be the worst summer of my life, Nevaeh thought.

No. It was worse than that.

This was the start of every summer for the rest of her life being awful.

3

Colin, the Three Brothers, and Tupperware

"Today's an easy one," Mom said, guiding her SUV through a gauntlet of badly parked cars in an unfamiliar neighborhood. "Mrs. Kruger needed to move into an assisted-living facility, so we already pulled out what she wanted to take with her. Everything left behind is garbage, recycling, or donations. And I hired these new movers I've been working with to help us."

"Movers?" Colin repeated, trying not to sound disappointed. "It's not just you and me?"

It wasn't that Colin was shy, exactly. But meeting new people always made him feel awkward, like he didn't know what to do with his hands or feet.

Or his mouth. He never knew what to say.

"Mrs. Kruger lived in the same house for sixty years," Mom said. "I promise, you'll be glad you and I don't have to carry out every single thing she accumulated in all that time."

They pulled up in front of a two-story yellow house with a wide front porch. Someone had left the blinds on the upstairs windows half-open, and a red porch swing rested against the railing, alongside a neat stack of white garbage bags. Colin only had to squint a little to make his eyes see the house as something else: a sleepy yellow dog with its tongue lolling out over its teeth, maybe?

"Is Mrs. Kruger nice?" Colin asked. What he really wanted to ask was, *Was she happy here? Were those sixty years good ones? Did she have kids? Did other kids in the neighborhood like hanging out here? Or did they cross the street to avoid it?*

"Uh, sure, she's nice," Mom said, even as she scanned a checklist on her phone. Mom was good at multitasking. "But don't worry—you won't have to meet her. She's already moved into her new home. Believe me, this part of the process is much easier if we don't have the client watching and second-guessing themselves: 'Maybe I do still need that broken mixer from forty years ago, after all. . . .' It's hard for people to let go. That's why they hire me. *I* don't have sentimental attachments to any of their things." She met Colin's eyes and grinned. "That's why they hire *us*, I mean."

Mom got out of the SUV, and Colin trailed after her. They'd just stepped into the house when a green pickup pulled up to the curb. It had a laminated sign on the door: Three Brothers Moving Company.

"Right on time," Mom said approvingly, glancing at her watch.

Colin slid over behind the doorframe, but peeked out. Three guys got out of the truck. Even at a distance, Colin could tell they were all built differently (one, tall and lanky; one, middling height but muscular; one, short and slight) and all had different skin tones (dark brown, light brown, and the kind of pale white skin that looked like it would burn easily). They all wore T-shirts and khaki-colored shorts. While Colin watched, all three of them shucked off their T-shirts, threw the T-shirts into the cab of the truck, and pulled on red polo shirts instead.

"You're making them wear shirts with collars, too?" Colin asked.

"It was a request, not an order, but they say they're fine with it," Mom said. She was down on her hands and knees, taping down a paper path across the carpet. "I like these guys a lot. They're hard workers."

Maybe Colin should have known to hold down the other end of the paper roll she was unspooling?

"Hey! You brought your son today!" one of the movers called as they crowded into the house behind Colin and Mom.

Colin guiltily stepped away from the window. He didn't want them to think he'd been spying on them. Even though he had.

"Sure did," Mom said. "This is Colin. Colin, meet Daryl, Derek, and Deepak."

Each of them gave a mini-wave in turn, and Colin did, too.

"Just say 'D,' and one of us will answer," Derek said. He had red hair and freckles, and a deeper voice than Colin would have expected.

But up close, it was also clear that Derek wasn't much older than Colin, and neither were the other two, taller guys. These weren't professional movers. These were teenagers.

Colin glanced back toward the Three Brothers sign on their truck.

"Are you really—" he began.

"Ooh, he's going to ask the question," Daryl said. He shook back dreadlocks and stooped a little to lean closer to the other two.

"Will he actually do it?" Deepak asked. He stroked the wispy beginnings of a mustache on his upper lip. "Or is it just a fake-out?" He sounded like a sports announcer doing a play-by-play. "The whole crowd is waiting to see his strategy. This is the next generation we're watching here."

"This could set the tone for the whole season," Derek agreed, as if he and Deepak both worked for ESPN.

"You get one personal question, kid," Daryl said, as if he were a coach. "What's it going to be? What are you *really* interested in finding out?"

Colin felt his face turning red with embarrassment. They didn't want him asking if they were brothers. He could tell.

"What was on the T-shirts you took off when you changed shirts?" he blurted, the first backup question he could think of.

"Ooo—good one!" Deepak congratulated him, even as he reached up and down to high-five Daryl and Derek in turn. "Nice recovery there!"

"For your information, it was band names," Derek said solemnly. "We're all musicians. On the side, I mean."

"See?" Mom said. "You found out something I didn't know. I'm old. What are the cool kids listening to, nowadays?"

"Wandering Vector," Daryl said.

"Stilt Opera," Deepak said.

"Krill River," Derek said.

"Proves my point—I've never heard of any of them," Mom said. She held up her phone. "Now, for assignments . . ."

After that, Colin might as well have been a robot. He carried trash bags. He carried boxes. He carried tables and chairs, headboards and footboards and pillows. Even he could see how well Mom and the three movers worked together as a team. There was never a point when any of them just stood around waiting for the truck or the SUV to get back from the dump or Goodwill or the recycling bins at the fire station. Anytime anybody stopped beside a piece of furniture too heavy for one person to carry alone, someone else appeared seemingly out of nowhere to pick up the other end of the bookshelf or couch.

Meanwhile, Colin kept tripping over his own feet. He kept having to back out doorways and down the stairway to let someone else past. He kept picking up boxes that were too heavy for him and having to put them right back down.

And he kept thinking too much.

Was Mrs. Kruger sad about leaving her house after sixty years? Did she cry?

What pictures did she have hanging on her walls for so long that they left those darker squares on the faded wallpaper?

Does she have all those pictures hanging in her new home now?

By late afternoon, Colin was so tired that he could barely even hold his head up as he trudged up and down the stairs, across the now-tattered paper path, out to the porch. . . .

"Young man!"

"What? Oh! I'm sorry!"

He dove to the side to narrowly avoid colliding with a gray-haired woman he hadn't even noticed standing on the emptied porch. She clutched the handles of a walker, and lifted the walker toward Colin like a shield. Beside her, a second woman—with the same squint, but fewer wrinkles—fended Colin off with a large cardboard box.

"Sorry! Sorry! I didn't see you!" he apologized even as he slammed into the wooden railing. He barely managed to hold on to the lamp he'd been carrying.

"You could have knocked my mother down her own porch stairs!" the younger woman scolded. "Don't you know that for elderly people, falls can be—"

"No one fell," the woman with the walker said. "He apologized. And *he's* the one who got hurt. Is your shoulder okay, young man?"

"I'm fine," Colin said, even though his shoulder already ached.

Mom appeared in the doorway.

"Mrs. Kruger and Marie! What a nice surprise! I see you've met my son, Colin. We were just finishing up—was there anything else we could help you with?"

"She insisted on bringing this Tupperware back to you," the younger woman—Marie?—said, holding out the box. She rolled her eyes behind her mother's back.

"You were right—it didn't all fit in my new cupboards," Mrs. Kruger told Mom. "And then Marie bought me new containers for Mother's Day."

"I told her *we* could just throw these away ourselves," Marie said, with another eye roll. "We didn't need to come over here and get in your way. Look how stained and nasty this is." She put the box down on the porch and flipped open the flaps as if Colin's mother needed proof. "My mom's been using this since I was a kid. It's probably the kind of plastic that's toxic—wasn't all plastic toxic back then?"

"Wouldn't it have killed me already if it was toxic?" Mrs. Kruger asked. Her voice quavered. "I just thought, why throw it away if someone else could use it? Mrs. Creedmont, you said you were donating as much as possible. I *want* someone else to use all the things I don't need anymore. It just doesn't seem right otherwise. I grew up during the Depression, you know, and 'waste not, want not' was what got us through. . . ."

"I'll make sure these get to the right place," Mom said, smiling warmly at Mrs. Kruger, even as she took the box from Marie.

Mrs. Kruger kept pushing her walker forward.

"Oh my," she said, inching through the open door. "It really is empty now, isn't it?" Her voice echoed off the bare walls. "This is how it looked when Edgar and I moved in. He stood right there and handed me the key." She pointed at a worn spot on the carpet. "Sixty years ago. He was just back from the navy. Young men got drafted back then, remember? We're just lucky that was between the wars. . . ."

Colin wasn't sure which wars she might be talking about.

"Mother, I told you this was a bad idea, coming back here," Marie said, stepping forward to take Mrs. Kruger's arm. "You'll wear yourself out."

"Oh, what am I saving my energy for, to do instead?" Mrs. Kruger snapped.

"You take all the time you need to say goodbye," Mom

told Mrs. Kruger. She handed the box of old Tupperware to Colin so she could pat Mrs. Kruger's shoulder. She laid a sympathetic hand on Marie's arm, too. "We'll let ourselves out the back. Colin, could you please take this box to the truck while I go tell Daryl, Derek, and Deepak the change in plans?"

"To . . . the truck?" Colin asked. The truck was for garbage, not donations. "But—"

"Yes, thank you, Colin," Mom said firmly, steering him toward the door. "The truck. Thank you for your help."

Colin stumbled—again—but took the lamp to the SUV and the box toward the truck. He saw what was happening. Mom was only pretending to Mrs. Kruger that someone else would ever use the Tupperware. It was like she was lying, and doing what Mrs. Kruger's daughter wanted, instead.

Colin liked Mrs. Kruger a whole lot more than her daughter.

He put the box down on the ground and eased open the flaps. He felt like someone about to rescue kittens or puppies some cruel person had dumped out by the side of the road.

But with the box open, he could see: Marie was right. This was a box full of nasty.

Some of the old plastic containers were ringed with orangish stains, the ghosts of some long-ago lasagna or spaghetti leftovers, maybe. The lids were dimpled and bulging, as if they'd contained science experiments that had climbed out. Or as if the containers themselves were science experiments:

What would happen if you microwaved a plastic container again and again and again?

Nobody in their right mind would want these containers.

Through the open window he could hear Mrs. Kruger saying wistfully, "That dent on the floor is because we always put the Christmas tree there. . . . Marie, remember how many people we always fit into this house every Thanksgiving?"

Colin squinted down into the box, and the overlapping pattern of ghostly orange plastic looked more like rose petals. Colin was *twelve*—much too old to believe in magic. But with Mrs. Kruger's voice in his ear, it felt for a moment as though he could see the old plastic containers the same way she did. Maybe she remembered how good a particular lasagna dinner had tasted all those years ago at—what? A birthday party? A graduation? Maybe that was all she was trying to share: good memories.

Good times.

It seemed wrong to just throw these containers away.

But it wasn't as though Mom would let him keep them.

Colin eased his phone out of the back pocket of his shorts. He held the phone directly above the top of the box and took a picture.

The picture showed a boxful of old, nasty Tupperware. Garbage.

Colin softened the lighting of the picture. He brightened the color. He kept tinkering with the exposure and contrast until he didn't have to squint to see the orange stains as rose petals.

There. That was how he wanted to remember this box.

"Colin! Time to go!"

Mom was walking toward the SUV, keys in her hand. Daryl, Derek, and Deepak were walking toward the truck. Quickly, Colin put his phone in his pocket and the box in the bed of the truck.

"Oh, sorry," he called. "I—I got a text I had to answer."

"From a lady friend, maybe?" Derek asked. "You're blushing."

Daryl gave Derek a playful slug in the arm.

"Dude! You do not ask a twelve-year-old about romantic entanglements! Don't you remember anything about middle school?"

"Ignore them both," Deepak advised. "Some people haven't matured past the middle school stage. Even though they've had years to do it." He glowered at Derek, then grinned at Colin. "Good working with you today. See you next time?"

"Uh, I guess . . ."

There was no way any of the older boys had caught a glimpse of Colin's phone screen, was there?

Colin scrambled over to the SUV and got in. Mom turned up the air-conditioning full blast. Colin felt like he might just melt into the seat. His body felt like it was made of nothing but sweat. His muscles ached. He might never be able to walk again.

"Good day, huh?" Mom said, pulling away from the curb. "Very satisfying, wasn't it?"

The smile she flashed him was infuriating.

"Mom, you *lied* to that old lady!" he complained. "You made her think you were going to donate her old Tupperware to someone who would treasure it, and then—"

"Colin, I did my job," Mom said. "I made decisions she didn't want to handle herself. And decisions she didn't want to fight about with her daughter." Mom was silent for a moment. "It was, at worst, a white lie. Anyhow, Mrs. Kruger didn't really care that much about the Tupperware. It was just an excuse to get her daughter to drive her to visit her house one last time. You can see that, can't you?"

Colin hadn't. Did that mean he'd been foolish, taking the picture? He eased his phone out of his pocket, just enough so that he could see its screen, but Mom couldn't.

He still liked the picture.

"Do *you* know if Daryl, Derek, and Deepak are really brothers or not?" he asked. "I mean, like, adopted, or stepbrothers, or half brothers, or something like that."

"I don't, sorry," Mom said.

"But you're their boss!" Colin protested.

"That doesn't give me the right to ask personal questions,"

Mom said. "Colin, sometimes you just have to let people keep their own secrets."

That made Colin feel even better about the picture he'd taken.

Now he had a secret, too.

4

Nevaeh and the Mongold Unit

"Storage unit day—whoo-hoo!" Dad cried, twisting the steering wheel to the side to veer suddenly from the road onto a concrete drive.

"Dad, you could have warned us you were going to turn," Nevaeh complained, rubbing her shoulder where she'd slammed into Prilla beside her in the back seat of the truck. "You didn't have to keep *that* a secret. You're making me feel like I'm being kidnapped or something."

"Bwaa-haa-haa-haa!" Dad fake-cackled.

"Wait, Dad—did you get the Mongold unit?" Axel asked from the front passenger seat. "*That's* what you were hinting about saving for Nevaeh's first day on the job?"

Dad backed the truck onto a concrete square in front of an orange garage door. It was one of about fifty orange garage doors that all looked identical to Nevaeh. But evidently it meant something to Axel and Dad. They were grinning at each other as though they'd reached the end of a rainbow and discovered a leprechaun with a pot of gold.

"Okay, I'll bite," Nevaeh said. "What's the Mongold unit?"

Axel turned toward her, clutching his chest as though he'd had a heart attack.

"She doesn't know about the Mongold unit?" he asked. "Nevaeh, are you even part of this family?"

Do I have a choice? Nevaeh thought.

"Hey, hey, she's new to this," Prilla spoke up, slinging her arm protectively around Nevaeh's shoulders. "Back off. You've been doing this longer than she's even been alive, remember?"

"But she sits at our dinner table every night," Axel countered. "She's heard Dad's stories her whole life. Nevaeh, don't you pay attention?"

Not if I can help it, Nevaeh thought.

"Axel, Prilla, simmer down," Dad said. He turned in his seat to face Nevaeh directly. "Nevaeh, I would be delighted to tell you the story of the Mongold unit again. We've got to wait for the key, anyhow."

"Dad, you're going to kill the environment if you sit here with the air-conditioning running while you wait," Prilla interrupted.

"That wasn't my plan," Dad said, even as he shut off the engine. "Nevaeh, you've got to stand right in front of that doorway while you hear this story."

Nevaeh stifled the impulse to cross her arms, sink down

into her seat, and protest, *Oh, no. I'm savoring every last breath of air-conditioning I can.*

Dad climbed out of the truck and hit the seat release so Nevaeh could slide out behind him. He put his arm around her shoulders and guided her to stand in front of the padlock on the orange garage door. It was right at her eye level.

"To the best of my knowledge, nobody has opened that door since 1989," he said.

"Nevaeh, this is like the Holy Grail!" Axel exclaimed behind them. "I can remember Dad talking about the Mongolds my whole life! This could be, like, our own personal gold mine!"

Dad silenced him with a look.

"Show some respect, son," he said. "You do not speak of the Holy Grail and 'our own personal gold mine' in the same breath."

He paused, as if to give Axel time to ponder his mistake.

Nevaeh felt a little sorry for him. She knew the engagement ring Axel just bought for his girlfriend had cost a lot of money.

And, really, it was annoying how Dad acted like being the Junk King wasn't just a way to make money, but a higher calling, practically a sacred quest—like how knights in legends searched for the "Holy Grail," the cup that Jesus had supposedly drunk from at the Last Supper.

Even if we owned a gold mine, Nevaeh thought glumly, *Dad would still make us work this summer.*

"The Mongolds," Dad went on, "lived in a big house on the other side of town. They were *serious* antique collectors. Then, in 1989, they moved to Florida. Rumor has it Arthur Mongold wanted to golf and fish every day, but Maribel hated sand and fire ants. She insisted on putting most of their possessions here into storage—she was sure even Arthur would get tired of Florida and they'd be right back. But their first day in Florida, a ninety-five-year-old man didn't see a stop sign, and plowed right into the Mongolds' car. On the passenger side. Maribel died instantly."

"Do you think she had a premonition?" Prilla asked. "Do you think *that's* the reason she didn't want to move to Florida?"

Does Prilla believe in premonitions? Nevaeh wondered. She stifled a shiver despite the heat. *Do I?*

Dad was still telling his story.

"Nobody knows, honey," he said. "But Arthur was grief-stricken. For about six months, anyway. Then he remarried. He and the new wife had kids. He started a new business that made a lot of money. It was nothing to him to just keep paying forty dollars a month, eighty dollars a month, a hundred dollars a month—whatever the rates went up to—so he didn't have to come back and deal with everything in this storage unit. Fifteen, twenty years ago, I put out feelers—in a sensitive way, of course—to say *I'd* clean out the storage unit for him. I'd deal with the personal effects any way he wanted, and we could split the profits from selling the valuables. But he didn't want that. Then a few months ago, Arthur died. Apparently his second wife and the kids hadn't even *known* about this storage unit. And apparently Wife Number Two hated even the mention of Maribel's name. It gave her great pleasure to just stop paying the fees."

"But that wasn't logical! *She* could have hired us and taken a share of the profits!"

Nevaeh turned—she hadn't realized Roddy and Dalton had arrived, too, in the second truck. Roddy was shaking his head. He was the one who always wanted things to make sense.

"Thanks, Roddy, for teeing up a teachable moment for Nevaeh," Dad said. He put his hands on Nevaeh's shoulders and turned her toward him so she could peer straight into his eyes. He was holding her so close that his beard tickled her face. "Honey, people are almost never logical about their possessions. Or their spouses' possessions. They think with their hearts way more than their brains."

"It made Arthur Mongold's second wife *happy* to think of the first Mrs. Mongold's precious possessions going into arrears and being treated like garbage," Dalton said, picking up the story.

"But it's not garbage to the Junk King!" Dad, Axel, Dalton, Roddy, and even Prilla chanted together. This was a line Dad used in his TV commercials.

Nevaeh realized belatedly that she should have joined in, too.

"Ah, my favorite trash pickers." A man in a Cincinnati Reds cap and a "Steve's Self-Storage and Moving" T-shirt came around the corner. "I always wanted you to get this, Lloyd."

"You can't possibly know how grateful I am that we worked out our special deal," Dad said. "If this had gone to auction—"

"You talked him into selling us the Mongold unit *before* the auction?" Axel marveled.

Prilla elbowed Nevaeh.

"Usually if someone stops paying for a storage unit, they have, like, two months to make up their payments," she explained in a whisper. "If they don't pay, Steve puts up the unit for auction, and anyone can bid on it."

Nevaeh nodded. She'd heard Dad talk about auctions before.

"Selling to you saved me a lot of paperwork," Steve said with a shrug. "And a lot of time opening the unit and letting strangers traipse through, when I *know* Arthur Mongold hasn't been back to even look at the unit since 1989, so it's all preserved, exactly as is. . . ."

"And you and Dad must have worked out a split of the profits that you really liked, right?" Dalton asked, squinting suspiciously.

Steve held up his hand like he was taking an oath.

"You know I don't reveal my secrets of the trade," he said.

He reached into his pocket and pulled out a tarnished key. "Here's your prize."

"She gets to do the honors," Dad said, pointing at Nevaeh. "Remember my daughter Nevaeh?"

"*That's* Nevaeh? Your *youngest* is old enough to help out now?" Steve asked. He looked from Axel to Dalton to Roddy to Prilla as if he were counting. Finally his gaze reached Nevaeh. "Kiddo, I remember when you were born. Wasn't that just two or three years ago?"

He held out the key to her, and Nevaeh took it.

"Uh, thanks?" Nevaeh said.

She felt strangely nervous. But that was ridiculous. It wasn't as though opening a padlock took any special skill.

Everyone crowded around, Steve seeming just as eager as the rest of the Greeveys. Nevaeh took a deep breath and put the key in the lock.

"If you need any WD-40, I've got some on the truck," Dalton said.

"And I've got a blowtorch, if we have to resort to that," Axel said.

"If the key doesn't turn easily, don't force it," Roddy advised. "You don't want to break off the bottom part in the lock and get it stuck forever."

Good grief. Maybe it did take special skill to open a padlock after more than thirty years.

Nevaeh turned the key slowly to the left. A few flakes of rust or dirt fell out of the keyhole. But then the lock clicked open. Everyone cheered.

"Let's see, let's see, let's see," Dad chanted, pulling the padlock off and yanking away the metal bar it had held in place. Everyone, even Steve, joined in grabbing the bottom of the rolling door and lifting it high. Prilla backed up to take pictures of their first glimpse of the inside of the Mongold unit.

And then everyone froze.

Nevaeh had been watching her family, not the storage unit, but now she too turned to peer past the open door. She could see all the way to the back of the space ahead of her. She could see all four flimsy metal walls. She could see the full span of the concrete floor. She could see all that perfectly well because . . .

The Mongold unit was completely empty.

No, wait, not completely, Nevaeh thought. *Because isn't that . . .*

"An envelope?" Nevaeh asked. "The only thing that's in there is an envelope?"

Colin at Home

Colin dropped his clothes to the floor and stepped into the shower.

"There's nothing like cleaning up after a long day of hard work, is there?" Mom called to him from the kitchen. "Just leave some hot water for me!"

Colin had no trouble hearing her over the drumming of the water. Their house was so small that either of them could stand in any room and hear the other person anywhere else, even if they whispered. Colin turned, back to front, front to back. The water pooled at his feet, perfectly shaped droplets on perfectly clean tile.

He'd been in friends' houses. He'd seen how other kids' bathrooms were crowded with shampoo bottles and deodorant cans and soap dispensers, with older siblings' razors hanging perilously from shelves. He'd seen the rust stains under old cans of shaving cream, the water stains under wet towels left too long on the floor, the caked-on toothpaste residue the other kids didn't bother rinsing out of their sinks.

He'd never felt compelled to take a picture of any of it.

Colin finished his shower. He tied his towel around his waist and dropped his dirty clothes in the hamper. He went back to his own room. He collected underwear, gym shorts, and a T-shirt from his dresser and put them on. He hung the towel on the rack inside his closet door.

And then he stood there, peering into his perfectly tidy closet. Three shirts with collars hung on the rod beside four shirts without. A single small box nestled on the shelf above, labeled in Mom's firm hand "Colin's Memorabilia." The wood floor was completely bare.

Are you poor?

Colin's friend-in-kindergarten Brewster had asked that the first time he'd come over to play at Colin's house. Brewster had been staring at Colin's small tub of Lego, his single Hot Wheels car, his solitary stuffed animal (a rabbit Colin had named Growls, for some reason even Colin had forgotten). But Brewster could just as easily have been looking at Colin's half-bare bookshelf, his single pair of shoes, his board game collection that fit into his nightstand with room to spare.

"Poor?" Colin had replied, totally baffled. "No, my mom has lots of money. In her purse. I've seen it."

"But you don't have *anything*."

"My mom hates clutter," Colin explained. He'd been

quoting. "She says everybody would be happier if they got rid of their clutter. That's her job, telling people that."

Brewster kept gazing around, as if a second or third glance at Colin's room would reveal some hidden stash of toys and games. It was like he didn't even see that everything Colin owned was "clean and new and high quality"—the way Mom described Colin's possessions. Brewster had been a little kid with big ears and spiky hair. He and Colin had bonded at the kindergarten art table. But in Colin's room, he kept staring at Colin as if Colin were from another planet.

"I don't know what clutter is," Brewster had said. "But if clutter's everything you don't have, then I *love* it."

Brewster hadn't lasted as a friend. He'd moved away a few months later. It was kind of the start of a trend for Colin—he seemed to have a knack for making friends with the kids who didn't stay. Colin already knew that his best friends from sixth grade, Anthony and Nazeem, were both going to go to the other middle school in Groveview next year. They'd been more play-on-the-same-soccer-team-at-recess friends than anything else, so he didn't mind that much.

But he'd also thought he would go to his usual day camp all summer, and hang out with kids there.

Colin shut his closet and went out into the combination living room/kitchen. Mom sat at the kitchen table, typing away at her laptop.

"Shower's open now," Colin said. "Your turn."

"Mm-kay," Mom said, without looking up. "Might as well finish these emails first. But don't worry. Dinner will still be on time. I already put it in the oven. Are you starving?"

"I'll live," Colin said. He pulled a bowlful of grapes from the refrigerator anyway, and sat down opposite his mother.

Mom's posture at the keyboard was perfect, even after the long day of moving boxes. Her eyebrows danced up and down as she muttered, ". . . guarantee you won't regret decluttering . . . a way to rethink your life, not just your belongings . . ."

"Mom," Colin said, talking around a mouthful of grapes, "why'd you choose this? Why 'Possession Curation'?"

"You know the story," Mom said. "You've heard it a million times. I wanted to help people. If they curate their belongings the way a museum curates its collection, then they're in charge. Their possessions don't own them. And . . . seriously. You want me to go on quoting from my website?"

Colin chewed and swallowed, and grabbed another handful of grapes.

"No, I mean . . . there are lots of jobs that help people. You could have been a doctor or a nurse. Or a teacher or a firefighter or . . ."

It was hard to imagine his tiny mom as a firefighter. He pictured her standing in front of a burning building, clinging to a fire hose. It would have been like something out of a cartoon, the fire hose whipping her around above the flames like a kite in a stiff wind.

"I like running Possession Curation," Mom said. "It's what I'm good at."

But she dropped her gaze toward the laptop screen. A shadow crossed her face, as if something on the screen told her she wasn't as good at it as she'd thought.

"And . . . Colin, you know I couldn't afford to go to college." She gave a little shrug. A "can't change the past" shrug. "A doctor or a nurse or a teacher—that's a lot of extra school. It would have meant a lot of debt for someone like me. Even a firefighter, I think they have to get an associate's degree. When I came back here with you when you were a baby, I needed to start making money right away."

"That's the only reason you could have ever worked for the Junk King," Colin said. Because that was a part of the story he knew, too. Mom changed the channel every time the Junk King's cheesy commercials came on TV. She was kind to a fault and wouldn't let Colin make fun of anyone, but he'd still heard her mock the Junk King's motto under her breath when she saw it on yard signs outside houses that his company—not hers—had been hired to clear out. Granted, the worst thing she said was, "King? Who are you kidding, Lloyd Greevey? Junk Jester is more like it." But that was the equivalent of anyone else cussing for hours.

And yet, she'd once been a Junk King employee.

"Fortunately, that only lasted about five minutes before I went out on my own, or we might have killed each other," Mom said, making a wry face. "But, Colin—I love what I do. I'm making a difference for my clients, improving their lives. It all worked out." She snapped her laptop shut, as if she'd stopped caring so much about the emails. "And things will be even better for you. You'll have choices I never had. I'm putting money aside for you for college. And I'm paying you full wages this summer, and every dime is going into your college fund—you'll never feel trapped, the way I did."

She waved her arms so emphatically, her own sleeve bonked her in the face. She winced.

"Okay, just got a whiff of my own sweat—you also deserve not to have to sit downwind from this reek all through dinner. Thank you for coming to my TED Talk. Now I'll go take a shower."

She whisked past him. Colin chewed his way through another handful of grapes. Then, as soon as he heard the shower start in the bathroom, he swung Mom's laptop over to face him.

I'll just glance at her emails and make sure there's not anything to really worry about, he thought.

But Mom had logged off her account before shutting the

laptop. And Colin didn't know her password.

Colin sat staring at the lock screen for a long moment. Why did it feel so much like Mom was hiding something?

Why did it feel that way more than ever, every time she talked about the Junk King?

Colin, sometimes you just have to let people keep their own secrets. . . .

The words she'd spoken about Daryl, Derek, and Deepak had seemed like a comfort an hour ago, a way for Colin to justify keeping his own secrets. But thinking about those words now made Colin want to squirm.

Was he doomed to spending the whole summer around people who confused him? Who all held secrets he would never understand?

Actually, there is one thing I can find out on my own, he thought.

He opened his own account, went to the internet, and began typing the band names Daryl, Derek, and Deepak had mentioned: Wandering Vector. Stilt Opera. Krill River.

According to the internet, none of those bands existed.

Are the Three Brothers so cool they know about hot new bands even before the internet? Colin wondered.

Or was he just so clueless, he'd never be able to make sense of anything?

The Envelope

Nevaeh took off running toward the thin white envelope lying on the floor of the Mongold storage unit.

"Nevaeh, no!" Dad called. "I think . . . I think this is a crime scene! That's evidence! You have to think about fingerprints, and—"

This might have been Nevaeh's first official day of working in the family business, but she'd spent her whole life around the revolving collection of antiques that flowed in and out of their house. She knew how to touch something without leaving fingerprints.

She slipped her hand under the bottom of her T-shirt and, using the shirt like a glove, picked up the envelope.

"Should I call the cops?" Steve asked.

"Oh, right," Axel snarled. "What if you're the one who cleaned out this unit of all its valuables, and now you're offering to call the cops so we won't suspect you?"

"Steve, would you really have—no, no, of course not." Dad wiped a sleeve across his sweaty forehead. "Axel, apologize.

Right now. I *know* Steve never would have done that."

Nevaeh flipped the envelope over. The flap wasn't even sealed. Still using the bottom of her T-shirt to avoid leaving fingerprints, she inched a piece of paper out of the envelope and began unfolding it. But T-shirts don't actually make good gloves. The letter slipped out of her grasp and fluttered down to the floor, landing word-side-up.

Nevaeh bent over to read it:

> Dear Arthur,
> I always knew you loved your things more than you loved me. Now you don't have either.
> Don't try to find me. Or your former possessions.
> Not Yours,
> Maribel

"It's—it's— Did *Maribel* steal everything?" Nevaeh asked. "Before she died? Or, I guess it's not stealing if it's your own stuff . . . or stuff you and your husband own together. So Maribel took everything out of the storage unit before moving to Florida with Arthur and dying? Or . . ."

Everyone else crowded around the letter alongside Nevaeh. Axel started to reach down to pick it up, but Dad held him back.

"Evidence, remember?" Dad said.

"Dad, there's no crime if Maribel Mongold just—" Prilla began.

"You're crazy if you think this is real!" Steve declared. He began herding the Greeveys away from the letter as if his long arms could serve as some CRIME SCENE DO NOT CROSS tape. "I'm the one who sold the Mongolds this storage unit back in '89. The way that Maribel looked at Arthur . . . She was all, 'Yes, dear,' 'No, dear,' 'Whatever you think is best, dear. . . .' She was about to move to Florida for him. When she hated Florida! She wouldn't have double-crossed him! She wouldn't have written this letter!"

Or maybe she was only pretending to love her husband in front of other people, Nevaeh thought. *Acting.*

Her face flushed, and it had nothing to do with the heat.

She shouldn't be thinking that she and Maribel had anything in common. Nevaeh was just a kid. Maribel had been a grown woman. She could have said whatever she wanted without pretending.

"If this letter's fake, when do you think everything was stolen?" Roddy asked, rubbing his shaved head as if that would help him think. "Back in 1989? Or more recently? Like, after Dad got the bid to clean this place out?"

"I've had security cameras for the past decade," Steve said. He shoved the bill of his baseball cap back. "I review the footage every morning. Anyone taking anything out of this unit in the past ten years, I would have seen that."

"Dad, Dad!" Axel said, stopping in his tracks. His foot was still just inches away from the letter on the floor. "Remember the summer I was Nevaeh's age? Almost *thirteen* years ago? Remember who was always so interested in the story of the Mongold unit? And then she just up and quit, and somehow had enough money to start her own business?"

Roddy and Prilla looked as puzzled as Nevaeh felt. But Dad and Dalton answered in unison: "Felicia Creedmont."

Steve tilted his head back so far his cap fell off.

"You think that awful Possession Curation woman did this?"

7

The Shoebox

Colin's first week of the summer passed in an exhausted blur. Was it Tuesday or Wednesday when he tripped over a shoelace he hadn't realized was untied, and almost dropped a whole box full of glasses? Was it Wednesday or Thursday when he and Mom worked with Daryl, Derek, and Deepak again, and they kept telling jokes he didn't understand? (What made it worse: when they would try to explain, and he still didn't get it.)

But each day he had a moment when he was carrying something out to the garbage, and he looked down and thought, *No. I shouldn't be throwing this away. I want to remember it, even if nobody else does.*

Once it was a flower suncatcher that had been hanging in a window for so long that almost all the color had bleached out of it—it was a suncatcher destroyed by the sun.

Once it was an old-fashioned tricycle that was warped so badly that it looked like anyone riding it would do nothing but go around in circles. Even riderless, it made Colin think of a cat chasing its tail.

Once it was a lopsided clay pot that Mom had hesitated over and asked the woman who hired her, "Did one of your kids make this?" And the woman had practically snarled back, "No. My *mother* did. After the stroke. When she was relearning how to use her hands. That's an awful memory. Get rid of it."

But Colin thought the clay pot was . . . what? Not pretty. With a crack running down the side and down the bottom, it wasn't even useful.

He still thought it was memorable.

When he was sure he was out of sight of Mom, the three "D" boys, and whatever client they were helping, Colin took pictures of the suncatcher. He took pictures of the tricycle. He took pictures of the crooked clay pot.

By late Friday afternoon, Colin was feeling almost proud of himself that he hadn't found anything he wanted to take a picture of that day. This taking-pictures-of-weird-things wasn't going to turn into anything embarrassing. He could delete all the pictures from his phone, no problem. He wouldn't take any more ever again.

Today they were clearing out a house for a woman who'd inherited it when her grandparents died. Daryl, Derek, Deepak, and Colin were dealing with the attic, which felt about seven thousand degrees hotter than anywhere else in the house. Mom had given them their assignment with the words "Mrs. Seville says her grandparents didn't move into this house until they were in their eighties, and they both had arthritis and barely ever stepped foot in this attic. So all this stuff belonged to previous residents. I took out everything that could possibly have any value already, so the rest of this—straight into the garbage."

Daryl, Derek, and Deepak began chanting, "Trash it! Trash it! Trash it!" while they worked. They pushed out a vent at the end of the attic and rigged a chute out of plastic sheeting to run down to the bed of their truck, parked on the grass below. That way, they didn't have to run up and down the stairs to get rid of the lighter items. They could just shove everything down the chute: the old clothes that had disintegrated into rags, the plastic toys that had melted together in the heat of who knew how many brutally hot summers, the collection of fake flowers that had somehow morphed into looking like they'd been exposed to radiation.

The three older boys began taking bets on who would be the first to find a dead mouse somewhere in the mess.

"You *know* there had to have been an entire mouse civilization living up here," Derek said.

"Mouse civilization? I bet it was a rat civilization," Daryl said.

"Or both," Deepak said. "Or worse. Raccoons? Skunks?" He went back into announcer mode, but this time he sounded like he was narrating a documentary. "We are standing here on the site of the Giant Rodent Wars of . . . Remind me, audience, what year were the Giant Rodent Wars?"

"Colin, you take this one," Derek directed.

"Um, I don't—" Colin began.

"Just say any year," Daryl whispered, passing him with a bag of old clothes under each arm. "It doesn't matter."

"Er—which decade?" Colin asked, teetering on one of the attic's wood beams. "Which century?"

"Ah, yes," Deepak said, still using his announcer voice. "As my research assistant reminds me, the Giant Rodent Wars are eternal, present in every century. . . ."

"Why do you get a research assistant?" Derek asked. "Why isn't Colin *my* assistant? Or Daryl's?"

"Last time I checked, Colin was the boss's son, and we're just the hired help. So I think you've got the relationship backward," Daryl said. "Right, Colin?"

"Uh . . . er . . ." Colin could tell the other boys were just joking around. About everything. But what was he supposed to say? If he went with *Yeah, you're not the boss of me. I'm the boss of you—get back to work*, that would sound ridiculous. He was twelve and they all had to be at least sixteen, since they could drive. They could clear out a whole section of the attic while he was still standing there figuring out which box to pick up first.

He wasn't their boss.

"I'll go clean up that corner," Colin blurted, pointing to an alcove at the back of the attic. "The roof's lower there, and I'm shorter than all of you and . . . yeah. That seems like a good idea."

And it was far enough away that they wouldn't try to talk to him for a while.

Colin didn't wait for them to answer, but started racing across the beams.

The flooring in this attic was strange—someone had put down plywood across some of the beams but not others. And it was hard to see which spot was which when Colin was also dodging piles of sagging boxes and split bags.

Just stay on the beams and you'll be fine, he told himself. *You'll be off in a corner and nobody will bother you and it's only another hour until we're done for the day and . . .*

Colin's foot slipped.

He tried to right himself, stomping down hard with the other foot. But he was at the spot where the alcove met the rest of the attic, and Colin realized too late that the pattern of the beams changed in the alcove, running perpendicular instead of parallel to the rest.

His foot broke through the floorboard, and there was

nothing but air and wispy pink insulation below.

Colin let out a yelp.

"Did you see a mouse or a mouse carcass?" Derek called from across the attic. "Who had Colin for their bet to find the first mouse?"

"Kid, you okay?" Daryl asked.

"I'm fine! I'm fine! I just . . . tripped."

"Tripped" didn't quite describe Colin's dilemma, but he didn't want the older boys swarming toward him if he could get back up on his own.

It took him a minute just to figure out how he'd landed, and where each of his hands and feet and knees and elbows had hit. He was crouched on the rotting plywood like a runner about to take off from a starting block. But his back foot—the one that he would have pushed off with the hardest, if he'd actually been a runner—was trapped beneath the plywood.

And it *hurt*.

Colin winced and looked for blood. Nope, there was none of that. He slid his hands into the hole and felt around his ankle. He was no medical expert, but as far as he could tell, all the bones in his ankle were as solid as usual.

I'm just going to have a weird-looking bruise, and I'm acting like a baby about this and . . .

And what if he actually started crying?

Colin decided to focus on maneuvering his foot out of the hole. He swung his hands around, trying to make the hole a little bigger. His foot still felt jarringly numb from the impact, so he dug his hand under the heel of his sneakers.

His knuckles brushed something under the floorboard that was too solid to be insulation.

He stifled another yelp.

But he also jerked back so instinctively that his foot and his hands came up out of the hole, only scraping a little against the broken plywood.

He hesitated for only an instant. Then he pulled out his phone and turned on its flashlight. He aimed the flashlight down into the hole and pressed his face as close to the hole as he could.

There, under the floorboard, just beyond the hole, was a dark-colored shoebox.

Why would someone hide a shoebox under a floorboard when it's already hidden in an attic? Colin wondered.

The dust he'd disturbed danced in the beam of light from Colin's phone. It made the ordinary brown shoebox seem mystical. Maybe even supernatural.

Colin reached down into the hole and tugged the shoebox toward the center of the hole. Now he could see the shoebox's lid, with remnants of some ancient dried-out rubber band zigzagging across its surface.

Colin blinked at the stirred-up dust rising from below. Now he could make out faded words on the shoebox lid, too, words clearly written by a kid:

This belongs to Rosemary.
Everyone else KEEP OUT!

Nevaeh's Secret

Nevaeh closed the door of the bedroom she shared with Prilla. She hesitated for a minute, listening to the rest of the family downstairs. Axel was arguing too loudly, "*I* think there's enough evidence. Someone should go ask her questions, anyway," and Dad replied, "You heard Steve say he wants this handled quietly. It'll hurt his business if people think he doesn't guard his storage units well enough."

Dalton said, "Didn't that woman go by the nickname 'Fleas' when she worked for you, Dad? And then suddenly she became Fe-lee-see-uh Creeeeed-mont, and her company's got some hoity-toity name and all her customers are 'clients' who 'only deserve the best'? Who does she think she is?"

Mom said something, too, but her voice didn't carry as well as the others'.

It didn't matter. Nevaeh was only listening to make sure there were no footsteps behind her, no one who'd followed her up the stairs.

She stepped over a pile of Prilla's clothes heaped on the floor and slid back her side of the closet door. Nevaeh gritted her teeth, as she always did peering into the closet. It was like watching a slow-motion horror movie: Prilla's jumble of clothes and shoes and books and backpacks and beloved stuffed animals from childhood—and everything else she crammed into her side of the closet—kept oozing farther and farther into Nevaeh's territory.

"I'm just sharing," Prilla was prone to saying lately. "You're welcome to borrow anything you want. It's only fair, since my stuff will never stay where it belongs."

And then she'd smile so disarmingly that Nevaeh couldn't gripe, *Your stuff doesn't have legs. It doesn't decide where to go on its own. If it's not where it belongs, whose fault is that?*

Now Nevaeh put her back against Prilla's mountain of stuff and shoved. Just for a moment, Nevaeh could see how she wanted her side of the closet to look: the shoes in tidy rows on the floor, the hangers of every shirt or dress spaced evenly, the books on the shelves at the side of the closet arranged alphabetically by author.

Then Nevaeh stepped toward the shelves. Prilla's stuff toppled onto Nevaeh's side again. Nevaeh sighed and reached behind the top row of books, the one that started with Louisa May Alcott and ran through Suzanne Collins.

She had to stand on tiptoes, but that was enough for her

to wrap her hand around a small wooden box behind the books. It was about the size of a Whitman's Sampler of candy. Nevaeh drew the box out and took it over to her bed.

In a family that applied the word "treasure" to everything from antique plumbing fixtures to ancient doorknobs, Nevaeh used this box for every "treasure" she valued. Which . . . wasn't much.

She flipped open the lid and pulled out a page she'd cut from a magazine.

A pretty woman smiled out from the center of the page. She had porcelain-pale skin and dark curly hair—but *tamed* curly hair; curly hair that followed instructions. Behind her, a tidy room positively gleamed. It had spotless white couches, a spotless white rug, silver accent pillows, a silver vase containing a single red rose. And everything matched. Everything coordinated. Everything was clean.

Everything was new.

This was how Nevaeh pictured heaven.

Above the woman's smiling face, elegant print announced, "You Deserve Only the Best." Below it, in smaller print, were a series of questions: "Is the clutter in your home driving you crazy? Do you dread going home to all the mess? Do you feel as though you are fighting a constant battle to keep your home neat and tidy—and always losing? Do you long for a different way? You *can* rethink your belongings—and redefine your life. Possession Curation is the answer."

And then, in a smaller version of the elegant script at the top, it said, "Felicia Creedmont, Founder."

Nevaeh raised her head and looked toward her own closet again. All her clothes had been worn by someone else before her—at least Prilla, if not Prilla and one or two other girls before that. All her books had been read by someone else before her, and many of them were missing spines or front covers; it was a rarity if Nevaeh *didn't* find someone else's crumbs in her books or somebody else's crumpled bookmark or the crayon scribbles of someone else's younger brother or sister. She'd lost count of how many times she'd gotten halfway through a book only to discover pages missing; she still didn't know what happened at the end of *The Parker Inheritance*. Nevaeh had never owned a stuffed animal without matted fur or a doll without tangled hair from some earlier child loving on it too much. When she'd gotten her first cell phone—the one she still used—it had arrived with the screen already cracked from someone else dropping it.

Just once, Nevaeh wanted to own something that had never belonged to anyone but her. Just once, she wanted to own something that was brand-new and spotless and perfect and . . . and curate-able. Was that a word? If it wasn't, Nevaeh wanted to make it one.

Nevaeh had found this ad for Felicia Creedmont's Possession

Curation in a pile of old magazines her dad had gotten from a dentist's office that was closing. The dentist had been a bit of a hoarder; he'd always thought that eventually he'd read all the magazines that had sat in his office waiting room over the years. But he'd died before that happened. Sometimes old magazines were valuable: Dad had once gotten fifty dollars for a *Time* magazine still in perfect condition from when Barack Obama was elected president. But that meant that their living room was often an obstacle course of stacks of old magazines Dad was slowly sorting.

Nevaeh had seen the Possession Curation ad in a local magazine, one she knew Dad wouldn't resell. But she'd sneaked it up to her room; she used a razor blade to cut out the ad because she didn't want to ruin it with jagged scissor cuts.

And then she kept it secret.

Nevaeh didn't want the rest of her family laughing at her the way they laughed at Felicia Creedmont. It wasn't mean, exactly—no one in Nevaeh's family was *mean*. The worst thing she'd ever heard anyone say about Felicia Creedmont was "She's like a cut-rate Marie Kondo." And then Nevaeh had had to look up who that was. (It turned out that Marie Kondo was a woman known worldwide for teaching people to pare down their belongings to only those that "sparked joy." Nevaeh liked that idea, too. But what if nothing you owned ever sparked joy?) Anyway, Marie Kondo lived all the way away in Japan. Felicia Creedmont lived right here in Groveview, Ohio, just like Nevaeh.

When Nevaeh stared at this ad, it felt *possible* that Nevaeh could grow up and live in a house like Felicia Creedmont's. It felt possible that Nevaeh could change her life, too. It felt possible that she could do something important and be someone who mattered, not just a girl who wore hand-me-down clothes and read hand-me-down books. Not just the Greevey everyone referred to as "the caboose."

Someday.

But was that still possible if Felicia Creedmont, the woman she admired, had gotten her start by stealing all the valuable antiques from the Mongold storage unit nearly thirteen years ago?

The very antiques that Nevaeh's father had hoped would bring his family a lot of money this summer?

9

Colin's Secret

Colin had to twist the shoebox this way and that to pull it out of the hole in the attic floorboard. The shoebox was old—really old—and he had a few moments of fearing he might crush it just trying to get it out to see it properly.

He also kind of thought the whole thing could disappear in a poof of dust, and he'd discover he was only hallucinating it because the attic was too hot and he'd gotten dehydrated.

But the cardboard held together. The box stayed solid in his sweaty hands.

He placed the shoebox on a non-rotted section of plywood.

"Sorry, Rosemary," he muttered, brushing dirt and crud off the top of the long-ago girl's scrawled KEEP OUT message. Whoever Rosemary was, she was probably dead by now. The box looked *that* old. And if she'd really wanted other people to stay out, she wouldn't have left the box behind in this attic.

At least, that was what Colin told himself as he opened the lid.

He braced himself for the box to contain something boring or useless or nasty—one of those mouse carcasses Daryl, Derek, and Deepak had been joking about, maybe? It might even contain *live* mice, nestled together in Rosemary's valuables-that-weren't-so-valuable-anymore. Whatever he did, Colin had to make sure he didn't scream. If it was mice, he could be really cool about it, and carry the box over to the older boys and say offhandedly, "Is *this* your mouse civilization?"

It wasn't mice inside the shoebox. It was papers.

No—Colin angled his phone flashlight a little better—it was letters.

Balancing the phone on his knee, Colin reached into the box and pulled out the top letter, the only one he could see that wasn't in an envelope. He unfurled the lined notebook paper:

Dear Rosemary,
Please please PLEASE don't hate me anymore!
I'm sorry! I didn't mean it! Will you ever talk to
me again?
Toby

Who was Rosemary? Who was Toby? What had he done? *Had* she ever stopped hating him?

"Colin?" Derek called from the other side of the attic. "Did the winner of the Giant Rodent Wars trap you over there, and are you being held down with tiny ropes like Gulliver in Lilliput?"

"Dude!" Deepak scolded Derek. "School's out! You are not impressing anyone with those AP Lit references!"

Gulliver? Lilliput? AP Lit?

Colin didn't have a clue what Derek and Deepak were talking about. But they had to be wondering why he hadn't yet carried a single load of garbage from the alcove to the plastic chute.

"I'm fine!" he called back quickly. "Just . . . finding stuff that's too heavy to go down the chute. I'll have to carry it downstairs myself."

He stuffed the letter back into the shoebox and replaced the lid. To avoid making anyone curious, he also grabbed a bag of ancient-looking, threadbare towels. He tucked the shoebox into the towels and headed for the rickety attic ladder. He scrambled down the ladder and then down the stairs from the second to the first floor.

Mom and Mrs. Seville were in the kitchen, and Colin could hear Mrs. Seville complaining, "Why should I care if my stepgrandmother's family wants any of her dishes or not? They didn't even bother coming to the funeral!"

Mom would be busy for a while.

Colin went out the front door and stepped behind an overgrown evergreen that he'd heard Mrs. Seville complain she'd have to have cut down. For now, he was hidden.

Colin took the shoebox back out of the bag of towels.

Now that he was in daylight—shady daylight, anyway—he could see that the shoebox was both green and brown. And it said "Thom McAn's" on the sides. That must have been some shoe company from a billion years ago. He opened the shoebox again and pulled his phone back out of his pocket, ready to start taking pictures. But there had to be at least twenty or thirty envelopes in the box. By the time he opened every envelope and took a picture of every letter, Daryl, Derek, or Deepak—or maybe even Mom—would surely realize he was missing and come and find him.

But how could he just throw away the box without knowing what the rest of the letters said?

Colin glanced back over his shoulder. Through the nearest window, he could see straight through to the kitchen. Mom and Mrs. Seville were both turned away from him. He could see the empty stairway, proving none of the older boys were on their way down with heavy loads of trash of their own.

Colin dropped the bag of towels. Then he took off running toward Mom's SUV. He opened the door and tucked the shoebox under the seat he always sat in.

It fit. Because this was Mom's car, and of course there wasn't any clutter crammed in, blocking the way.

"Just stay out of sight until we get home," he whispered, as if the shoebox had ears and could hear him. Then he felt ridiculous. The shoebox wasn't alive. Neither were the letters it contained.

Colin still couldn't throw them away.

10

Nevaeh's Non-Weekend

Dad was even making everyone work on Saturday.

Nevaeh sat at the breakfast table, hunched over burnt toast. (Whatever Roddy had done to the toaster made it burn everything.) She was primed to snarl at whoever stepped into the kitchen next. Her muscles already ached from five days of carrying heavy boxes and having to stretch up on tiptoes to match Prilla's height and pace when they worked together carrying two-by-fours that could be reused and twisted metal bedframes deemed recyclable and . . . well, Nevaeh couldn't even remember what all else she'd carried with Prilla that week. Her head throbbed because she hadn't gotten enough sleep. It hadn't even been daylight yet when Dad yelled up the stairs, "Kiddos! Everybody up! Our Junk Kingdom awaits!"

Down the hall, Axel and Dalton were huddled with Dad in Dad's office. Nevaeh thought about yelling at her brothers: *Seriously, Ax? Seriously, Dalt? I'm just a kid, so I kind of have to do what Dad tells me. But you're* adults! *You could move out! You could tell Dad you quit! You don't have to do this!*

Axel and Dalton both already had second jobs they worked on the side. Axel was apprenticed to an electrician, and Dalton helped a plumber friend of Dad's whenever the plumber needed a second set of hands around. But all Axel and Dalton ever talked about was how they could grow the Junk King business so they could do that full-time.

Now Axel and Dalton and Dad were talking too loudly. It made Nevaeh's head hurt worse. And it didn't improve the taste of her burnt toast.

"Yeah, we lost a whole morning dealing with the Mongold unit mess," Dad was saying. "Even catching the crook who did that may not help us. And here I thought that was going to be pure windfall. Guess I shouldn't have counted those chickens before they hatched."

Dad . . . didn't sound like Dad.

Normally he was like the Energizer Bunny, bounding from project to project, exploding with joy about how this load of junk a customer had been about to just dump out had actually contained hundreds of dollars' worth of scrap metal. And how that old, falling-down house that the city was just going to bulldoze had actually contained doors and other antique woodwork that Dad had been able to sell to buyers as far away as California. . . . Prilla had found a meme once showing a large, bearded man wearing a pink tutu and ballet shoes and doing the splits in midair. The man's expression had been pure joy. It also held a hint of *Don't you tell me who I'm allowed to be and what I can and can't do!* The meme had cracked up all the Greeveys, because the man looked so much like Dad—just as big-bellied, just as bearded, just as joyful. And just as determined not to care about what anyone else might think. Nevaeh couldn't imagine her father being caught dead in a pink tutu, but the meme-man's attitude about ballet was just like Dad's attitude about junk.

He really did love it.

He really did act like he thought he had the best job in the world.

Had Nevaeh ever heard him sound so discouraged before?

"Dad, I've been over the numbers," Axel was saying. "We can still make this a profitable summer if we double down. If we just catch a break or two, make a few lucky finds, line up some extra contracts . . ."

"Yeah," Dalton agreed. "It's possible. We're already working faster, now that we've got Nevaeh helping us."

Dalton was pretty much Nevaeh's least favorite sibling. Was he actually . . . praising her?

"Yeah, she's a hard worker," Dad said. "All you kids are. I'm a lucky man. And the harder we work—"

"The luckier we get," Axel and Dalton finished in unison. This was one of Dad's favorite sayings. Nevaeh had been hearing it her whole life.

She sat up a little straighter, Dad's words echoing in her head. *She's a hard worker.* Did Dad really think she was doing a good job? It would have helped if he'd just said that directly to her face, but still . . .

Dad thinks I'm doing a good job! Dalton thinks I'm doing a good job! Probably Axel does, too! They need me!

Her muscles ached a little less.

Prilla stumbled into the kitchen. It looked like she was having trouble even getting her eyes to open. Prilla wasn't a morning person. She slumped against the refrigerator as if she needed a moment to gather her strength before walking the rest of the way into the kitchen.

Then she seemed to notice Nevaeh watching her.

"Look," Prilla said, setting her jaw. "I know this is awful, getting up so early on a Saturday morning. It's going to be hot, and that house we're going to probably won't have air-conditioning. But we can't complain. We can't let the *boys* think we're weak."

"I wasn't going to complain," Nevaeh said. She put the last bite of burnt toast in her mouth, chewed, and swallowed.

Prilla did a double take and blinked, wide-eyed now.

"Oh," she said. She gave Nevaeh a weak fist bump. "Then . . . you go, Nevaeh."

Had Prilla *expected* Nevaeh to complain?

It felt too weird to ask. It wasn't like Nevaeh could say,

How do you see me, Prilla? Do you think I'm a hard worker? Do you ever see me as myself, Nevaeh, and not just your little sister?

These were such strange thoughts to have at six a.m. on a summer Saturday. Nevaeh might just as easily ask Prilla, *Would it be possible for a Greevey like me to grow up to be more like Felicia Creedmont? I mean, if she's a good person, after all—not a criminal?*

Nevaeh *really* wasn't going to say that.

For a moment, Nevaeh just stared at her big sister, who had the same brown eyes as Nevaeh did, and the same stubborn chin and the same ponytail-rubber-band indentation in her messy hair and the same kind of worn-threadbare jeans. Then it got weird that Nevaeh was staring at Prilla for so long.

"A word of advice," Nevaeh said, looking back at the black crumbs on her plate. "Don't use the toaster."

"Wasn't planning to," Prilla said. She pulled a can of ravioli from the cupboard and held it up like she was toasting Nevaeh. "Breakfast of champions." She dug in the nearest drawer for the can opener. "You know, Dad acts like if we'd gotten to clear out the Mongold storage unit, we would have been able to afford a new toaster. And a new microwave, a new refrigerator, and new couches for the living room, and—"

"Do *you* think Felicia Creedmont stole everything?" Nevaeh asked.

Prilla shrugged. "Dad'll find out, don't you think? He got his friend at the newspaper looking up old society-page pictures of what the Mongolds' house looked like inside. He's asking his friends at antique stores all over the place to trace certain kinds of furniture, the pieces that were really rare or unique. He'll track down who sold what when."

Nevaeh put her finger down on the flower pattern in the center of her plate. It was a new-old plate, from the set Dad had just added to their cupboards this week. She traced the spiral chain of the flowers, making a matching path through the burnt crumbs she'd scraped off her toast. It could have been a maze for ants, a labyrinth for spiders.

The crook won't be Felicia Creedmont, she told herself. *If Dad's trying to prove she's guilty, then . . . then I've got to prove she's innocent. I've got to be a hard worker at that, too.*

Somehow.

The Start to Colin's Weekend

Mom gave Colin Saturday off.

"You've worked hard all week—go! Be a kid!" she told him after breakfast. "I've got paperwork to catch up on, but I can drive you to meet up with a friend at the park or something like that, if you want. Or do you need me to text Anthony's or Nazeem's mom and let them know you have permission to have a friend over?"

The problem with being twelve, Colin decided, was that adults could never decide if they wanted to treat you like an adult or a five-year-old.

"That's okay," Colin said. "I think I'm just going to hang out."

He went into his bedroom and shut the door. He pulled down the plain blue backpack he'd brought home from school the last day of sixth grade and cleaned out immediately. He'd intended to leave it hanging empty on its hook on the wall the entire summer. But last night while Mom was in the shower, he'd sneaked out to the car and brought in the shoebox he'd smuggled out of Mrs. Seville's inherited attic. And then he'd frantically tried to figure out where to hide it—living in a clutter-free house meant that there was nowhere to hide *any-thing*. He'd resorted to using the backpack because it seemed like the only possible choice. But even then, Colin was sure that Mom would notice how the backpack hung lower on the wall, how it pooched out more than it had the day before.

To avoid having her come into his room, he'd gone to bed early. He'd thought that would give him a chance to ease the shoebox out of the backpack so he could read its letters by his phone flashlight. But he chickened out. What if Mom had seen the light through the crack under his door and come in while he least expected it?

Now he took the backpack to his bed and sat down. He started to unzip the backpack, but turned coward again. What if Mom unexpectedly burst into his room now? She did that sometimes. She'd call out, "Hey, want to make cookies?" or "Want to take a walk?" or "Are you still playing on the laptop? Don't you think you've been staring at a screen long enough?"

How had Colin never noticed before that he didn't have any privacy?

He rezipped the backpack and slid an arm through one of the straps. He went back out to the kitchen.

"I'm going to take a bike ride," he told Mom. "I'm just . . . taking my backpack with me so I can carry snacks and a water bottle."

To make his cover story convincing, he opened the cupboard and pulled out a box of wheat crackers.

"Want to wait until the afternoon, and maybe I'll be done with all this and can go with you?" Mom asked, gesturing at the laptop before her.

No, Mom—I want to be alone!

What he said was, "Oh, I can go again then, if you want."

And then he escaped.

He rode straight to the library and sat at a cubicle in the back, hidden behind a tall shelf full of books. He still looked around three or four times before he dared to pull Rosemary's shoebox out of the backpack, and three or four more times before he lifted the lid.

And still he hesitated. He'd been so concerned about his own privacy—what if reading these letters violated Rosemary's privacy? And Toby's? And whoever else had written these letters?

These letters are old. Probably everyone who wrote and received them has been dead for years. They don't matter to anyone anymore.

Except Colin.

He reached into the box and pulled out the whole stack.

And then he read them straight through, one after the other.

All the letters were from Toby to Rosemary. Every single one.

At first, he read from the top down, but then he realized that that put them in backward order. Some of the letters were dated, and the oldest one was from 1973.

The newest was from 1977.

So these letters were all about fifty years old. Practically a half century had passed since Toby wrote even the last one. It could have been just as long since Rosemary—or somebody else?—had tucked the letters away, hiding them in the attic that would eventually come to belong to Mrs. Seville's grandparents and then Mrs. Seville.

Colin couldn't quite wrap his head around how long ago fifty years was. His mom hadn't even been born yet, fifty years ago.

Colin was halfway through the stack of letters when it occurred to him that if Rosemary and Toby were kids when Toby wrote to Rosemary, that meant they were probably only about sixty now.

Sixty was old, but lots of people made it that far.

Rosemary and Toby probably *were* still alive.

But if these letters meant anything to Toby and Rosemary, they would have kept them. These letters were left behind. They were going to be thrown away. It's not going to hurt anyone if I read them.

Colin looked back at the top letter, the one where Toby begged Rosemary to forgive him.

He had to know what happened.

But the letters talked about things Colin had never heard of. What was Skylab? What was a mood ring? What was a pet rock? (It couldn't just be a rock that people treated like a pet—it wouldn't be that simple, would it?) What was a Sleestak? Who were Mr. Kotter and Vinnie Barbarino? What was the ERA? Colin started out looking things up on his phone, but that took too long. He switched to taking notes on his phone of all the things he didn't understand, to look up later.

Toby seemed to write more letters in the summertime, and it took until the 1974 letters for Colin to understand why: Toby's parents sent him away every summer. Once, Toby wrote, "I wish it didn't cost so much to call long-distance."

Long-distance? Colin thought. *Why would that matter? With a cell phone you can just . . .*

Oh. There probably weren't cell phones way back in 1974.

And then Colin reached the end of the letters, and he still didn't know why Rosemary had started hating Toby or whether she ever forgave him.

"Nooo . . . ," he moaned, shoving the shoebox across the cubicle desk.

He'd accidentally moaned too loudly. A library worker who was reshelving books nearby glanced at him curiously.

She looked older than Mom and had streaks of gray in her hair—for all he knew, *she* could be Rosemary, and she had all the answers he wanted, and he would never find them out.

Colin got up and pretended he needed a drink from the water fountain. He walked past the library worker and glanced at her name tag.

Her name was Linda, not Rosemary.

Colin sat back down.

He looked past the cubicle and the bookshelves to the row of sleek library computers, all in use. They looked strange now—wrong, even. It was almost like the Toby letters had taken Colin back to the 1970s for real, and now he had to readjust to the twenty-first century again.

Reading Toby's letters had made him feel like the 1970s were a different world, not just a different time.

What did Toby say or do, to make Rosemary hate him? Did she ever stop hating him in the past fifty years?

Colin felt like he had that time he'd actually dared to ask Mom, "Um, if I ever wanted to go meet Dad—just to see what he's like, not anything else—would you let me?"

Mom had looked at him for a very, very long time.

Then she'd said, "No. That's not a good idea. You'll have to trust me on this one."

Colin didn't even know where his dad lived.

He didn't know where Rosemary and Toby lived now, either.

Wait a minute. . . .

He dug back through the stack of letters. There. He found the letter with a P.S.:

I'm coming home next week, that's why the return address says Groveview. Don't come over and look for me there, yet! Wait for September! Then we can talk and talk and talk. . . .

Colin never wrote letters. He could barely remember what a return address was. But didn't that mean the address on the outside of the envelope that wasn't Rosemary's would be the one where Toby had lived in 1975?

It was 895 Willow Street. In Groveview.

Toby might still live in that same house, Colin thought. *Or his parents or some other relative might . . .*

It wasn't as though Colin would have the courage to go up to the door and knock. That wasn't a smart thing to do, anyhow—kids weren't supposed to talk to strangers.

Colin started to stuff the letter back into the envelope from nearly fifty years ago. But he hadn't folded it right this time, and it wouldn't go in straight.

Oh. That was because there was another page Colin hadn't noticed before. It was only a half sheet, where Toby had added a second P.S. And this one said:

I'm going to be like you and hide all my letters,
too, when I get home. Remember when we
figured out that we had a loose floorboard
in the exact same place in both of our attics?
(I mean, mine was loose after we used the
crowbar. . . . But I'm not telling if you don't tell.)
Remember when we used to hide treasures
there? That's where I'm going to keep your
letters. Just like you're keeping my letters in
your attic.

Toby had hidden Rosemary's letters in his attic, just the
same as she'd hidden his in her attic. Toby's letters had still
been in Rosemary's attic fifty years later.

Would Rosemary's letters to Toby still be in his attic?

Colin looked at the address again: 895 Willow. He looked
it up on his phone. It was only ten blocks from the library.

*I'll just go and look at the house. I can at least find out
if the house is still there.*

He shoved all the letters back into the shoebox and the
shoebox back into the backpack. Back on his bike outside,
he started breathing hard even before he'd gone one block.

He really, really, really wanted Toby's house to still be there.

Three blocks from the library, the houses all looked too
new to have been built before the 1970s. But then he turned
a corner, and the houses looked older again.

Five more blocks, and he was turning onto Willow.

Looking around at all the houses, he almost ran into a huge truck that said "JUNK KING" on the side.

A girl about Colin's age was walking down the sidewalk toward the truck. She carried two huge bags with handles. While Colin skidded the heels of his sneakers against the pavement to stop his bike, the girl hoisted the bags into the back of the truck. A brown shoebox slid off the top of one of the bags just as she let go.

A shoebox.

A *brown* shoebox.

The girl frowned at the shoebox and puffed out her cheeks to let out an exasperated sigh. The burst of air blew her thick, blondish-brown hair back from her face. She snatched up the box from the floor of the truck bed and reared her arm back like she was just going to throw it toward the boxes and bags heaped at the other end of the truck bed.

Colin dropped his bike and ran over and jumped in between the girl and the truck.

"Stop!" he yelled. "Don't throw that away! It's important!"

12

Nevaeh the Bold

Nevaeh stared at the boy who'd suddenly appeared in front of her. Where had he even come from?

Then his words registered. The shoebox in her hand was *important*?

"What—do you collect grocery receipts from five years ago?" she asked. The guy whose house her family was clearing out had been a total pack rat. It seemed like he'd kept every piece of paper anyone had ever given him. Dad, of course, thought that was great, because, as he put it, "That means he must have saved something valuable at some point!" But all morning Nevaeh had been carrying out bags and boxes full of junk that decidedly wasn't valuable.

"Grocery receipts? No—just let me look. . . ." The boy in front of her was practically begging.

Nevaeh thought about how many sayings Dad had about people acting crazy about possessions. She'd never quite believed them until now.

"Be my guest," she said with a shrug.

She flipped the lid of the shoebox off and hurled the lid into the truck. It spun and cartwheeled end over end before landing perfectly at the top of the pile—maybe Nevaeh was showing off a little. Then she held out the rest of the shoebox toward the boy as if she were offering him a box of chocolates.

One of the thin papers from the box started to blow away, and Nevaeh caught it in midair.

"So," she said. "Looks like ground beef and potato chips were both on sale at Kroger on July third, five years ago."

"That's just what's on top," the boy in front of her insisted. "Rosemary's letters could be—"

Nevaeh dumped the whole shoebox into the sack it had fallen out of. One grocery store receipt after another fluttered down.

The boy rocked back on his heels.

"That whole bag is shoeboxes," he said. "I'm being stupid. The letters could be in any . . ."

He glanced back at the house where Nevaeh had been working all morning. Axel and Dalton walked out carrying a giant mirror. The boy stepped back, as if afraid of getting in their way. But of course Axel and Dalton were going to the other Junk King truck, the one they'd parked in the driveway to hold things that were actually valuable.

The boy looked like he really wanted to run away. But he

peeked into the bag of shoeboxes again.

"Did any of these come out of the attic?" he asked. "Anywhere *hidden* in the attic? Like . . . under a floorboard?"

Nevaeh looked at the boy in front of her a little more closely. He had short, dark, curly hair, and dark eyes that still looked like they were begging. Some of Nevaeh's friends at school had gotten really interested in boys this past year (though Prilla had told Nevaeh, "Sixth-grade boys? Don't bother."). Nevaeh could hear Stella or Cicely or Ava's opinion in her head—all of them would tell her, "He's *cute*." And that was true. But there was something else about this boy, something that made Nevaeh think that she'd met him before.

Something that made her think she already liked him.

Even if he was acting crazy.

"We've got enough junk to clear out of that house that's just lying around in plain sight," Nevaeh said. "We are *not* prying up floorboards in the attic looking for more garbage."

The boy raised his eyebrows, which made him look hopeful again.

"Then the letters could still be there," he said, peering back toward the house again. It was a gray two-story, and as simple as something a little kid would draw with a triangle on top of a square. The boy seemed to be staring at the roofline, and his expression squeezed into a puzzled squint. "But there's no alcove and . . ." He dropped his gaze toward the house number beside the front door. "Wait a minute. That's not the right house."

"Of course it's the right house," Nevaeh began indignantly. "We've been here for hours. You're not going to tell me we've been cleaning out the wrong house all along, and—"

The boy was peering farther down the block.

"You mean *you* have the wrong house," Nevaeh said. "You mean it's some other house where there are these mysterious letters you're looking for hidden in a shoebox under a floorboard in the attic." Nevaeh looked up and down the street, too. "Which house is it?"

The boy backed away from her.

"Never mind," he said. "Forget it."

He tripped over a bike someone had left lying in the street—the boy himself, maybe? Nevaeh grabbed his arm so he wouldn't fall. The boy's face flushed with embarrassment, which he covered with a smile so quickly that it was like he'd put on a mask.

"Thanks," he mumbled.

But Nevaeh stared. Because suddenly she understood why he looked so familiar. And why she already felt like she liked him.

"Are you . . ." She cleared her throat. "Are you related to Felicia Creedmont?"

13

The Discovery

"Um. Yes?" Colin hated himself for making it sound like he wasn't sure.

"I knew it!" The girl was watching him now as if he were some sort of celebrity, and she was only a minute away from asking for his autograph. She pointed to herself. "Nevaeh Greevey."

"Oh. I'm Colin. Colin Creedmont. Felicia's my mom."

Colin swept his gaze toward the two Junk King trucks behind Nevaeh. She'd hoisted the bags of garbage as effortlessly as if she'd been working in junk removal her whole life, but she didn't look any older than him. Was she maybe related to the Junk King? Like, possibly, his daughter?

Colin thought about how much his mother despised the Junk King, and how she never said his name as much as she spit it out like it tasted bad in her mouth.

Colin was, essentially, in enemy territory. He'd been too focused on the shoebox and the letters to really think about that before. But Mom and the Junk King were practically like the Hatfields and the McCoys: feuding families.

Did that make him and Nevaeh like Romeo and Juliet?

Colin did not feel like dropping to his knee and shouting up to Nevaeh on some balcony while she shouted back, "Romeo, Romeo, wherefore art thou Romeo?"

He felt more like melting into the pavement in embarrassment.

"Okay, uh, sorry I bothered you," Colin said. "Sorry I had the wrong house."

He turned to go—hopefully without tripping over his own bike this time. But Nevaeh was still holding on to his arm.

"I could help you," she said. "You're looking for letters hidden in someone's attic? In one of the houses on this street?"

"The letters may not even be there anymore," Colin said. "They're from fifty years ago. Anyway, it's not like I could just knock on someone's door and talk them into—"

"Why not?" Nevaeh asked. "*I* could."

How crazy was this? Colin almost believed her.

The two guys beside the other Junk King truck were watching him and Nevaeh. They had the same blondish-brown hair, the same dark eyes, the same kind of muscular build as she did—were they maybe her brothers? Or cousins?

"Nevaeh, there are still a lot of bags left in that back

bedroom," the taller of the two called to her. "Tell your friend to come back after you're done."

Colin saw Nevaeh roll her eyes, but her brother or cousin was probably too far away to get the full effect.

"I'm taking my lunch break now, *Axel*," Nevaeh said. "I'll get the rest of the bags after lunch."

"You aren't eating," the other guy said.

"That's because my *friend* and I have an errand to do first, and then I'll eat," Nevaeh said. "I'll just eat fast." She tugged on Colin's arm and muttered to him, "Do you have older brothers who try to run your life?" Before Colin could answer, she added, "And please tell me the house you're looking for is in this direction, because I am not turning around and walking the other way while Axel and Dalt are watching."

"Uh, right," Colin said. "It is." He craned his neck to stare at house numbers. They passed six houses, and then he froze in place. "It's 895. This one."

The house in front of them was yellow with brown shutters, and much smaller than the one where Colin had found the Toby letters. But its layout seemed familiar, with a wing that jutted out beside the front walk. That made Colin think of someone hiding his face with an arm—someone keeping secrets.

But wouldn't that extra wing also mean that the attic

would have a section branching off to the side? Just like back at Rosemary's house?

"My dad says almost all the houses on this street have turned over in the past few years—older people moving away, younger people moving in and fixing them up," Nevaeh said. "He's cleaned out a lot of them. And I think this one . . ."

Nevaeh didn't even bother finishing her sentence. She just walked up the front walk and rang the doorbell at 895 Willow.

Colin really felt like running away. But he scrambled up onto the concrete porch alongside Nevaeh.

Colin could hear someone crying deep inside the house. The cries seemed to be getting closer and closer.

"This probably isn't a good time to—" he began, tugging on the sleeve of Nevaeh's T-shirt.

But then the door opened. A harried-looking woman stood there, holding a baby in each arm. One of the babies was sleeping. The other blinked in the sudden sunlight, mouth open, as if the next wail was startled right out of him.

"Oh, thank goodness!" the woman said. "This is the first time he's stopped crying all morning! Whatever you're selling, I'll buy it . . . Oh, wait. You're Nevaeh, right?"

"Mrs. Torres?"

"You know each other?" Colin asked incredulously. "You knew all along whose house this is?"

"Everybody knows the Greeveys," Mrs. Torres said.

"My sister babysat for Mrs. Torres once," Nevaeh explained. "I helped."

"It was when these rascals were newborns and I was desperate to get out of the house," Mrs. Torres added. "And I was so grateful Prilla and Nevaeh both came, because, you know, double trouble." She held the babies up higher, as if maybe Colin hadn't noticed there were two of them. "Nevaeh, I thought those were your family's trucks down the block, and I was going to come down and say hello just as soon as things quieted down."

"But your sons are practicing to be opera singers," Nevaeh said.

"You remember," Mrs. Torres said, making a face. "Listen, my mom's healed from her back surgery now, so I won't need a babysitter anytime soon—not one I can pay, I mean. But if you want me to put a good word in with any of my friends, then—"

"This isn't about babysitting," Nevaeh said, looking pointedly at Colin.

Was that the cue for Colin to explain what he wanted? He couldn't. He just stood there, as open-mouthed and gawping as the baby.

He could almost see Nevaeh wanting to roll her eyes at him, but deciding not to.

"So my friend Colin here thinks someone left something

hidden in your attic fifty years ago," Nevaeh said. "I know this sounds kind of weird, but we wondered if you would mind letting us come in to look."

Colin half expected Mrs. Torres to slam the door in their faces, but she didn't do that. She just looked puzzled for a few seconds. Then she grinned.

"If you find a hidden treasure that would let us start a college fund for these boys, I'd love you forever," Mrs. Torres said. "Heck, if there's a hidden treasure that could help us pay for diapers, I'd still jump for joy."

"It's just old letters," Colin said. "Not a treasure. I mean, not as far as I know."

"This is still the most interesting thing that's happened to me all day," Mrs. Torres said. "Come on in."

She nudged the door open farther.

It was that easy?

Colin followed Nevaeh into the house. Mrs. Torres was explaining that there was a pull-down ladder on the second-floor landing to get to the attic, and she'd help, but she really needed to put the babies down for their nap. . . .

"I can't believe the right house was the one where you knew someone!" Colin hissed as Nevaeh climbed the stairs ahead of him and then reached for the string for the pull-down ladder. "And she trusts you!"

Nevaeh shrugged.

"I would have known someone in almost any of these houses," she said. "Or they would have known my dad, anyway. Because of his job. Isn't it like that with your mom and what she does?"

"Uh, no?" Colin said, and again, it sounded like he wasn't sure.

He remembered what Mrs. Torres had said: *Everybody knows the Greeveys.* Why wasn't it also *Everybody knows the Creedmonts?*

Then he pushed that thought aside and focused on climbing up to the attic behind Nevaeh.

Mrs. Torres's attic was neater than any of the ones Colin had cleaned the past week. But he could see it aspiring to clutter—boxes marked "baby swing" and "twins' newborn clothes" clustered near the stairs.

The section at the front of the house was empty and open.

"Please tell me we're not going to have to pry up every floorboard," Nevaeh said. "I don't think Mrs. Torres would be happy about us hammering all the nails back into place afterward and waking up the twins."

"Just one floorboard," Colin said. "Over here . . ."

He headed toward the open section, hunching over where the roof slanted down above him.

One of the floorboards rocked slightly beneath his feet.

Colin bent down and turned on his phone flashlight.

This floorboard was already missing its nails at one end. It had nail holes in the right places, as if there had once been nails holding the board in place, but they were gone now.

"I think," Colin whispered. "I think . . ."

Nevaeh rushed to his side.

Colin tried to dig his fingers under the floorboard to lift it, but fifty years of hot summers and cold winters—if it really had been fifty years—had warped the board too much. It didn't budge. He remembered the line from Toby's letters about how the floorboard in his attic only came loose after he and Rosemary had used a crowbar on it.

Maybe that hadn't been a joke.

"Next time we go treasure-hunting in people's attics, maybe we should bring tools," Nevaeh muttered.

"I—didn't—really—expect . . ." Colin grunted as he kept trying to lift the floorboard.

Nevaeh wandered away. Moments later, she came back with a curved strip of metal.

"Luckily, I know how to take apart old Christmas tree stands," Nevaeh said.

She slid the edge of the metal strip between the warped floorboard and the one next to it. She leaned hard on the other end of the metal. The floorboard groaned—and gave way.

His hands shaking, Colin picked up his phone again and

directed the light below the floorboard. The circle of light landed on something red.

No—not just "something."

Red cardboard.

Red cardboard with a white Nike Swoosh.

This was another shoebox.

14

Nevaeh and the Shoebox

"Has Nike really been using the same kind of boxes for the past fifty years?" Nevaeh asked, peering beneath the floorboard alongside Colin.

Dad would be all over a question like that—he *loved* finding out about old corporate logos, especially if it gave him a good paycheck. Normally Nevaeh would have said the whole topic bored her to tears. But she did want to know if this really was the box Colin was looking for.

She also wanted to know why he'd been looking for it.

She'd kind of been showing off all along—this was someone connected to Felicia Creedmont! He was the *son* of Nevaeh's idol! And he wanted a way into an attic? He wanted to see beneath a particular floorboard? Sure, she could help. No problem.

It was what Greeveys did, anyhow. Greeveys *believed* in helping.

And maybe it would lead to Nevaeh clearing Felicia

Creedmont's name with her family. Maybe it would lead to Nevaeh actually meeting Felicia Creedmont.

But if someone had gone to the trouble of hiding a box under a floorboard fifty years ago and just left it there, and if Colin had somehow found out about it and cared enough to go into a stranger's house looking for it . . . how could Nevaeh *not* wonder what this was all about?

Nevaeh hated junk. She'd always thought that also meant she hated old things.

But she *had* to know what was in this box.

Colin lifted the box out of the hole they'd revealed beneath the floorboard. He handled it the way someone might carry a wounded bird. Or, actually, the way Dad handled any junk he thought he could resell.

"This has to be the right box," Colin whispered, practically sounding reverent.

He cradled it against his chest just as protectively as Mrs. Torres had cradled her babies.

He doesn't want me to see what's in it, Nevaeh thought. *After I got him in here, after I'm the one who actually pried up the floorboard . . .*

"Oh, no," Nevaeh said. "We can't go back down that ladder until we know for sure we have the right box. You think Mrs. Torres is going to let us traipse through her attic again and again and again?"

Colin winced as if she'd made a truly painful request—like *Hey, how about you let me throw your cell phone out the window?* For a second, he even looked like he might break away and run for the ladder.

But then he laid the box down and slid off the lid.

This time, Nevaeh was the one who switched on her phone flashlight.

A paper slipped out of the box alongside the lid. Nevaeh directed the beam of her flashlight to follow the paper. Her heart beat a little faster, as if she was present at the opening of King Tut's tomb, or with the farmer who uncovered the first of the terra-cotta warriors in China, or . . .

Dad really has made me watch too many of those Amazing Discoveries of History *shows on TV,* she thought. *This is just a shoebox. That's all.*

Then she saw what was written on the paper:

YOU'RE WRONG!
I am never speaking to you again.
P.S. I won't read any of your letters anymore, either. So stop writing.

"It's the right box," Colin said.

15

Colin's Deal

Colin just wanted to get away. He wanted to stuff the shoebox of Rosemary letters into his backpack alongside the shoebox of Toby letters. And then he wanted to go somewhere to read every single letter he could see stacked in the Nike box. He wanted to match them up with the letters he'd found at Rosemary's house, and read the conversation between Rosemary and Toby, back and forth and back and forth.

And he wanted to do that alone.

In private.

Without Nevaeh.

But Colin was a polite kid. And Nevaeh had helped him. He couldn't just *leave*.

"So, um, thanks," he said. "I never would have found these letters without you. Thank you for using part of your lunch break to help me. I don't want you to miss your actual lunch because of me. Or have your brothers get mad at you. We can just go and thank Mrs. Torres, too, and then—"

"And then we read the letters," Nevaeh said. "*Both* of us read the letters."

How could Colin stop her without just snatching the box and running away?

Mrs. Torres's head appeared at the top of the attic ladder.

"Okay, both boys are asleep now, so I can help you look," she said. "Just be really quiet over in that corner, because I swear, a pin drop could wake up Nathan, and—"

In one smooth move, Nevaeh grabbed the shoebox and its lid—and even the letter that had fallen out. Before Colin could so much as cry *Wait!* she was already carrying the box over to Mrs. Torres.

"Oh, we already found it," Nevaeh said. "Look."

And now Colin couldn't even scream, *No! Don't!* Because he was standing in the corner where Mrs. Torres wanted them to be quiet.

He tiptoe-ran after Nevaeh.

"I—I really don't think it's anything that's going to matter to anyone except me," he said.

Nevaeh ignored him. She crouched down beside Mrs. Torres and began showing her the box.

"See? Look at the postmarks on these letters," she said, riffling through the stack in the box. "Here's one from 1975. This one's 1974. And so on. These are really old!"

"And you know how they got under a floorboard in my

house?" Mrs. Torres asked.

"A kid named Toby lived here back in the 1970s," Colin said. "He hid his 'treasures' in your attic. Then I don't know if he forgot them, or if he just didn't want them anymore, or . . ."

"But, sorry, I don't think any of these letters actually do contain any treasure," Nevaeh said sadly. She lifted the whole stack of letters, as if there was a chance precious gems or gold bullion were hidden below. "Oh, wait. Maybe . . ."

"What did you find?" he called even as Mrs. Torres asked, "What is it?"

Now Nevaeh was squeezing each letter in turn. And then she pulled out . . .

A quarter. One that didn't even look real.

"You said you were hoping for diaper money," she told Mrs. Torres a little ruefully.

"I wasn't really expecting it," Mrs. Torres said. She brushed the hair back from her forehead. Colin could feel the air-conditioning seeping up from below into the hot attic, and Mrs. Torres seemed to be noticing the temperature difference, too. "Look, you kids can keep the quarter. I'd like to know what those letters say, but let's be honest here. Since the twins arrived, I've barely even had time to read text messages. Even the ones that are just a single emoji. And I really need a nap right now, since I have the miracle of both babies sleeping at the same time, and—"

"Got it," Nevaeh said. "We'll get out of here. Thank you so much for letting us in to look for these. We'll come back sometime after we've read these letters and let you know what they say."

"Especially if they provide any explanation for the weird wallpaper in our dining room—and why it was apparently put up with Elmer's glue," Mrs. Torres said. She was already backing down the ladder, and Nevaeh followed her, still clutching the box of letters.

Colin could do nothing but follow along.

Mrs. Torres led the two kids back to the front door.

"Nice to meet you," she told Colin, and Colin jumped, because he'd been letting Nevaeh do all the talking.

"Oh, yes, you, too," he said. "Thank you."

There was an awkward moment, and then Nevaeh said, "You know, we really do owe you. How about if Colin and I come back sometime and babysit for a couple hours for free to repay you?"

"I don't—" Colin began. He'd never held a baby in his life. Nevaeh dug an elbow into his side.

"What Colin's trying to say is, yeah, we know we're kind of young for babysitting. We can do it more as a 'mother's helper' kind of situation, if you want." Nevaeh completely talked over him. "We can watch the babies while you're just in the next room, taking a break."

"That . . . would be amazing," Mrs. Torres said. She practically had tears in her eyes. "Could it be a Tuesday night? My husband always has to work late those nights, and my mom has church choir practice, and—"

"How about this coming Tuesday?" Nevaeh said. "Six o'clock? I'll get your number from Prilla and text you, so you can reach me if you want to change the time."

"This . . . this is better than any treasure you might have found in my attic," Mrs. Torres said.

And then she stunned Colin by giving him and Nevaeh both a hug.

"Have a good nap!" Nevaeh told Mrs. Torres as they walked out the door.

Colin barely managed to wait until Mrs. Torres went back into her house and shut the door before he spun toward Nevaeh and protested, "I don't know how to babysit!"

"I'll teach you," Nevaeh said. She lowered her voice. "Don't you want another chance to get back into that house, in case there are *other* letters you might want to look for?"

Colin's jaw dropped.

"You were just scamming her!" he accused.

"No, she really does need help," Nevaeh said. She glanced over her shoulder, then tugged on Colin's arm, pulling him toward the sidewalk. "That's one frazzled new mom. And her babies really did scream the whole time Prilla and I were there. So you and I are going to pay big-time for these letters."

She held up the red Nike box as if Colin might have forgotten about them.

Once again, Colin had to resist the urge to snatch the box out of her hands and take off running.

"Why do you care?" Colin asked. "Why would you sacrifice two or three hours of having to listen to babies scream—and having to teach me how to babysit—for a box of letters you don't know anything about?"

For the first time since he'd met her, Nevaeh seemed briefly at a loss for words. She wrinkled her brow. She opened her mouth, and then she shut it. She wiped sweat from her forehead before trying again.

"Maybe I'm like Mrs. Torres," she said. "Maybe finding these letters is the most interesting thing that's happened to me all day, too."

Why did it feel like she was lying? Or at least not telling the whole truth?

But how could Colin call her out on that after she'd helped him so much?

"You know. I don't actually care about five-year-old grocery receipts," Nevaeh added. Then she had to point at the Junk King trucks ahead of them for Colin to remember the boxes she'd been dealing with earlier.

"Right," Colin said. He reached for the Nike box. "Well,

after I read these letters, I'll tell both you and Mrs. Torres if I find anything you'd be interested in."

"Oh, no," Nevaeh said, actually swinging the box to the side, out of Colin's reach. "You shouldn't have to do everything by yourself." She smiled sweetly, the same way she had when she offered to babysit for Mrs. Torres. "We'll split the letters in half. I'll start reading my half during the rest of my lunch break. We can trade off when we meet back here on Tuesday."

Nevaeh was already pulling the top half of the letters out of the box.

Colin wanted to scream, *No! That's the half I'm most interested in!* He wanted to protest, *But you didn't read the Toby letters first! You don't know anything about Rosemary and Toby! You don't have any right to those letters!*

He didn't have any right to the letters, either.

He did the same move Nevaeh had done a moment earlier: opening his mouth, shutting it, opening it once more.

He glanced toward the Junk King trucks again. Nevaeh's older brothers—Axel and Dalt?—were taking their lunch break now, their legs dangling off the end of one of the trucks as they pulled containers out of a big cooler. A boy who looked a lot like them except for having a shaved head was crouched down by the cooler, too, alongside a girl who looked like an older version of Nevaeh. And a heavyset man who Colin recognized from TV commercials as the Junk

King himself was pacing beside the truck, saying excitedly into a cell phone, "Yes, we're ahead of schedule, so we'll be there first thing Monday. . . ."

None of them were looking toward Colin and Nevaeh. But Colin felt outnumbered anyhow. Nevaeh had a whole family behind her. She had *Everybody knows the Greeveys*; she had *I would have known someone in almost any of these houses*.

Colin swallowed hard.

"Okay," he said. "See you Tuesday."

16

Nevaeh and the Rosemary Letters

Nevaeh had Colin Creedmont's phone number now. And he had hers. They'd had to exchange numbers so they could make arrangements for both the babysitting and the letter handoff.

Am I a genius or what? Nevaeh wondered.

She felt a little silly about her glee. She was acting like some of the girls Prilla told her about, the ones who made Prilla shake her head and mutter, "If they only had brothers like we do, Nevaeh, they wouldn't go all googly-eyed every time some boy looks at them. Boys aren't *gods*."

But Nevaeh wasn't excited about having Colin's number because she was in *love*. It was because he was connected to Felicia Creedmont. Maybe he'd invite Nevaeh over to his house, and she'd get to see that perfect living room for herself. Maybe he'd introduce Nevaeh to his mom, and Nevaeh could tell her . . .

What would I tell her? "I want to be you when I grow up"? "I think you're right about how people should arrange their houses, and my dad is totally wrong"?

Nevaeh felt disloyal even thinking that.

Would I warn her that Dad thinks she stole everything from the Mongold storage unit almost thirteen years ago? Why? So she could run away before Dad's friend the sheriff arrests her?

Nevaeh decided she was being ridiculous.

She tucked her portion of the letters under her seat in the truck and went to grab a sandwich from the cooler while there were still some left.

"Who was your little friend, Nevaeh?" Dalton asked through a mouthful of peanut butter.

"'Little'?" Nevaeh repeated, totally deflecting. "He's almost as tall as you!"

Dalton was sensitive about being the shortest of the three Greevey brothers.

"Boundaries, Dalton," Prilla said, giving him a slug in the arm. "Nevaeh doesn't have to get your permission for everyone she hangs out with. Not unless you want *us* to start vetting your next girlfriend."

"*Next?*" Nevaeh asked. "Oh, Dalton. Did Sadie dump you?"

"By text," Roddy said. "Ten minutes ago."

"We're just on a break," Dalton said. But his lower lip trembled.

Nevaeh slung her arm around Dalton's shoulders.

"Oh, Dalton," she said again. "Sadie's gone crazy. She'll come to her senses."

"You hurt one Greevey, you've got to answer to all of us," Axel said fiercely.

Nevaeh leaned against Dalton's right side, while Prilla propped him up on the left. Roddy and Axel leaned in, too. One for all, and all for one—it was like the Greevey kids were the five musketeers.

Nevaeh sniffed, getting a whiff of how much five Greeveys could stink after working in an un-air-conditioned house all morning.

Oh no, Nevaeh thought. *Did I stink this bad all by myself, when I was with Colin Creedmont?*

She had the impression that somehow, magically, Felicia Creedmont wouldn't sweat.

The rest of the day felt interminable, but finally the house was emptied out and the Greeveys could just go home. Nevaeh waited until everyone else was out of the truck before she slipped the letters from Mrs. Torres's house out from under her seat. She hid them under her T-shirt as she tiptoed up to her room. But Prilla was sprawled across her bed, watching something on her phone while she waited for her turn in the shower. Every other room in the house felt too open and public and occupied, too. Was there nowhere Nevaeh could go to read the letters in private?

She finally ended up walking out to the barn where Dad kept furniture he hadn't sold yet. She felt like Goldilocks sitting on one couch or overstuffed chair after another: too hard, too soft, too deep in a dark corner, too close to the glaring sunlight. . . . Eventually she settled into a cozy love seat that Dad had probably forgotten about—it was that far back in the barn. The love seat was mauve, which probably meant that it was nearly as old as the letters clutched in her hands—Dad said that mauve was the color of the 1980s and early '90s, while practically everything in the 1970s had been harvest gold or avocado green.

Does Felicia Creedmont force Colin to know useless information like that? Nevaeh wondered.

She thought about texting him to ask, but he'd probably think that was a strange question out of the blue.

Or he'd just demand his letters back.

Nevaeh dropped her phone, put her head back on the arm of the love seat, and started reading.

The first letter she opened was dated December 27, 1975, and it began:

Dear Toby,

How was Christmas at your grandparents'? Did you hear the news? Girls are going to be allowed to play Little League now!!!! We can be on the same team! I bet by the time we're grown up, women will be allowed on professional baseball teams, too. I'm going to be the first female pitcher for the Cincinnati Reds. You'll see. Want to be my catcher?

Huh, Nevaeh thought.

This Rosemary kid had to be grown up by now, and no, as far as Nevaeh knew, women weren't allowed to be on professional baseball teams with men.

It made her kind of sad for Rosemary, as if she was still some naïve little kid, and Nevaeh was older and wiser.

I know Rosemary's future, Nevaeh thought.

Except, that wasn't really true, either. Nevaeh knew what *hadn't* happened for Rosemary. But she didn't know what *had* happened to her.

She kept reading.

She was only on the second letter when she started thinking that she and Rosemary would be BFFs if they'd been kids at the same time. Rosemary was funny and feisty and all about what she called "women's lib." Which meant . . . (Nevaeh had to google it on her phone) liberation? Was it like women were prisoners back in the 1970s? Nevaeh googled that, too. Women didn't used to be able to get their own credit cards, only with their husbands' or fathers' permission. Employers could say they didn't want any women to apply for a particular job, only men. In the 1970s, a woman had been fired for not making coffee for the men in her office.

"No way," Nevaeh muttered.

In the third letter, Rosemary had a whole paragraph about how stupid it was that married women were referred to as "Mrs. John Smith," instead of by their own name.

Did that really happen? Nevaeh wondered. She peered at Rosemary's next words:

When I'm grown up and famous, people are still going to know me as "Rosemary," not "Mrs. Whatever." Everybody will know my name. My real one.

Just then, a band of light flashed across Nevaeh's eyes, temporarily blinding her. Someone had opened the door at the front of the barn.

"What did you want to tell me that you needed this much privacy?"

Mom's voice. Definitely not talking to Nevaeh, since Nevaeh was so far back in the barn, and hidden behind so many couches and chairs.

Should Nevaeh pop up her head and say, *Oh, hey—no privacy here! I'm listening!*?

While she was still deciding, she heard Dad say, "It's about Felicia Creedmont and the Mongold unit."

Nevaeh slid her head down, pressing her face flat against the love seat cushions. Mom and Dad wouldn't be able to see her now unless they were standing right beside her. And they were still far across the barn.

"That nonsense again?" Mom asked. "Lloyd, you're being ridiculous. And sexist! Felicia didn't steal all the Mongold antiques and sell them to start her business! It *is* possible for a woman to build a successful business on her own, without cheating!"

Of course that's possible! Nevaeh thought. *Of course that's what Felicia Creedmont did!*

But because she'd just been reading Rosemary's letters from nearly fifty years ago, she heard Mom's words a little differently.

We may not have female pitchers for the Reds yet, but all that other stuff has changed for females since the 1970s, she told herself. *Hasn't it?*

"You've gotten Axel and Dalton so fired up about this, I'm worried they're going to go all vigilante on her, and do something really stupid," Mom was saying. "Remember what a hothead *you* could be at their ages?"

"I remember a certain girl who was a real spitfire back then, too," Dad teased.

Ugh, ugh, ugh. If Mom and Dad were going to get all flirty like that, Nevaeh really would have to stop listening.

Fortunately, Dad's next words were serious.

"That's why I'm telling you this, not them," Dad said. "Nothing's going to happen until there's proof. But we're on the road to proof. Proof's coming. That one-of-a-kind table I told you was in the Mongolds' foyer? It's been located."

"So?" Mom said. "That only proves *someone* sold it at some point since 1989. You're not going to find Felicia's fingerprints on this, Lloyd!"

"Why do I feel like you're rooting for her, not me?" Dad asked. And even though Nevaeh had her head down and was far across the barn from Mom and Dad, she could totally picture how Dad must have looked, saying that. He had a mock-pout he put on when he thought anyone else in the family was being unfair—when he wanted to pretend to be a powerless victim, not the one in charge. He let his jowls droop, his eyebrows sag . . . Nevaeh didn't know how he did it, but he could make even his beard look sad. When Nevaeh was little, that look would always make her fly to his side and throw her arms around him and promise, "Daddy! I'm sorry! I'll do whatever you want! I'll help you feel better!"

She braced herself for Mom to go all gushy again. To be like little-girl Nevaeh, and vow to do whatever she could to make Dad happy again.

But instead, Mom countered, "Why can't I root for you both? Why can't I want both of you to succeed?"

"Brutal facts." Dad wasn't pretending anything now. This wasn't how he ever talked to the kids. "When the economy's bad, people aren't as likely to pay for junk removal of any kind. Groveview's not big enough for that woman and me to both stay in business."

Nevaeh didn't hear what Mom said next. Nevaeh was too busy scrambling away. She rolled down to the floor and crawled between the couches and chairs to the hole in the siding at the back of the barn where it was possible to sneak out. That hole had made Nevaeh a champion of hide-and-seek games in the barn when she was little—it had taken her friends a long time to realize it was there.

But she needed this escape now. She couldn't stay here listening to Mom and Dad. Not if they were going to sound so grim.

Not if what they said made it impossible for *Nevaeh* to be loyal to Dad and Felicia Creedmont, both.

Nevaeh squeezed out through the hole at the back of the barn, scraping her arm on one of the old beams. The hole was a tighter fit than it had been when she was eight or nine. Once outside, she stood for a minute with her back against the barn wall, listening in case Mom or Dad had heard her and shouted out, "Who was that? Is someone there?"

But no shout came. Their voices now were only a distant, indecipherable murmur.

Nevaeh gulped in air as though she'd done something much more strenuous than crawl.

She looked down at the Rosemary letters she still clutched in her hands. The late-day sunlight caught them, making Rosemary's childish handwriting glow. It felt like a trick of the eye, as though Nevaeh could literally see the exuberance of that girl from so long ago who was so excited about her future.

I'm loyal to you, too, Rosemary, Nevaeh thought.

17

Colin and the Rosemary Letters

What could possibly have happened to make Rosemary stop speaking to Toby? Colin wondered. *They were such good friends!*

He was back at the library, back in his same cubicle. He'd texted Mom to say his bike ride was taking longer than expected, so he wouldn't be back in time for lunch.

Don't worry, he'd written. I have snacks.

And Mom had written back, That's okay. My paperwork's taking forever. I won't be done until 4 or 5. Enjoy the bike ride for me!

So he had hours to read through his portion of the Rosemary letters. He'd read them all, and then he'd sorted them by date and placed them in between the Toby letters, in order. Then he read everything all over again, the back-and-forth between Toby and Rosemary, Rosemary and Toby, the entire conversation.

Some spots made him laugh, and some spots made him

add to his long, long list of things about the 1970s that he needed to look up.

But mostly, the Toby and Rosemary letters made him jealous.

Reading their letters was like stepping into a river of friendship, a bubbling, frolicking torrent of inside jokes and longing comments like "I wish you were here" and "I really wanted to know what you thought." The letters held so many shared ideas and plans, hopes and fears and reassurances. They were full of scrawled "I couldn't wait to tell you . . ." and "You should have seen . . ."

Colin had never had a friendship like that.

The most he'd ever written to his friends were text messages, and usually those were just "ok" or some goofy emoji.

Even when he and his friends talked, it was usually just "Hey" or "Are you playing Fortnite tonight?" or "What'd the teacher say we're supposed to do for math?"

Toby and Rosemary had whole conversations in their letters. It was so much easier to see, having Rosemary's letters, too.

Some of Rosemary's letters, anyway.

Nevaeh had the letters he really wanted to see, the ones that must have led up to Rosemary vowing to never speak to Toby again.

Colin had to know what had happened, how two kids who were such good friends had stopped speaking.

He read back through the letters one more time, but he saw no clues, no hint whatsoever of why Rosemary would eventually give up on Toby.

But she never threw away his letters, Colin reminded himself. *Toby never threw away hers.*

No, they both just abandoned the letters in attics where they wouldn't be discovered for nearly fifty years.

"This library will be closing in ten minutes," he heard over the public address system. "Please take your library materials to the checkout counter now."

How had it gotten so late?

Colin had nothing to check out, but he sorted the letters back into a Toby pile and a Rosemary pile, and returned them to their original boxes. Then he hid them again in his backpack and left the library.

Back at home, he parked his bike in the shed in the back-yard and silently eased open the back door into the house. If he was lucky, he could hide the backpack in his room again before Mom even knew he was home. She'd still be at the kitchen table, wouldn't she? Staring at her computer screen?

But as soon as he had the door open, he heard Mom talking.

"Thanks for the heads-up," she was saying. "I really appreciate it."

Colin froze. She had to be on her phone. But she wasn't quite using her Professional Voice, the one she reserved for clients. So he couldn't be sure if she would have her head bent over the computer, taking notes for some new job, or if she'd be up and pacing around the house.

He stayed frozen.

"No, no, I understand," Mom said. "I get it."

Who did Mom ever talk to by phone, besides clients? The parents of his friends occasionally, every now and then a random friend of her own. Very, very rarely an ancient great-aunt who used to send Colin presents when he was little, but who now only sent cash.

This wasn't the voice she used with any of those people.

Whoever was on the other end of Mom's phone call was doing most of the talking.

"Right," Mom said grimly. "And of course I'll keep this secret, that you called me. It's the least I can do after everything you did for me all those years ago. I'll keep your secret, you keep mine—nobody else needs to know about any of it."

What did that mean?

What "secret" was she talking about?

Mom finished with a "Thanks. Bye," but Colin stayed frozen a moment or two longer. He didn't move until a car door slammed somewhere down the block and he worried, *Will Mom notice that that's louder than it should be with all our doors and windows shut?* That unfroze him to step into the house and pull the door silently shut behind him.

All the way home, Colin had been toying with the notion of just telling Mom about the Toby and Rosemary letters—and maybe asking her advice about how to find out more about the two kids from fifty years ago. But that would require also telling about meeting Nevaeh, about going into Mrs. Torres's house, about taking the Toby letters from a client's house in the first place. . . . None of those were things Mom would approve of.

All the way home, he'd still thought he could tell Mom. But not now. Not when Mom seemed to be keeping so many secrets of her own.

Colin sneaked his backpack into his room, waited a few more minutes, then went back to the door. This time he opened and shut it as emphatically as he could, so hard he made the doorframe shake.

"Hi, Mom," he called, as if he'd just arrived. "I'm home! What's for dinner?"

18

Nevaeh and Rosemary. And Colin.

Nevaeh had plenty of friends. Of course Nevaeh had friends. She was her father's daughter, and he was friends with everyone in town. (Except Felicia Creedmont, anyway.) Nevaeh had probably been about a week old the first time her mom or dad plopped her down alongside some other baby in a Pack 'n Play at some town picnic or church ice-cream social or family reunion. She had three older brothers and an older sister—she'd pretty much inherited all the younger siblings of all her older siblings' friends. Just as Nevaeh's kindergarten teacher had recognized Nevaeh right away as a Greevey, Nevaeh had been able to look around her kindergarten classroom and pick out all the kids she knew from church, all the kids she'd played with during Roddy's science fairs, all the kids she'd met at Axel's and Dalton's high school baseball games or at the back of the theater while Prilla had play practice.

But Nevaeh knew everyone also thought the Greeveys were a little . . . odd. And something with Nevaeh's friends had changed in sixth grade. Nobody had actually been mean to her—not the way Nevaeh defined "mean," anyway. But there'd been little comments, little slights. She hadn't been invited on certain shopping trips, not even the ones when her friends went thrifting up in Columbus, because "You always tell us if something's overpriced or not, and Nevaeh, that takes all the fun out of it." Other times, her friends had said, "You always have family stuff going on when I invite you over. That's why I stopped."

Was it weird that Nevaeh now wished she could trade her actual friends for Rosemary—not Rosemary *now*, but Rosemary as she'd been about fifty years ago when she was Nevaeh's age?

Was it weird that Nevaeh also wanted to be friends with Colin Creedmont?

Meeting up with Colin again *was* the only way she could get the rest of the Rosemary letters.

What does Colin know about Rosemary and that Toby kid she was writing to? How did he know Rosemary's letters were in Mrs. Torres's attic? Why does he care so much about Rosemary?

Sunday and Monday, Nevaeh texted back and forth with Mrs. Torres, nailing down the babysitting plans. She talked Prilla into agreeing to drop her off and pick her up afterward Tuesday night (even though Nevaeh had to give Prilla the impression that it was a paying babysitting job, and Prilla still said, "Better you than me. Those twins guaranteed *I'm* never going to have kids!"). And Nevaeh texted back and forth with Colin to make sure he'd be there, too. He sent her so many one-word answers—"Ok"; "Yes"; "Fine"—that she decided to wait to see him in person for all her important questions.

So Tuesday night, she was antsy standing on Mrs. Torres's doorstep as Prilla pulled away from the curb behind her in one of the Junk King pickups.

What if Colin doesn't even show up? Nevaeh wondered.

Just then he came speeding around the corner on his bike.

He parked the bike neatly beside Mrs. Torres's garage, flipped down the kickstand, and blurted out even as he took off his bike helmet, "You brought back the letters, didn't you?"

Hello to you, too, Nevaeh thought.

But what she said was, "Of course. Did you?"

Colin nodded so eagerly that he bonked himself on the chin with the bike helmet. His face turned red—even redder than it had been from riding around in the heat—and Nevaeh felt sorry for him.

"We can trade letters now, before we go in," she said. "I haven't knocked yet."

She drew out the large Ziploc bag she'd stored the Rosemary letters in, before putting the whole thing in an old drawstring bag Prilla had made in 4-H years ago. Since the Ziploc bag came from the Greeveys' house, of course it was one that had been used before and rinsed out for reuse. But Nevaeh had chosen carefully, making sure the bag contained no leftover crumbs or nearly microscopic traces of old mayonnaise or mustard.

Colin twisted his backpack around sideways, unzipped it, and pulled out one of those cloth bags that people (people who weren't the Greeveys, anyway) bought for grocery shopping.

"Mom and me, we don't do plastic," he said apologetically, stepping forward to hand her the bag. "So you'll have to make sure this doesn't get wet or anything."

Of course Felicia Creedmont wouldn't use plastic. Nevaeh felt more elegant just by association.

"I'll be careful," Nevaeh promised, trading her bag for his. They each tucked the letters out of sight. "Do you think—"

She had so many questions. But just then the garage door of the Torres house started rolling upward. Mrs. Torres was inside the garage, holding both twins—who were crying, of course—as she nudged a double stroller forward with a gentle kick of her foot.

"You two are even early!" Mrs. Torres enthused. "I am so grateful to you for doing this!"

She bent down and strapped first one, then the other baby into the double stroller.

"Um, I thought we were going to—" Nevaeh began, even

though she wasn't sure Mrs. Torres could hear her over the babies' screaming.

Mrs. Torres pushed the stroller forward, and . . . the babies' cries subsided into whimpers.

"I made an amazing discovery yesterday," Mrs. Torres said. She rolled the stroller back and forth, back and forth, keeping it in motion. "*This* is what Nathan and Mateo are crying for when they've already been fed and they've already had their diapers changed. They want to move, and they like their stroller so much better than their car seats. But I walked them probably two miles to get them to sleep for their morning nap and another mile or two to get them to sleep for their afternoon nap, and I am so tired. . . . I don't need you to stay for two hours, babysitting. If you could just walk them around for half an hour or so until they're asleep, that would be great."

Nevaeh couldn't exactly say, *But we wanted to snoop around your house to see if we could find any other letters!*

"Sure," Colin said, before Nevaeh could answer. He looked insanely relieved. Nevaeh couldn't tell if it was because this meant he wouldn't actually have to touch a baby—or because he wouldn't have to spend two whole hours with *her*.

"We're on it," Nevaeh said, going over to wrap her hands around the rubber grip of the stroller.

"Oh, thank you," Mrs. Torres said. "I'll leave the garage

door open. Just text me when you're back."

Mrs. Torres turned around and went back into the house. Nevaeh gingerly propelled the stroller down the driveway and along the sidewalk. As soon as she picked up any speed, the babies stopped crying altogether.

Colin caught up with her.

"This is . . . quieter than I expected," he said.

"That's a relief," Nevaeh agreed.

One of the babies—Mateo?—let out a contented sigh. The other one gave a gentle coo.

"I don't get it," Colin said. "We could be kidnappers. How'd she know we wouldn't just steal her babies and never bring them back? I mean, I guess she knows you, but . . . I could be anyone."

"I vouched for you," Nevaeh said.

"But why?" Colin asked. "You don't know me either."

"Don't you ever just trust people?" Nevaeh asked. She sneaked a sidelong glance at Colin. He was red-faced again. "You do! You trusted me with half of Rosemary's letters."

Colin opened his mouth like he was going to object.

"Besides, this is Groveview," Nevaeh said, gesturing at the houses they were passing, including the one she and her family had just finished cleaning out on Saturday. "Everybody knows everybody, everyone sees everything, everyone gossips about everybody—we'll be lucky if we get off this block before someone stops us and asks if Mrs. Torres knows we're pushing this stroller this fast or this recklessly or this *something*."

Nevaeh was exaggerating. It was a hot night, and as far as she could tell, everyone was actually inside their air-conditioned houses and probably staring at TVs or computer screens, not acting like a Neighborhood Watch. But Colin gazed around in horror, as though he was a fugitive from the law and feared spies everywhere.

"Does your family know you're with me?" he asked. "When they saw me on Saturday, did they know who I am? Who I'm related to?"

"I don't know," Nevaeh said. "Who cares?"

She meant to sound defiant and unconcerned. But her voice came out sounding as if she was actually admitting, *Yeah, I'm worried about that, too.*

"Your dad, my mom . . . ," Colin said.

Nevaeh squinted at Colin.

"Wait a minute," she said. "Could she possibly hate my dad as much as . . ."

She stopped herself at the last minute before the words "he hates her" slipped out. That would have been so rude. But Colin was already saying, "So he doesn't like her either?"

Either had to mean Colin's mom hated Nevaeh's dad, too.

"Why would your mom hate my dad?" Nevaeh asked.

At the same time, Colin asked, "Why wouldn't your dad

like my mom?" This made Nevaeh laugh, that she and Colin were thinking so much alike. One of the babies in the stroller actually joined in. Nevaeh eased the stroller a little more gingerly over a cracked place in the sidewalk.

"I guess it's just because they're competitors," Nevaeh said. "My dad thinks everybody should give their junk to *him*. I mean, he's the Junk King. Kings don't—"

"Share?" Colin asked, his face twisting.

"That wasn't what I was going to say!" Nevaeh protested. "My dad shares a lot! He donates stuff to charity!"

She clutched the stroller handle like it was a weapon she might swing at Colin. That Greevey loyalty—it was like lighting a fuse. She thought of Axel saying, *You hurt one Greevey, you've got to answer to all of us.*

But then she thought of her dad being so certain that Colin's mom had stolen everything from the Mongold unit. She thought about Dad telling Mom she couldn't root for both him and Felicia Creedmont, because with the bad economy, only one of their businesses would be able to survive.

Nevaeh couldn't tell Colin any of that.

"*Are* they competitors?" Colin asked. "Really? My mom's making me work for her this summer. And mostly what she does, she helps people sort through their stuff and figure out what they want to keep and what they want to give away. That's different than being Junk King. Or, uh, Junk Queen?

She usually hires movers to actually haul the junk away, if there's a lot of it. Your dad, what he does is take away people's junk and resells it, right?"

"The stuff that's worth reselling," Nevaeh said glumly. "If you're working for your mom, you've seen what it's like— most people's junk is just junk. My dad's always telling us one man's trash is another man's treasure, but even my mom says most of what he does is like putting lipstick on a pig. I'm working for my dad, too, this summer. You saw all those grocery store receipts. Why would anyone spend their entire life saving those? You know, I close my eyes at night, and all I see is garbage. It's like there are swirls of garbage inside my eyelids all the time."

It was okay to confess that to Colin since he was dealing with junk, too. Wasn't it?

"'Swirls of garbage'?" Colin repeated. "That almost sounds . . . poetic."

And then he blushed again, as if it were embarrassing for a boy to use the word "poetic."

Honestly, Nevaeh couldn't imagine Axel, Dalton, or Roddy saying that. Or any of the boys she went to school with.

But the girls she knew weren't really into describing things as poetic, either.

She shot Colin a curious glance. He was different from anyone she'd ever known. Was it just because he was a

Creedmont? Because he was his mother's son?

Nevaeh remembered the mocking, hoity-toity way Dalton had said Colin's mother's name: *Fe-lee-see-uh Creeeeed-mont.* It'd been like he was really saying, *She thinks she's better than us, and she's not. She's so not.*

Why couldn't the Creedmonts just be different from the Greeveys and not better or worse?

Nevaeh wished she could ask Colin if he ever thought about questions like that.

Rosemary and Toby asked each other questions like that all the time, she thought. *You could tell from the letters.*

But Colin and Nevaeh weren't Rosemary and Toby. Colin and Nevaeh barely even knew each other.

Colin kept his face turned away from her. All she could see was his dark, curly hair. He bent his head forward, like he was going to cover his embarrassment by pretending to be really, really interested in how the babies were doing in the stroller. Then he jerked back.

"Whoa," he said. His voice started as a whisper, but arced higher with surprise. "They're asleep already."

Nevaeh checked, and it was true. Both babies had their eyes closed.

"Prilla—that's my big sister, the one who taught me about babysitting—she says even after it looks like a baby's asleep, you have to keep rocking them for a while, to make sure they won't wake up the minute you put them in bed," Nevaeh said. "I guess pushing the twins in the stroller is like rocking."

"Oh, right," Colin said. "We should keep going then."

Nevaeh knew she wasn't imagining things: he sounded relieved.

He wants to keep walking and talking to me, too! she thought.

Nevaeh kept pushing the stroller. One of the babies snuffled happily in his sleep.

Sometimes things came together in Nevaeh's head. It felt like she'd been staring at the jumbled-up pieces of a jigsaw puzzle ever since she'd met Colin and they'd found Rosemary's letters. But now all the pieces seemed to click into place, everything she wanted fitting together. There was a way to get to spend more time with Colin, and maybe even meet his mom. That could go along with solving the mystery of the Mongold unit, too—Nevaeh was surer than ever that it wasn't connected with Felicia Creedmont doing anything wrong.

And there was a way to find out more about Rosemary, and to learn what she had been able to do with her life, even if she hadn't become the first female pitcher for the Cincinnati Reds.

And somehow, if Rosemary had managed to do great things with her life, even after growing up in a time when women could be fired for not making coffee, wouldn't that mean that Nevaeh could do something besides just being a Junk Princess her whole life?

"You know what we have to do, don't you?" Nevaeh asked Colin. "We have to find Rosemary—the grown-up Rosemary. We have to find her and give her her letters back. We have to do that together."

And then she bit her lip. Colin could refuse. She knew that he hadn't even wanted to let her read Rosemary's letters in the first place.

He hadn't wanted to share.

But Colin jerked his gaze back to meet hers. His eyes were wide with surprise—and excitement.

"And Toby's," he said. "We have to find Toby and give him his letters back, too."

19

The Deal

"You have letters that belong to Toby, too?" Nevaeh exploded. "*You have Toby's letters?* Why didn't you tell me that before?"

Her voice rang out too loudly on the quiet street. One of the babies—Nathan?—startled at the sound. He screwed up his face and began screaming.

Colin cowered, frozen in place.

"Seriously, dude?" Nevaeh muttered. Colin couldn't tell if she was talking to him or the baby. She started running, propelling the stroller faster and faster toward the end of the block.

The baby stopped crying.

Nevaeh was three sidewalk squares ahead of Colin. Now five, now seven, now nine . . .

I could turn around and run away while she's not looking, Colin thought. *I could go back and grab my bike and be on my way home before she even notices.*

But Colin didn't do that.

His feet stayed pointed forward, toward Nevaeh, as if they understood what he wanted before his brain did.

He didn't want to run away from Nevaeh, even if it involved being around crying babies. He did want her help finding Toby and Rosemary. He wanted to talk to her about every question he had about Toby and Rosemary, every line in every letter he couldn't quite figure out: *What do you think Toby meant here? What do you think Rosemary meant there?*

He wanted to keep talking with her about how working for her dad was and wasn't like working for his mom.

He wanted them to be friends the way Toby and Rosemary had been friends.

(Before those two got into a fight and Rosemary said she was never speaking to Toby again, anyway.)

He wanted to ask Nevaeh what she thought about that, too.

And I could ask Nevaeh if, working for her dad, she's ever wanted to pull out her phone and take pictures of everything she sees, all those "swirls of garbage" that are ugly and beautiful all at once. . . .

Colin had too many thoughts scrambled together in his brain now. He couldn't get his feet to move in any direction.

But it didn't matter, because when Nevaeh reached the end of the block, she spun the stroller around and jogged back toward Colin.

"Fair's fair," she said. "It's your turn to push the stroller.

And, really, you should have to push it farther, because you didn't tell me sooner that you have Toby's letters. . . ." She lifted her hands from the stroller handle, and for a second it seemed like Nevaeh might be about to slug him. But instead, she surprised him by throwing an arm around his shoulders.

"This is going to be so much fun!" she exclaimed. "We're going to have such a great time tracking down Rosemary and Toby!"

She sounded exactly the way he imagined Rosemary sounding.

"We will?" Colin squeaked. He tried again, and somehow the words came out in a totally different way. "We will. You're right. We will."

Somehow he sounded resolute now. It was like Nevaeh's certainty was contagious.

Nevaeh was already pulling back from the impromptu almost-hug. She gave him a gentle shove, and Colin took over pushing the stroller. It wasn't as hard as he'd expected. Nevaeh bounced along beside him, her ponytail flopping up and down, her eyes dancing. She looked so overjoyed, it reminded Colin of the Junk King in all those TV commercials where he'd throw his arms out wide and cry, "Got junk you don't want anymore? I'll take it! I looooove junk!"

The commercials my mom can't even stand to watch, Colin thought. *Because she sees Nevaeh's dad as her worst enemy.*

"Only, we can't tell our parents what we're doing," Colin added quickly. "We can't let them know anything."

He expected Nevaeh to protest. She didn't seem like the type who needed to keep secrets from anyone. She seemed more like the type who would march right up to her dad and say flat out, "Colin's my friend. Deal with it."

But Nevaeh stopped bouncing.

"You're right," she said. "We'll keep this secret." She put a hand over Colin's for an instant, quickly brushing her fingers against his. "Pinkie promise."

And then she giggled.

The giggle made fun of things like pinkie promises. It made fun of parents who disliked each other for stupid reasons. It was a giggle that was just between her and Colin, that only the two of them would understand.

And that made her promise into something serious.

"I promise, too," Colin said quickly.

This is what it was like, he thought. *This is exactly what it was like for Toby and Rosemary. Being friends.*

20

Blind Alleys, False Starts . . . and a Breakthrough

The internet is useless.

Colin texted that to Nevaeh on Wednesday, in a long chain of back-and-forth conversation they had in between breaking down empty boxes from an old lady's attic for recycling (Colin) and scrubbing tarnished forks with silver polish on an old toothbrush (Nevaeh). It made Nevaeh happy that he was saying more than "OK" or "Fine," but sad, too, because he was right.

It did seem like the internet was useless for finding out anything about Rosemary or Toby.

They'd both tried googling "Toby Carter" and "Rosemary Buvon" with and without qualifiers like "Groveview, Ohio" or "Groveview" or "Ohio" or even Toby's and Rosemary's old addresses, 895 Willow and 108 Haven. And they'd found plenty of Toby Carters, but none of them were the right Toby.

Looking for Rosemary, mostly what they found were recipes. And though Nevaeh thought rosemary-bacon nut mix or rosemary, bacon, and tomato frittatas sounded tasty (especially as Wednesday morning wore on, and she got hungrier for lunch), recipes didn't move them an iota closer to finding out anything else about the two kids from the 1970s.

Nevaeh kept pressing the toothbrush harder and harder against the discolored fork tines she was polishing, as if the answer to finding Toby and Rosemary would come to her as soon as all the forks were shiny and bright once more.

"Okay, spill," Prilla said, taking the toothbrush from Nevaeh's hand and replacing it with one whose bristles weren't as splayed. "That's the second toothbrush you've worn down to nothing, and you keep sneaking away to check your phone. Which of your friends are you fighting with?"

"I'm not fighting with any of my friends!"

"Come on, Nevaeh," Prilla said. "I remember what middle school was like. What's that quote about believing six impossible things before breakfast? In middle school, my friends could have six impossible arguments before homeroom. And even if I was like, 'Nope, I don't want to take sides. None of this matters to me,' that would just mean they *all* got mad at me."

"Thanks for making middle school sound so appealing," Nevaeh said. "Maybe I'll drop out before I get there and work for Dad full-time."

She pretended to admire the sheen on the fork handle she'd been scrubbing.

"I'm just saying, it wasn't until the end of seventh grade when I felt like I'd found my *real* friends," Prilla said. "My people. We theater kids, we're dramatic, but it's for a reason. Whatever you're going through, it'll get better. You'll find your people, too."

Nevaeh flushed, because how much had Prilla noticed? Did she know how things had changed for Nevaeh in sixth grade? How Nevaeh's friends had stopped inviting her over?

Maybe Colin is my people, Nevaeh thought. *Maybe it's with Colin and his mom and the way they live that's more where I belong.*

"Or . . ." A smirk traveled over Prilla's face, making her look more like Axel or Dalton. "Is it a *boy* you're texting back and forth with? Is that what's going on?"

The way Prilla said "boy" made it so Nevaeh couldn't even look her in the eye. A moment earlier, Nevaeh might have thought, *Maybe Prilla would know how to find Rosemary and Toby. Maybe I could ask her, and just tell her not to tell Dad.* But now . . .

Nevaeh remembered something Rosemary had written in one of her letters: "Why does your mom always say, 'Toby, it's your little girlfriend,' every time I call? She knows my name. Doesn't she know a boy and a girl can be friend-friends, not just boyfriend-girlfriend? Doesn't she know things are different now than when she was growing up, when girls weren't even supposed to call boys? (Yeah, she tells me that all the time, too.)"

Rosemary had written that way back in 1976. But people still acted like, if a boy and a girl hung out together a lot, it was probably a boyfriend-girlfriend thing. Even Prilla did that.

That meant Nevaeh couldn't tell Prilla anything about Colin.

Which also meant she couldn't ask her anything about finding Rosemary and Toby.

"How's my silver-polishing team coming along?" Dad said, walking into the kitchen. He strolled over to the sink where Nevaeh and Prilla were working. "We just got a call to pick up a load of junk over on Strivers Road, and it would be great if we could drop off that silverware on the way."

"Give us another half hour," Prilla said, gesturing at the tarnished spoons and knives still lying beside the sink. "Though, we'd be faster if you had Roddy or Axel or Dalton come in and help us."

"Enh, you know none of them are any good at this," Dad said.

"Why, because they're boys?" Nevaeh asked. It was like she still had Rosemary's voice in her head, talking about people treating males and females differently. "*I* wasn't any good at this either, until Prilla showed me how. Are you letting Axel and Dalton and Roddy get away with not having to do this because you think it's a girl job?"

Prilla flashed Nevaeh a "You go, girl" look. Dad's jaw dropped. But then he recovered.

"I'll have you know, *I'm* really good at polishing silver," he said. He picked up a spoon. "Tell you what, let's race. Me against the two of you. See who's fastest, with points deducted for any left-behind streaks of tarnish. On your mark, get set—"

"Don't fall for it, Nevaeh!" Prilla cried. "This is like the Tom Sawyer thing where he cons his friends into painting the fence for him. Dad thinks we'll work faster if he makes it fun!"

Dad brandished the spoon at Prilla like a weapon.

"When did you get so smart?" he asked. "And anyhow, what's wrong with having fun?"

And then he went into hyperdrive, scrubbing the spoons at top speed. Prilla laughed and sped up, too. Nevaeh followed suit.

They were done in ten minutes.

They were also all three panting and gasping by the end. Dad rubbed his arm muscles like he'd just finished lifting weights.

"You two tricked *me* into helping," he complained jokingly. "Curses on your diabolical girl power."

Nevaeh felt like she had too many things jumbled in her head at once. Dad did make her laugh. But he *hadn't* made

Axel, Dalton, and Roddy help. And the silverware was shinier now, but it was still banged up and old, no matter how much they'd scrubbed.

Nevaeh held out a spoon and pretended to inspect it for any last traces of tarnish. How many other people had touched this silverware over the centuries? For all she knew, maybe even Toby or Rosemary had used it, once upon a time.

"You already know who you're selling this to, right?" she asked Dad. "Does that guy know who owned it before us? I bet it'd be worth more if you knew its whole history. What if, say, George Washington once ate off this spoon?"

Dad kissed her on the top of her head.

"You are a true Junk Princess!" he announced. "You've only been on the job a week and a half, and you're already thinking about provenance!"

"I am?" Nevaeh said. "What's provenance?"

"Where something came from," Prilla told her. "Like, if you found a Picasso painting, you'd want documents proving who bought it from Picasso, who that person sold it to, and on and on, right down to when *you* picked it up and held it in your hand."

"But forks aren't Picasso paintings," Axel said, conveniently strolling into the kitchen now that work was finished. "Nobody would bother keeping track of who all owned that silverware over the years."

"But how would you find out something like that if you wanted to?" Nevaeh persisted. An idea was growing in her head. What if she could get Dad to tell her how to track down Rosemary and Toby by making him think she just wanted to know how to track down the history of *things*?

Dad slung an arm around her shoulders.

"Kiddo, you just earned the right to ride up front with me on our next junk run," he said. "I'll tell you all about it."

"That's great," Nevaeh said.

And for once, she wasn't even pretending to be excited for Dad's sake.

Heading out to the truck, she texted Colin one more time before climbing into the cab: **Don't worry. I think I've got a lead on how to find R and T.**

21

Traces of the Past

"Ta-da!" Nevaeh said, gesturing at the computer screen before her.

It was the following Saturday morning, and Nevaeh and Colin were huddled together at the back of the Groveview library. Colin had ridden his bike again. Nevaeh said she'd convinced her mom she had an urgent need to check out all her summer reading books right away, and arranged to be dropped off.

She'd also been very mysterious about what she planned to show him, saying she didn't want to spoil the surprise.

So now Colin squinted confusedly at the computer screen. A moment ago, Nevaeh had been on some dry, boring site that said something about a county auditor. Now she was clicking back and forth between a list of names in regular computer typeface, and a picture of some ancient document with sloping, old-fashioned handwriting and a list of dates beginning in 1920.

"See, this is everyone who's ever owned the house where we found Rosemary's letters," Nevaeh said. "The lists weren't kept on computers until the 1990s, so somebody scanned all the old documents, too. You can look at these names and know we have the right house."

She pointed to the top of the first list, where the names "Hugo and Sara Torres" appeared. The parents of the crying twin babies had evidently bought the house on Willow Street only a year earlier.

Nevaeh clicked back to the picture of the old, handwritten document.

"And this," she said, pointing to the middle of that list, "is who lived in that house when Rosemary and Toby were writing letters to each other."

The name was Robert Carter. It stood beside the date June 4, 1971.

Carter.

"Toby's dad, don't you think?" Nevaeh asked.

Colin felt dizzy.

"That's proof," he said. "Toby's real." Which was such a silly thing to say—of course Toby was real. Colin had held letters in his own two hands that Toby had written; he'd touched the smear of eraser marks over penciled words Toby had changed his mind about. Colin had seen where Toby had written to Rosemary, "You're my best fiend" (when Toby must have been only eight) and then "You're my best freind" later on, with the *e* and the *i* crossed out and the words "I don't think that's spelled right, but you know what I mean" scribbled above it. That alone had made Toby seem real from the very beginning.

Colin braced for Nevaeh to laugh at him.

Instead, she turned her head toward him and her eyebrows shot up and she breathed, "That's exactly what I thought, seeing this! Just . . . exactly . . . the same."

For a moment neither of them said anything. Then Nevaeh pointed to the computer screen.

"It looks like Toby's dad sold the house to some bank in April 1977," she said. "So he didn't live there long."

Colin thought about the last dated letter he'd seen between Rosemary and Toby. It was from Easter 1977.

Of course, the last notes the two kids had written to one another—with Rosemary telling Toby to never write to her again, and Toby begging for forgiveness—didn't have dates on them at all.

At least, Colin assumed those were their last notes.

Something else struck Colin.

"It's only his dad who owns the house?" he asked. "Toby says things in his letters like 'My mom's making me take out the trash,' and 'Mom's making me a chocolate birthday cake right now,' so it sounded like he lived with both of them."

"Well, *I* didn't know that, because you didn't give me Toby's letters until today," Nevaeh grumbled. But she offset it with a grin, so Colin knew she wasn't really upset. They'd negotiated the handoff of the letters in a way that reminded Colin of the way his (former?) friend Anthony had talked about his divorced parents negotiating which part of Thanksgiving he'd spend at whose house.

Colin had never told Anthony that the only reason he didn't have to deal with the same situation was because Colin never went to his dad's.

"Anyhow, I don't think it means anything that Toby's dad's name is the only one listed here," Nevaeh said. "From the other records I looked at, I guess back then wives' names may or may not have been included. Remember how Rosemary was always complaining about how things weren't fair for women?"

"Yeah . . ." Colin wanted to say something cheerful like *Isn't it great that things are fair now?* But he remembered his mom saying that it was harder for her to borrow money for her business than it would be for a man. He remembered her saying that she had to work harder to convince people to hire her, because people wouldn't think she was any good at moving boxes, just from looking at her.

"I guess you looked up Rosemary's house, too, huh?" he asked instead.

"Yep." Nevaeh reached for the keyboard again. "And this is kind of strange. It looks like Rosemary's family moved away in 1977, just like Toby's."

"Hmm." Colin squinted at the new records Nevaeh called up. Rosemary's parents—Lawrence and Annette—had moved into their house in 1962. "This is cool and all, and you did better than I did finding out anything, but . . . how does this help us find Rosemary and Toby now?"

Nevaeh leaned over and took out a spiral notebook with a giant black X on the cover. The X didn't quite cover the words "Biology II/Period 2/Prilla Greevey."

"Yeah, yeah, it's a hand-me-down notebook, but look . . ." Nevaeh flipped open the cover to reveal page after page of addresses: 889 Willow, 883 Willow, 877 Willow . . . Most of them had the word "NO" written alongside the address, but every now and then the address included names and dates: Anthony and Stella Ionio, 1972; Carol Haynes, 1968 . . . "Some of the people who lived by Toby or Rosemary fifty years ago are still there now. Still in the exact same houses. And we can go talk to them."

"We can?" Colin squeaked.

"We'll do it together," Nevaeh said. "And it's not like we'll go *into* anybody's house. We'll just ring the doorbell and step back and ask questions. That'll make it safe."

She was acting like the only reason he might object was

the whole "Don't talk to strangers" thing.

"It'll be no different than selling Band Booster candy or Boy Scout popcorn," Nevaeh said. "Except we'll be saying, 'Tell us everything you remember about Toby Carter and Rosemary Buvon,' instead of 'Don't you want to waste money on overpriced food that's bad for you? Pleeeease?'" She gave him a beseeching smile and batted her eyelashes in a mocking way. "Axel and Dalton, Roddy and Prilla, they used to take me with them for selling things door-to-door back when I was little and cute. They said I was their secret weapon. Mostly, I think, I just kept talking and talking, and people would pay us to go away."

She flashed him another smile, but this one seemed a little evil.

"I've never had to sell anything door-to-door," Colin admitted. "My mom always said it would be kind of 'hypocritical,' for her own kid to ask people to add to the junk already in their homes."

"Oh, wow, I never thought about it that way," Nevaeh said. "So we Greevey kids, we were helping the Band Boosters or the Scouts or whatever *and* our dad's business!"

Colin wondered if he should say something about her "little and cute" comment. Something like "You're still cute"? Were boys supposed to talk like that to girls?

Ugh, ugh, ugh, he thought. *If Toby had written that to*

Rosemary, she would have told him she hated it.

That probably meant Nevaeh would hate it, too.

He felt a little bit like he'd just avoided falling into a hole.

"So . . . you want to start looking for these people now?" Colin asked, pointing to the list of addresses and names.

"We can't today," Nevaeh said, glancing at her phone. "It'll have to be next Saturday, if I can get a ride. Mom said she only had three errands to run, and then she'd be back to pick me up."

"You don't live close enough to walk?" Colin asked. "Or go back and get your bike?"

"No, we're too far out in the country," Nevaeh said. She rolled her eyes. "No one wants to live next door to the Junk King, you know? And before we lived there, it was my grandfather's place, and my great-grandfather's before that, and they ran an actual junkyard with old, rusty cars sitting around. . . . I've seen pictures. It wasn't pretty."

Colin barely managed to stop himself from saying, *I wish I'd seen that.* He thought about the pictures he'd been taking at the houses he and his mom cleaned out. He'd gotten one just this past week with an old, rusty fishing reel, and it'd made him so interested in rust that he'd looked up iron oxidation on Wikipedia.

But he couldn't tell Nevaeh that.

"Did you look up all the other people who ever owned your

house, when you were looking up Rosemary's and Toby's?" Colin asked.

"No, because I already knew," Nevaeh said. "It was one Greevey after another. My great-great-grandfather was the one who built the house I live in." She shrugged and began easing pages out of her notebook. "Look, I didn't have time to look up the owners for all the addresses around Rosemary's and Toby's houses, so I thought we could divide them up— you do half, I do half, and we can meet up next Saturday all ready to go."

She slipped the pages into Colin's hand. He saw that she'd written instructions at the top. It was like getting homework. But he peered back at the image on the computer screen, all those loops of old-fashioned handwriting, all the ancient dates. Someone had sat down with a pen and paper more than a hundred years ago, and then someone had sat down with a scanner probably about thirty years ago, and now anyone anywhere in the world could look up who had owned a particular wood-frame house on a particular piece of dirt in Groveview, Ohio, back in 1920 or 1948 or 2000—any year they wanted.

It was so orderly and efficient. Colin's mom would definitely approve. But it was also . . .

Haunting? Colin thought. If that wasn't the right word, it was as close as Colin could get. What had happened to all the people whose handwriting Colin was looking at right now? Had they been clerks in government offices, or were they the homeowners themselves? Which of the homeowners had children either when they bought the house or after they moved in? How many kids besides Rosemary had grown up in that house? It was a shame Colin couldn't tell which names had happy families, and which didn't. And . . .

"Colin?" Nevaeh said. "Want to try looking up a house yourself while I'm still here to make sure my instructions make sense?"

"Oh, sure," Colin said. "I'll do my own house. I don't even know when it was built."

He followed the directions Nevaeh had written, and maybe he'd been expecting too much. This was Groveview—it wasn't like he believed someone famous might have once owned his house. Groveview didn't have famous people. (Actually, now that he thought about it, Nevaeh's dad might be the closest thing Groveview had to a famous person.) But it was still a letdown that none of the names listed below his mom's meant anything to him.

"At least it's not all Greeveys," he joked, reaching for the mouse to click on "Historical Parcel Sheets" to go to the older records.

Nevaeh grabbed his wrist, stopping him.

"Wait!" she cried, so loudly that an old man at one of the

other computer terminals glared at her.

"Why?" Colin asked. "What's wrong?"

Nevaeh had one hand over her mouth. She let that hand slide down, then pulled it away to point at the list of names.

"Because it's not Greeveys, but that's still my family. On my mom's side," Nevaeh said. "Did you know your mom bought your house from my *other* grandfather?"

22

Surprises

"That's weird," Colin said. For a moment he looked as freaked out as Nevaeh felt, then he seemed to recover. "But it's just a coincidence, right?"

Nevaeh winced.

Like how Dad's stupid theories about Colin's mom and the Mongold unit are just a coincidence? she thought. *I can't tell Colin about any of that, but . . . how could there be* another *connection between Colin's mom and my family I didn't know about?*

Just that morning, she'd overheard Dad telling Axel and Dalton about a new way he was looking for proof: with a handwriting analysis of the letter Nevaeh had found on the floor of the Mongold storage unit. Dad was expecting fingerprint test results, too.

"Betcha anything we'll find out that letter was written by Felicia Creedmont just over a decade ago, not Maribel Mongold back in the eighties!" Dalton had crowed.

All those tests are going to prove Colin's mom is innocent, not guilty, Nevaeh told herself firmly. *And that somebody else wrote that letter and took those antiques.*

But it *didn't* seem like just a coincidence that Colin's mom had bought a house from Nevaeh's grandfather.

"My mom worked for your dad for a while," Colin said. "Maybe it was just because of that that she heard your grandfather was selling a house."

"Oh, right," Nevaeh said. She gave a "no big deal" shrug. At least, she hoped it looked that way. "Grandpa Landman died when I was little, so I never really knew him. Or saw any house he owned. I think he used to have two or three houses he'd rent out? Maybe—"

Her phone buzzed with a text. Mom was telling her, In parking lot now. Hurry—I have ice cream in trunk.

Nevaeh groaned.

"Ugh. I thought she had *three* errands—how'd Mom do them so fast?" She began stuffing her notebook back into her bag alongside the Toby letters Colin had given her. "Look, I'll see what I can find out about this, too. You look up your set of house records, I'll look up mine, I'll read the letters. . . . We'll figure out everything!"

"Okay, um, text me about next week," Colin said. He was blushing again, for some reason.

Nevaeh was halfway across the library parking lot before

she remembered she hadn't checked out any books.

Oh well. Mom will think I just have them in my bag. And I can get them for real next week when I'm here. . . .

Still, Nevaeh felt a little guilty when she slipped into the car and Mom rewarded her with a tired smile. Working nights at the hospital meant Mom was always tired.

"You're going to have to talk to me the whole way home to keep me awake," Mom said.

That was like an invitation to ask questions about Colin's house and Nevaeh's grandfather. But how could Nevaeh do that without giving away that she'd been hanging out with Colin? (And looking up Colin's house . . . what excuse could she give for *that*?)

Nevaeh tilted her head to the side, pretending to search for some random topic.

"Dad had so much work for us to do this week," she said. That was a way to start, wasn't it? By pretending to complain? "How'd he get anything done before even Axel and Dalt were old enough to help? He had to hire other people, right?"

"Oh, has Dad been telling you about all the characters who used to work for him?" Mom said, even as she pulled out of the parking lot. "You know, we didn't have much money for paying workers back then. So lots of times, I was his main assistant. Before I went back to school and all. When I was pregnant with you."

Nevaeh had heard that story before, but it had always seemed about as real as a fairy tale—just like everything else that happened before Nevaeh was born. Prilla had said to Nevaeh once, "You know Mom was basically Superwoman, right? Going back to school when she had four kids and was pregnant with her fifth? That's pretty amazing."

That wasn't the story Nevaeh wanted to hear right now.

"Did you ever work with Felicia Creedmont?" Nevaeh asked. She tried to make the question sound casual, as if she didn't care much about the answer. "Did you know her very well when she worked for Dad and they . . . didn't get along?"

A long moment passed before Mom answered. And it wasn't even like Mom needed to focus on driving—they were stopped at the red light between the Walmart and the Home Depot now.

"Yes, I knew Felicia," Mom finally said. Was it Nevaeh's imagination, or did Mom's casual tone sound as forced as Nevaeh's? Mom started tapping her fingers against the steering wheel. "Nevaeh, I know your dad talks bad about her, but it's not really fair. He put up with the worker who overslept every single day, and the worker who always had reasons he couldn't actually carry a single box: 'Oh, that will rub the place where I just got a new tattoo,' 'I got a bee sting last week, and I'm being careful so it doesn't get infected. . . .'

But *Felicia* was the one he wanted to fire?"

Nevaeh gasped.

"He *fired* her? I always thought—"

The light changed, and Mom hit the accelerator a little too hard. Nevaeh jerked back in her seat.

"Technically, no," Mom said. "She quit before that could happen. But, Nevaeh . . . oh, never mind. This is all ancient history. Felicia has her own business now, and she's doing what she wants. And your dad's living his dream, with his family by his side. He said you were even asking him about provenance the other day? He was so proud!"

A wave of guilt hit Nevaeh. She'd asked that question because of Colin and Rosemary and Toby, and Dad thought she'd done it because she was like him, a true Greevey, falling in love with junk.

She couldn't ask Mom anything else about Felicia Creedmont right now.

"Dad's dream was always to be the Junk King, huh?" Nevaeh said. She could imagine him being like Rosemary, planning his future when he was only ten or eleven or twelve.

But Rosemary hadn't achieved her dream of becoming the first female pitcher for the Cincinnati Reds. Nevaeh now knew that Rosemary's other letters talked about other dreams, too: She was going to compete in the Olympics. She was going to be a world-famous actress. She was going to be president of the United States.

The fruitless internet searches Nevaeh and Colin had done proved none of those dreams had happened for Rosemary, either.

Nevaeh looked at her mom through lowered lashes.

"Mom, what was *your* dream when you were my age?" she asked. "When you were a kid, what did you want to be when you grew up?"

Wasn't it weird that she knew that about Rosemary—a girl from fifty years ago that she'd never even met—but didn't know it about her own mother?

Mom laughed.

"A wife and a mother and an X-ray tech, of course," she said. "See? I'm living the dream, too. I just thought it would involve a little more sleep."

Mom's not going to tell me, Nevaeh thought. *I'm her own kid, and she doesn't want me to know.*

This made her feel even weirder. They got home and Nevaeh helped Mom unload the groceries. But then Mom said, "Ah, now I get to go to bed!" as if that was all she'd ever dreamed of. Nevaeh took the letters Colin had loaned her and sneaked out to the barn, where no one would interrupt her.

The air in the barn was hot and still. Nevaeh's weird mood made her see all the furniture that had once belonged to other people like something out of a time capsule. Who had propped up their feet on that brown La-Z-Boy recliner so many times that it was worn ragged? How many kids had secretly jumped on that flowered couch often enough to bust its springs?

It was like the barn was full of ghosts, not just old furniture.

She tiptoed toward the couch she'd lain on before, to read Rosemary's letters. Nevaeh didn't want to be haunted by anyone right now except Rosemary and Toby.

It was so dim at the back of the barn that she had to turn on her cell phone flashlight to navigate through the furniture. But she was awkward shifting between the letters and the phone—she accidentally flashed it into her own eyes.

So she was temporarily blinded when she brushed the foot dangling off the couch.

"AHHH!" Nevaeh shrieked.

"AHHH!" someone else shrieked.

Nevaeh whipped her phone around, aiming the light at the screaming.

It was only Prilla.

Prilla's eyes were wide and terrified, and then they turned squinty and amused.

Nevaeh dropped down onto the couch beside Prilla. Prilla was laughing hysterically now, and Nevaeh began giggling, too. When one of them stopped, the other one set them both off again. They hugged each other, Nevaeh bracing her forehead against Prilla's shoulder and laughing until she had tears in her eyes.

"I . . . was so scared!" Nevaeh sputtered, as Prilla admitted, "You . . . terrified me!"

This made them laugh even more.

Finally Prilla calmed down enough to say, "You know how much Axel and Dalt would make fun of us for this?"

"Oh, come on," Nevaeh countered. "They'd have screamed, too!"

"Even louder!" Prilla agreed.

Nevaeh pulled back.

"What were you doing out here?" she asked.

"Listening to music." Prilla shoved her hair back, revealing earbuds. "It's a band a few of my friends started, and I wanted to listen . . . intently. Alone."

"Oh, sorry," Nevaeh said. "I interrupted. I didn't know you ever came out here except, you know. To work. You were here first. I'll just go and let you have your own . . . hiding place . . . to yourself."

She'd never thought about Prilla needing a break from the rest of the family, too.

Somehow that made Prilla seem like a totally different person.

"No, you know what? You stay—I'll go," Prilla said. "I'd forgotten . . . I was about your age when I started needing this place." She dug into her shorts pocket and pulled out a set of car keys. She jingled them like a prize. "But I have lots of other places I can go now, on my own, and you don't yet."

She stood up, smoothed down her hair, and flapped her T-shirt a little where it stuck to her skin with sweat. She began threading her way through the crammed-together furniture. Then suddenly she stopped and turned back toward Nevaeh.

"Oh, and, while no one else is around . . . I owe you an apology," Prilla said.

"For finding this place as a hideaway before I did?" Nevaeh asked. "You're five years older than me! I'm always the last one in the family to find anything!"

"No, for the other day. When you were texting with some friend, and I was all, 'Oh, is it a *boy*?' I hated it when I was your age, and Dad or Axel or Dalt did that to me," Prilla said. "I hated them teasing me all the time about boys and who I was or wasn't falling in love with. . . . They made me feel so *silly*. So it's stupid that I did that to you, too."

Nevaeh noticed whose name she'd left out.

"Roddy didn't tease you like that?" she asked.

"Nah, I was still bigger and more muscular than Roddy when we were twelve. He knew I would have punched him."

"Nobody teases you like that anymore," Nevaeh said. "How'd you get them to stop?"

"I punched them."

"But—"

"Kidding," Prilla said. She flipped her hair over her shoulder. "I'd go into acting mode and say things like 'If my only function in this family is to be married off like some medieval princess making an advantageous match with a rival kingdom, then mayhap I should put down this filthy box of old canning jars. You wouldn't want me to break a nail and diminish my appeal.' They got so sick of hearing stuff like that, they finally shut up."

It was on the tip of Nevaeh's tongue to say, *Rosemary would have loved that!*

But she still couldn't talk about Rosemary with Prilla. Not without also telling about Colin.

"And, Nevaeh? When I was your age, I thought however things were, that was the way they'd always be," Prilla went on. "But it's not like that. Next year, well . . . Roddy hasn't talked about this with Dad yet, but he's going to go to college. You know, with that big science-y brain of his."

"He is?" Nevaeh said.

She didn't know why she sounded so surprised. Lots of people went to college right after high school.

It just wasn't how Greeveys did things.

Did going off to college mean Roddy would stop working for Dad?

It did. That was what Prilla was trying to tell her.

"I didn't know they taught toaster repair in college," Nevaeh joked.

"See, that's exactly the kind of comment Roddy's scared of hearing from Dad," Prilla said. "Roddy's teachers—who are also my teachers—they say Roddy's not so great at hands-on science, but the ideas in his head . . . pow!" She clutched her head, then jerked her hands out to mime an explosion. Like, *Mind blown*. "And once Roddy started talking about college, I started thinking . . . maybe . . . maybe I'll go, too."

She lowered her head, like she'd suddenly gotten all shy.

Prilla? Shy?

She couldn't be worried about what I might say, could she? Nevaeh wondered.

"Really?" Nevaeh could hear the doubt in her own voice. She tried again, flipping to hyper-enthusiasm. "Really! Oh, yeah, that's great! You could study acting, and get even better at it, and then go to Hollywood and— Prilla, you'll be a star!"

"No, that's not what I want," Prilla said. "That's not my goal at all. I was thinking I could be a . . . a . . . theater teacher."

And then she cringed.

It was so odd to see Prilla hunched over, as if *she* feared being punched.

"Prilla, that would be so perfect for you," Nevaeh said. She didn't have to fake enthusiasm this time. She could see it so clearly. "You'd be a great teacher!"

"You think so?" Hope traveled across Prilla's face. "You're not just saying that?"

Nevaeh shook her head, and Prilla beamed.

"Don't say anything to Mom or Dad," Prilla warned. "Nothing's for certain yet. I'm pretty sure Roddy will get all the scholarships he needs, but I'll have to get grants and loans and, and . . . next year I'll *have* to get a job that pays better than working for Dad. I mean, nothing against Dad, he pays us what he can, but . . . there are five of us. I've been thinking about this a long time. I would have gotten a different job this summer and saved even more money, except . . ."

Except?

Prilla froze, midsentence. But suddenly Nevaeh understood what she wasn't saying:

Except this was Nevaeh's first summer working for Dad.

Prilla stayed for me, Nevaeh thought.

Her eyes clouded with tears, because working for Dad would have been so much harder without Prilla. It *would* be much harder without Prilla.

Next summer.

"Thank you," Nevaeh whispered.

Prilla glanced at her phone, and it was like a spell breaking.

"Ack! I'm late!" she wailed, spinning around and hopping over furniture. She turned back only once to holler before disappearing out the barn door, "Remember! Don't tell anyone!"

More secrets.

And then Nevaeh was left with the hot, still barn and the old couch and her own ghosts. Dust hung in the rays of light coming in through the cracks in the barn wall, especially where Prilla had jumped over furniture and disturbed the usual order of things, the places where the dust had settled and seemed like it would be layered forever. But now the dust spun and danced. It relocated. It was constantly relocating.

Nevaeh felt dazed.

I thought this was the start of every summer being the same, Axel and Dalton and Roddy and Prilla and me always working for Dad. . . .

Instead, this was both a first summer for Nevaeh and a last summer for Roddy and Prilla. Everything was churning; everything was changing. Constantly. Nevaeh just hadn't seen it.

Prilla's going to stop being a Junk Princess. Someday I'll stop being a Junk Princess. . . .

Nevaeh hadn't even wanted to be a Junk Princess in the first place. She'd never wanted to have anything to do with junk.

So why did this make her feel sad, as well as . . . freed?

Thoughtfully, she lowered her head to start reading Toby's letters, the other half of the conversation from the letters she'd already read of Rosemary's.

But maybe she was still influenced by the conversation

with Prilla, the conversation with Mom. Maybe that made her see things she wouldn't have noticed before.

Because she was only two or three letters in before she snatched up her phone and fired off a text to Colin:

Why didn't you tell me Toby kept so many secrets from Rosemary?

23

Colin's Confession

"I still don't see it," Colin said.

It was only Tuesday, but Nevaeh had finagled another meeting for them. As far as Colin was concerned, she'd put together a brilliant plan: she'd texted Mrs. Torres and told her Nevaeh and Colin needed to do a service project for some club they were in, and they'd chosen babysitting for the Torres twins every Tuesday night for free as their "gift to the world."

Colin never would have come up with that idea in a million years. His brain didn't work that way.

But he was glad Nevaeh's did.

And she wasn't exactly lying, because it did feel like he and Nevaeh had become a club—a Find-Rosemary-and-Toby club.

And Mrs. Torres did act like it was a huge gift, to have Colin and Rosemary push the twins around the block in their stroller again and again.

But Colin still didn't see why Nevaeh thought Toby kept

so many secrets in his letters. She'd given up trying to explain it to him by text. And now, as they took turns maneuvering the Torres twins' stroller over the uneven sidewalk, he was a little afraid she'd give up on him completely.

"I mean, I get that he talks about TV shows all the time instead of his own family," Colin said. "But that's just because TV was more important to kids in the 1970s." That was almost an exact quote from something he'd read online. "Like how video games are for kids now."

"Or TikTok," Nevaeh agreed. "Because Rosemary and Toby didn't *have* video games or the internet yet. Or, I guess they had Pong, but—"

"But that was just *blip . . . blip . . . blip . . . blip . . . Ping! Blip . . . blip . . . blip . . . blip . . . Pong!*" Colin made his imitation slow and robotic. "Remember how Rosemary said, even though she was the first person in their class to get Pong, she thought it was boring? Because there's time to eat a sandwich and do her math homework *and* watch paint dry before the ball comes back to her side? No wonder she says she'd rather play Ping-Pong for real!"

Colin had read Rosemary's and Toby's letters so many times now, he practically had them memorized. He guessed Nevaeh had, too.

"I think she was just trying to make Toby feel better, writing that," Nevaeh said. "Because she had Pong and he didn't. Because . . . Colin, I don't think Toby's family could afford it."

"Oh," Colin said.

This was something else he never would have figured out in a million years.

He'd been thinking too much about how things were in his own house.

If he'd been a kid in the 1970s, Mom wouldn't have let him have Pong because it was *clutter*.

"So do you think everything Toby is hiding has to do with Rosemary's family having more money than his?" Colin asked.

"No," Nevaeh said. "You have to look at all the questions Rosemary asks that Toby never answers."

She pulled out an actual list and placed it on the stroller canopy, which was keeping the sun out of the babies' eyes. Colin let Nevaeh take over pushing while he read:

What did you get for Christmas?

How was your birthday party with your family?

How was the drive to Michigan?

Did you do your back-to-school shopping yet?

Does your family have Monopoly tournaments on vacation like mine does?

What do you want to be when you grow up?

Where is your dad going to work now?

What do you like best at the lake?

There were a dozen other questions—and even more on the back of the sheet. But Colin lowered the sheet of paper without reading them all.

"Maybe Toby just doesn't like answering questions," Colin said. "Or he forgets what she's asked, when he's writing back."

"Every time Rosemary asks a question about a TV show or a movie, Toby answers it," Nevaeh countered. "He wrote so much about the movie *Jaws*, I felt like I'd seen it myself. I got so mad at that mayor who said it was safe to go back into the water!"

"Yeah, me, too," Colin said.

"I figured out categories for the questions Toby never answers," Nevaeh said. "One, feelings. Two, his family. Three, family gatherings. Four, plans for anything besides him and Rosemary hanging out."

Colin started laughing.

"I bet your teachers always really like you," he said. "You're that kid in the class with your hand up, going, 'I know! I know! Let me answer!' And, 'Look, I did this color-coded chart with all the themes in—'"

"No, for your information, teachers *never* like me," Nevaeh said. "They always say I talk too much, and I shouldn't interrupt, and why don't I give the other kids a turn to express their opinions, too? And I say, 'Look, I'm the fifth kid in my family. If I didn't interrupt people, I'd still be waiting for my first chance to talk!'"

Colin waited politely for her to finish talking.

"And?" he said, because it seemed like she still had more to say.

She tilted her head to the side.

"And . . . I don't know that I would have noticed that Toby was keeping secrets from Rosemary if I hadn't already been thinking about . . . about how there are secrets all around me," she said. "People I thought I knew everything about . . . maybe I only knew the surface. The outer layer."

Colin thought about Mom never wanting to talk about Dad. He thought about her answering his questions about Daryl, Derek, and Deepak by saying, "Sometimes you just have to let people keep their own secrets." And he remembered her telling the mysterious person on the telephone, "I'll keep your secret, you keep mine—nobody else needs to know about any of it."

Of course, he was keeping secrets from Mom, too.

He'd let her think he was at the library again tonight. She didn't know he'd met Nevaeh. He hadn't told her anything about finding the Rosemary and Toby letters.

She didn't know he'd taken pictures of something every single day on the job—some object she would have insisted was just junk that had to be thrown away.

He was still doing that, and nobody knew.

"Everybody has secrets," Colin said impatiently. "It's just, like, privacy. Everybody has a right to keep their own personal stuff to themselves. We don't all walk around with signs around our necks, 'This is who I am. This is what I'm thinking about right now. This is what I believe.'"

He turned toward Nevaeh to make his point . . . and burst out laughing.

"What?" Nevaeh said.

"Your . . . your shirt," Colin snorted. "It says 'The Junk King is #1'—it's like you *are* wearing a sign that says who you are! Or at least who you're related to!"

Nevaeh crossed her arms over her chest.

"It's from when Dad sponsored Dalton's baseball team, years ago," she muttered. "They were league champions, and the T-shirt maker accidentally made too many—this is just what we Greeveys wear when we haven't had a chance to do laundry. It doesn't mean anything."

"But, see, that's not how it works in my house," Colin said. "My mom would have gotten rid of those mistake shirts, like, the very first day."

Mom also had a regular laundry schedule. She and Colin took turns doing it. Colin couldn't remember ever running out of clean clothes.

He wasn't going to say that to Nevaeh.

Nevaeh kept her arms crossed.

"Yeah, I'd have thrown away the shirts, too, if it'd been

up to me." She scowled. "So, see? Even though I'm wearing actual *words*—"

"In neon orange," Colin added.

"Okay, sure," Nevaeh said grudgingly. "Even in neon orange. That still doesn't mean you can look at me and know anything *important* about me. Or any of my secrets."

Was she mad at him now?

"I'm not saying there's anything wrong with your shirt," Colin said quickly. "The fact that you're wearing that . . . it's like you're braver than I am. I stopped telling kids at school what my mom does after I got called 'Garbage Boy' all through second grade."

"Seriously?" Nevaeh said, rolling her eyes. She let her arms dangle again. "Why would they call you that? What your mom does, that's classy. 'Possession Curation'—it's like she runs her own museum. But I'm *not* ashamed of what my dad does. He hustles. He works *so* hard. When I was a little kid, I thought he was like that guy in the fairy tale— Rumpelstiltskin. The one who spun straw into gold. My dad turns junk into a paycheck."

She sounded so fierce. Colin said, "Is that your secret? That you're proud of your dad?"

He'd never had a conversation like this with anyone. Not even Mom.

Nevaeh and me, we are *like Rosemary and Toby,* he thought.

But Nevaeh only shrugged.

"I guess it's a Greevey thing," she said. "We're all proud of Dad. At least, I thought we were. What if everyone else in the family is only pretending? Like I pretend to be excited to be a 'Junk Princess'?"

Like I pretend for Mom that I don't mind working for her this summer, Colin thought.

But that was a good secret to keep. Wasn't it? It would have hurt Mom's feelings if she'd known how much Colin dreaded going to work with her that first day. Mom already felt bad about not being able to send him to his usual day camp.

Working with Mom wasn't as awful as Colin had expected, but still.

Looking every day for something to take a picture of—that keeps the job from being awful, Colin thought.

He hadn't really thought about it that way before.

"What if I don't even know the people in my own family?" Nevaeh asked. "What if Rosemary and Toby weren't even as good friends as we thought? What if we just *want* to think that?"

"But they tell each other so much," Colin argued. "So many other secrets. Rosemary even told Toby her mother thinks Richard Nixon is handsome and never should have resigned."

Nevaeh giggled.

"Right, and have you *seen* a picture of Richard Nixon?" she asked. "Who would admit that, except to a really close friend? Toby tells Rosemary he stands in front of a mirror and practices saying, 'Heyyyy,' like Fonzie in *Happy Days*. For *hours*."

"Rosemary tells Toby she tried breathing like a Sleestak in *Land of the Lost*, and it scared away the neighbor's dog when he was about to bite her," Colin said.

"Toby tells Rosemary it's kind of a shame that Billie Jean King beat Bobby Riggs in that 'Battle of the Sexes' tennis game, because he thought *Rosemary* would be the one to prove girls could be as good as boys in sports," Nevaeh said.

"And Rosemary said, 'Take it back! You are *never* allowed to say anything bad about Billie Jean King!'"

Colin grinned at Nevaeh, who grinned right back at him. It was like they had their own private language now, like they'd *both* memorized Rosemary's and Toby's letters, and looked up all the 1970s references. At first it had all seemed so long ago, so far away.

But not now.

"Did you watch any of that Billie Jean King–Bobby Riggs game online?" Nevaeh asked. "She *killed* him. And did you watch any of the TV shows Rosemary and Toby talk about? Like *Happy Days*?"

"Heyyyy," Colin said, leaning back and giving a double thumbs-up, doing *his* best Fonzie imitation. He felt ridiculous and cool, all at once. "Of course I did. It's kind of stupid, but . . . now I really want a black leather jacket."

"Is that the secret you keep from everyone?" Nevaeh teased. "The secret *you* would share if you were Rosemary or Toby, writing letters to your best friend?"

"Ha," Colin said. "No, it's—"

And then he stopped, because he really had been about to tell Nevaeh his biggest secret.

"You could tell me, you know," Nevaeh said. She didn't sound like she was about to laugh anymore. "I mean, I pretty much told you *my* biggest secret."

"You did?" Colin asked.

"Yeah." Nevaeh slowed down, barely easing the stroller forward. "It's that I love my dad, I love my whole family—but I hate being the Junk King's daughter, the youngest 'Junk Princess.' Because I hate junk."

Colin didn't laugh. He stopped in his tracks.

"It's like we were switched at birth or something," he said. "Because my mom's whole job is, like, a war on junk. She hates it, too. She hates clutter. She hates old stuff. She hates anything that doesn't have a purpose. But the more time I spend working for her this summer, the more I love all of that. I love junk! I—I even take pictures of it! Because I think it's beautiful!"

Colin clapped his hand over his mouth. How could he have said that? Especially just a minute after Nevaeh said she hated junk?

Nevaeh stopped beside him. One of the babies in the

stroller gave a little grunt of protest, but then he just sucked his thumb a little louder and went back to sleep. In the yard beside the sidewalk, an early firefly rose up from the grass. It was still bright enough out that Colin could see not just the firefly's light, but its striped body, its gossamer wings.

That's beautiful, too, Colin thought. *But fireflies are going to be ruined for me forever, because of this moment. Nevaeh's going to laugh at me, she's going to make fun of me, she's going to say that's the craziest thing she's ever heard. . . .*

Somehow Colin dared to look straight at Nevaeh anyhow.

"You take pictures of junk?" she asked. Her tone was curious, but not unkind.

"In every house my mom and I clear out," Colin said, talking fast now. "There's always something I want to remember. Something she thinks is nothing but garbage. Something nobody cares about but me. . . ."

It was like digging himself deeper and deeper into a hole. Deeper and deeper into losing Nevaeh as a friend. Deeper and deeper into her finding out how weird he was.

Deeper and deeper into not being able to *stop* being weird.

But Nevaeh still wasn't laughing. She wasn't grabbing the stroller and rushing away from him. She just stood there, waiting for him to finish talking.

And then she asked, "Can I see?"

24

Nevaeh Sees

"This isn't junk," Nevaeh whispered. "This is art."

Colin was holding his phone out for her, swiping through one photo after another. At first he'd kept a finger halfway over the screen, as if he didn't really want her to see. But every time she'd oohed or aahed, he'd seemed to relax a little more. Now he was letting her zoom in to look at each photo closely.

Somehow, in his phone pictures, crusty old Tupperware looked like a bouquet of roses.

A rusty fishing reel looked like a ladder.

A broken trike looked like a pet, like some creature you'd want to take home and nurse back to health.

"And you took all these pictures at houses in Groveview?" Nevaeh asked, still stunned. "I think you and your mom must encounter a different class of junk than we Greeveys do. *I've* never seen anything like this working for my dad. Or . . . maybe I just didn't look the right way? How do you do it?"

"I don't know," Colin said. He was blushing again, but it

seemed to be more from happiness now, not embarrassment. "I did change the—what's it called? Color saturation? —on some of the photos, and some other things I don't really understand, like this thing called vibrance. I had to play around a lot to get the pictures the way I wanted them. The . . . the way I saw them in my head."

"I could change the settings a million times on every picture on my phone, and I'd never get one that looks as good as this," Nevaeh said, pointing to a picture of toy soldiers jumbled together with jacks. "Sometimes Dad has Prilla or me take pictures of stuff we're trying to sell on Craigslist or eBay or wherever, and it takes us forever, and all we're trying to do is get one shot that isn't awful! It's a shame I can't just tell Dad to hire *you*! You're an artist! Or, I know, you should start an Instagram account. You'd get so many followers and likes, you'd become one of those influencers who actually get paid. And—"

"I couldn't do that!" Colin's voice arced high and panicky. "Mom would find out, and she'd say I was violating her clients' privacy."

"Why would they care, if it's stuff they're throwing away anyhow?" Nevaeh asked.

Colin's face got even redder.

"And . . . what if people laughed?" he asked.

"That doesn't matter, either," Nevaeh said. "It's on the

internet—you wouldn't hear them! You wouldn't even have to know they were laughing!"

"I could imagine it," Colin said. "And they might make really mean comments. People do that online. Trolls." He swallowed hard. "Anyhow, this is private. I don't *want* to show other people. I just take the pictures so I'll remember what I saw."

"But you showed me," Nevaeh said. And even though she was used to being loud and trying to make herself heard over a whole houseful of Greeveys, she let her voice drop low, so low it might as well have been a lullaby for the Torres twins. "You let me see."

"Yeah, but . . . ," Colin began. "You already know about the Toby and Rosemary letters. This is . . . like that. Something I can share with you, but I don't want to tell anyone else. I mean, even if you think Toby kept some things secret, don't you think Rosemary tells him everything?"

He means we're like Toby and Rosemary, Nevaeh thought. *He sees that, too!*

Except, she was still keeping secrets from Colin. Especially the one about how Nevaeh's dad thought Colin's mom might have stolen everything from the Mongold unit.

But if he knew that I want to clear her name, then . . .

The phone in the back pocket of Nevaeh's shorts began to vibrate. Nevaeh yanked it out: Mrs. Torres was calling.

Nevaeh tapped the screen and held it up to her ear.

"Hello?"

"Are the boys *still* awake?" Mrs. Torres asked. "I'm so sorry. It's going to be dark soon. Have they been screaming this whole time, and the neighbors are giving you dirty looks because they're so loud? You can just bring them home, and, I don't know, I'll rock them or something. . . ."

"Oh," Nevaeh said, glancing guiltily at the stroller, which she and Colin had left parked for at least the past fifteen minutes. "No, the boys are asleep now. That's just the wind you're hearing in the background. Everything's fine. We were just about to turn around and come back. So we'll be there in . . . let's say, ten minutes?"

She hung up.

"Oops," she told Colin. "We're not very good babysitters."

"The babies fell asleep, which was what Mrs. Torres wanted," Colin said, shrugging. "We've been right here beside them the whole time—they weren't in any danger."

He sounded so carefree. Which wasn't at all how he'd been the last time they'd babysat.

Or, really, any other time Nevaeh had been around him.

Is that because he told me his secret? Nevaeh wondered. *Because he trusted me?*

25

The Three Brothers Confess

Colin was walking on air.

It was the next day, and Colin was back in some stranger's attic. The attic was at least thirty degrees hotter than the rest of the house, and working with Daryl, Derek, and Deepak again just reminded him how much better they were at the job. Deepak could carry three boxes at once down the ladder, while Colin struggled to balance one without falling.

But Nevaeh liked my pictures! Nevaeh said they were art!

That kept singing through his brain. It made him feel like he was floating.

At noon, Mom said, "I'm going to work through lunch, so we can be sure to finish today. But if you want, come sit with me and keep me company while you eat."

Colin glanced at the card table set up in front of her. It looked like a jewelry store had vomited its contents into one gigantic heap. No, not just a jewelry store—the Walmart jewelry counter, the Target jewelry counter, and

Etsy, too. Mom was sorting through tangled necklaces and mismatched dangly earrings so the client could come back that afternoon and know with one glance what she did and didn't want to keep.

If Colin tried to eat at that table, he'd probably end up getting earring posts and charm bracelet figurines caught in his peanut butter sandwich.

Also, he would be so tempted to take pictures. He could frame the ballerina necklace alongside the boxing glove earrings. Or maybe the clunky button bracelet beside the pearl ring that still had a price tag on it—and the price tag was in yen. The sunlight was streaming in the window at the exact right angle that maybe he could make it look like the whole pile of jewelry was glowing. . . .

He really couldn't take pictures in front of Mom.

"Umm . . . ," he said.

"Little dude," Daryl called from the doorway. "Come eat with us. This room's like a bowling alley! How many chances do you get to eat in a bowling alley?"

"Uh, okay," Colin said.

He followed Daryl into the next room. This was another downsizing job—had the husband died and the wife was moving into assisted living, or was it the other way around? And was it the couple's daughter or daughter-in-law who'd hired Mom? Colin couldn't quite remember. But all the furniture was already gone from this room, and Daryl was right: the long, narrow expanse of empty wood floor did look like a good place to roll a bowling ball.

Derek and Deepak were spreading a length of thick plastic on the floor like a picnic blanket.

"Got to keep the customer happy," Derek said solemnly as he, Daryl, and Deepak all settled onto their own corners of the plastic. Belatedly, Colin sat down cross-legged on the fourth corner. "Always protect the flooring."

"This has been *Professional Movers Tips with Derek Greenlee*," Deepak intoned. "Tune in next time for his hour-long inspirational session, 'Don't Drop Anything.' You'll be stunned, you'll be awed, you'll be treated to insights you never could have discovered with your own puny brain. And—"

"Shut up!" Derek laughingly protested. He threw a potato chip at Deepak.

"Manners," Daryl scolded, shaking his head. "Management's eating with us today. Kid's going to think he's back in his middle school cafeteria."

Was Colin supposed to join in the joking and say something like, *That's right! Behave yourselves*? Or would it be better to protest, *No, I'm not management*? Or, *I'm not even in middle school yet. All I've ever seen is an elementary school cafeteria, and nobody threw food there*?

No. Colin wasn't as cool as Daryl, Derek, and Deepak,

but even he knew not to talk about elementary school.

It felt like everyone was waiting for Colin to say something, and it was awkward that he hadn't yet.

But Nevaeh liked my photos, he thought. *She called them "art"!*

That gave him enough confidence to say, "I thought you guys were really musicians, not professional movers. I mean, I know you do both, but . . . it's like actors who wait tables while they're going to auditions, right? This is just what you're doing while you're waiting for your big break?"

Colin saw the three teenaged boys exchange glances.

"That's right," Deepak said, his tone solemn again. "You should take notes on everything you hear us say this summer. Or, better yet, record us. You'll be able to say you knew us when. You might as well have footage to sell when the documentary about our careers comes out."

Daryl and Derek smirked.

Colin thought again about the pictures he'd taken.

"When you're playing music, when you're performing—how do you decide what you want to do?" he asked. "I mean, do you play only what *you* like, or are you trying more to make your audience happy? What if you play a song that you think is great, but people say mean things about it?"

It wasn't that he was really thinking seriously about doing what Nevaeh had suggested and posting photos online.

Or maybe he was.

"Ah, the eternal questions for an *artiste*," Deepak said, stroking his chin. "Are you asking if we would ever sell out and play only for money, not for love? Or to please ignoramuses—ignoramusi?—I mean, *critics* who have no taste? Never, my lad. Never."

Daryl and Derek began laughing so hard they both fell over. Derek landed on his bag of chips.

"Dee-man, you have to confess," Daryl said. "Even you can't keep this up."

"Confess what?" Colin asked, gazing around in bewilderment. Now Deepak was smirking, too. "You said you were musicians the first day. Aren't you musicians?"

"Right. We're in . . . we're in . . . *marching* band," Derek sputtered. "We're nerds! You're acting like we're, I don't know, the Rolling Stones, trying to decide whether to play 'Satisfaction' for the millionth time in concert, or whether to follow their artistic instincts and play something new."

In spite of his confusion, Colin felt a little burst of pride for knowing who the Rolling Stones were. Because of the Rosemary and Toby letters.

"You keep looking at us like you think we're cool, and, kid, that will get you in so much trouble in middle school. And high school," Daryl said. "I play the *xylophone*. The xylophone!"

"The . . . toy?" Colin asked, picturing the rainbow-colored wooden version he'd seen in his own baby pictures.

"This," Deepak said, holding out his phone. On the screen, about a dozen teenagers in ugly maroon uniforms clustered around Daryl, who was holding giant mallets above some musical instrument—evidently a xylophone—about the size of a piano keyboard. It was a still photo, not video, but Colin could still tell that Daryl's mallets had been flying. By the awe on the faces around Daryl, Colin could also tell that whatever he was playing was amazing.

But Derek started shaking his head. His red hair flopped around in a way that Colin did notice was a little nerdy.

"You've been hanging out with us for weeks now, Colin," Derek said. "You've heard us talking about AP Bio and SAT vocabulary words. And you still thought we were some cool musicians doing gigs every night?"

"How was I supposed to know? Three weeks ago I was still in elementary school!" Colin protested.

Oops. Hadn't he just told himself not to mention elementary school?

"Stop it!" Deepak thundered. At first Colin thought Deepak was yelling at him. But Deepak was actually glaring at Derek and Daryl. "You are falling for a false social construct. We can be cool and nerds, both. *You*"—he pointed at Daryl—"are going to be the next James Baldwin. And *you*"—this time he pointed at Derek—"don't have to follow your father into the fascinating world of gastroenterology unless you really want to. It wouldn't be an admission of failure to do that. Someone has to attend to the intestines of the hoi polloi of Groveview!"

"Intestines?" Colin said. "Isn't that—"

"Yep," Deepak said. "Dude thinks he doesn't have a choice but to be a poop doctor. But, Colin, the three of us—Daryl, Derek, and me—we do actually have a rock band, too. It's just not . . . widely known. Because we haven't decided yet if we're going to call it Stilt Opera, Krill River, or Wandering Vector."

So that's why I couldn't find any of those band names online, Colin thought.

"But you said those bands are what the cool kids are listening to now!" he protested.

"Right," Deepak said. "Because every single person who's ever heard our music absolutely loves it."

Daryl groaned. Derek rolled his eyes.

"That's because only one other person in the entire world has ever heard us," Derek muttered. "And Prilla's so nice, she'd have told us she loved it no matter what."

"Prilla?" Colin said. Wasn't that Nevaeh's sister's name? How many girls named Prilla could there be in Groveview? He glanced back over his shoulder. Mom had stepped away from her tableful of tangled jewelry. Where had she gone? He caught a glimpse of her through one of the windows. She was on the front porch, talking on the phone. So Colin dared to ask, "Do you mean Prilla *Greevey*?"

Daryl glanced over his shoulder, too, as if he knew not to talk about any Greevey near Mom.

"Do you know Prilla?" he asked.

"Not really," Colin said quickly. "I've just . . . heard the name."

"Because Deepak whispers it under his breath every time he starts daydreaming about her?" Derek asked. "Which he does all the time?"

"I never said I was in love with Prilla!" Deepak protested. "That time I asked her about her name—it was only because I thought it *could* be Indian. Or, you know, some white person's idea of 'Hey, let's give our kid a name from another culture.'"

"And then when she said it was actually short for 'Sarsaparilla,' you just stood there all lovestruck, and said, 'What a beautiful name.'" Derek imitated Deepak by gazing off into space and blinking dramatically.

"Prilla's real name is Sarsaparilla?" Colin asked, even as he wondered, *Is Nevaeh's name short for something, too?*

"Those Greeveys, they march to the beat of their own drummer," Deepak said. Now he was the one glancing into the other room, to watch for Mom. "You've got to admire that."

"Only, you admire some Greeveys more than others," Daryl joked.

"And now you've psyched yourself out so badly, you don't even dare to say anything to Prilla besides, 'W-w-will you listen to my band?'" Derek added.

Colin shook his head, trying to clear it. He'd misread Daryl, Derek, and Deepak entirely, the whole time they'd been working together. He didn't actually care if they were cool or nerdy, rock stars or marching band kids. Maybe he even liked them better, knowing they were nerds. But he'd thought they were . . . complete. He'd thought they knew who they were and what they were doing with their lives.

Instead, they were like him—still trying to figure that out. Deepak could talk a mile a minute, pretending to be some kind of announcer. How could he be terrified of saying more than six words to Prilla?

Maybe he should be like Toby, and start writing letters, Colin thought.

Then he got chills.

What if Rosemary and Toby were totally different in person than they seem in their letters? he wondered. *What if Nevaeh and I haven't figured them out at all?*

Daryl and Derek were still harassing Deepak, teasing him about being in love with Prilla. Colin eased his phone out of his pocket and typed a quick text to Nevaeh:

What if we find Rosemary and Toby—and we don't even like them?

What if finding them ruins everything?

26

What Nevaeh Figures Out

"I still want to know," Nevaeh said.

It was Saturday morning, and they were back together at the library. And Nevaeh was still disagreeing with Colin, just as she had with every text message since Wednesday.

"But it's fun enough right now, just with the letters," Colin said. "It's like we have our own secret language because of them. How else would you have found out about that 'zephyr winds' chant?"

Nevaeh wished she'd never told Colin how much she liked all the female superheroes she'd learned about in Rosemary's letters. Back in the 1970s, there'd been a Wonder Woman TV show, a bionic woman TV show, and—Rosemary's favorite— one about a teacher who found a magical Egyptian amulet that gave her the powers of "Oh, mighty Isis." That even included the ability to fly, when she chanted about "zephyr winds which blow on high." Nevaeh had joked that she'd tried that chant, hoping to get superpowers to deal with all the garbage she'd encountered last week.

Obviously it hadn't worked. But thinking about magical amulets had made her look at the garbage differently.

So had thinking about the photos Colin took.

And thinking about solving a mystery with Colin.

"Sure, we've had fun because of the letters," Nevaeh said. "So shouldn't we repay Toby and Rosemary by helping them? And . . ."

She clamped her mouth shut—she'd almost messed up and started talking about the *other* mystery: the one about the antiques missing from the Mongold storage unit. She couldn't tell Colin his own mother was a suspect. Or that, if Nevaeh was ever invited to Colin's house, her dad and brothers would want her to swipe evidence of his mom's fingerprints or handwriting.

At least Dad is considering *the possibility that it wasn't Felicia Creedmont, but Maribel Mongold who really did write that letter saying she took all the antiques,* Nevaeh thought.

But the fingerprinting had proved "inconclusive." The handwriting analysis kept getting delayed: Nobody could find anything else Maribel Mongold ever wrote, to compare with the letter.

Regardless of whether Maribel had loved her husband or hated him, she seemed completely . . . invisible . . . outside her marriage.

I can't believe that Rosemary could have become that invisible, too, Nevaeh thought.

She wanted to prove Rosemary had done something great, just as much as she wanted to prove that Colin's mom hadn't stolen anything.

"And . . . wouldn't you want your letters back if you were Rosemary or Toby?" Nevaeh finished weakly.

"They knew where the letters were, because they put them there themselves," Colin said. "They could have come back for the letters anytime they wanted, if they cared."

"What if they *didn't* know the letters were left in their attics?" Nevaeh argued. "What if they had mean parents, and the parents said they'd found the letters and burned them? What if they both died tragically, and they left behind kids who would be so, so happy to get these letters, and find out what their parents were like as kids?"

"How can you be so sure it'll be a happy ending if we find them?" Colin asked.

"You're calling it a happy ending that I'm imagining Rosemary and Toby both being dead?" Nevaeh said.

"You know what I mean," Colin said. "You're only seeing it as a good thing, finding Toby and Rosemary."

She did know what he meant. Even when they were disagreeing, they understood each other. The two of them hadn't even made it into the library lobby yet. She'd seen Colin at the bike rack, and they'd started talking right away.

This is how it was with Colin. The two of them could talk and talk and talk.

Nevaeh was certain that was how it had been with Toby and Rosemary, too.

So they deserved to get their letters back. No matter what.

"We might find out that something sad happened to Toby and Rosemary—or both of them—but I still want to know," Nevaeh said. "Because we won't find out anything that will make us dislike them. I just know it. How could they change that much from who they were at eight or ten or twelve?"

Colin went over and sat down on a bench partially hidden in tree branches.

"People can change," he whispered.

Nevaeh joined him on the bench. And then she waited. It wasn't like her not to fill up a silence with chatter. But for once, she didn't know what to say.

"You probably already know my parents are divorced, right?" Colin asked. "And the whole reason my mom started working for your dad was because my parents split up and she needed to do *something* right away?"

Had Nevaeh known that? She couldn't remember hearing anything, one way or another, about Colin's dad. She hadn't even thought about it. Secretly, she'd always thought that other people's dads were boring. Back in fifth grade, she'd been in the same class with a girl named Reagan who was always bragging, "You know my dad is the mayor of Groveview, don't you?" She was one of the worst kids ever for teasing Nevaeh about being the Junk King's daughter. Then the mayor was voted out of office. Nevaeh wasn't proud of this, but she'd run over to Reagan the next morning on the playground all ready to say, *At least my dad didn't lose his job!* But Reagan had been crying, so Nevaeh said, "Sorry about your dad," instead.

That was practically the only conversation Nevaeh could remember having about anyone else's dad.

"Lots of kids' parents are divorced," Nevaeh said now.

Colin winced.

"I guess it doesn't help to have me say that?" Nevaeh asked.

"No, it's okay," Colin said. "I don't remember a time when my parents *weren't* divorced, so it's not like I'm just getting used to it. I don't even remember my father, because I never see him. I just brought it up because . . . there had to have been a time when my mother loved my father, right? Because she married him? And now she thinks he's so awful she can't even talk about him? He *must* have changed."

Nevaeh tried to imagine being Colin. It was hard for her to imagine being anything but a Greevey. It was hard for her to imagine not having Dad always there, always filling up the house with his exuberance and his big plans.

And the trash that he saw as treasures.

"Maybe your mom is just waiting until you're older to talk about all that," Nevaeh said gently. "You're twelve, right? Like me? Sometimes parents forget how old that is. Maybe you just need to tell your mom you're ready to have your questions answered."

"But what if I'm not?" Colin asked. "What if I can't cope with whatever I'd find out?"

"Are you talking about your dad now, or Rosemary and Toby?" Nevaeh asked, because she was getting confused.

"Oh," Colin said. He bit his lip. "Maybe . . . both?"

A cicada buzzed in the tree behind them, and Nevaeh jumped. Cicadas always reminded her of the end of summer, of August and the countdown to school starting again. At the rate she and Colin were going, it would be August before they found out anything about Rosemary or Toby.

"Maybe finding out about Rosemary and Toby could be like your . . . test case," Nevaeh said. "You could work up to finding out more about your dad. And, with Rosemary and Toby, we'll be in it together. Even if we find out something bad about them, *we'll* still be friends."

Colin met her gaze. He had such dark brown eyes. They didn't remind Nevaeh of his mom's anymore. In the pictures Nevaeh had seen of Felicia Creedmont, she always looked so perfect, so mysterious, so unknowable. But Nevaeh knew Colin now. *He* was knowable. She even had a pretty good idea what he was about to say.

"Okay," he agreed. "As long as we stay friends."

27

Information

Old people remembered a lot.

The man at 895 Elm Street remembered that Toby's father had driven a black Ford the whole time the Carters had lived at 895 Willow.

The woman at 109 Haven remembered that Rosemary's mother had had beautiful dresses, always the latest style, and never stepped foot out of her house without perfectly curled hair.

The couple at 210 Haven remembered that Rosemary's dad had had some big important job at "the bank"—though they couldn't remember which bank it was, or what he'd actually done there.

And to get to that information, Colin and Nevaeh had also heard about random other kids, parents, grandkids, cars, dresses, dogs, cats, parakeets (and one ferret, one hedgehog, and one lost stuffed zebra), houses, garages, meals eaten, meals not eaten, good times, bad times, recessions, jobs lost, jobs found, graduation ceremonies, babies born, people of every age dying, ne'er-do-wells, hard workers, doughnut shops, health food crazes, bursitis, arthritis, diabetes, heart attacks, surgeries . . .

"Oh my gosh, that was like cleaning out an attic or a basement," Nevaeh giggled, once they were out of earshot of the man who lived at 742 Willow. "Except instead of having to shove aside fifty years' worth of mouse droppings to see if there's anything good underneath, we had to listen to stories about every 'bowel movement' he's had in the past fifty years!"

"At least he remembered that Toby's dad worked at 'the factory,'" Colin said.

Nevaeh giggled again.

"Did you see how he looked at me like I was crazy when I said, 'What factory?'" she asked. "How was I supposed to know there was only one factory in town fifty years ago?"

"And it shut down in 1977," Colin said, raising an eyebrow at Nevaeh. He knew she'd understand.

The two of them said, practically in unison, "The same year both Toby and Rosemary moved."

Colin had started the day knowing absolutely nothing about the Groveview Glass factory. But now he looked to the west, down Willow Street, and he could almost picture the factory gates the man had described. The man had said, "When I was a boy, I thought the factory looked like a castle," and that made Colin want to search for pictures of the old building. And the man—whose name was Mr. Robinson—had kind of tricked Colin and Nevaeh, because he'd said, "Of course, there are golden arches there now."

Colin was still trying to figure which building in Groveview was grand enough to have golden arches when Mr. Robinson had shouted, "Because they built the McDonald's there after the factory closed!"

Mr. Robinson had laughed much harder than the joke required.

"People just don't remember the *right* details," Nevaeh complained. "It's like Rosemary and Toby weren't even important to them."

"They were important to each other," Colin said. "They're important to *us*."

It kind of felt important to him now, to know that Groveview had once had a glass factory. He could squint and imagine men and women—er, no, almost all men, because it was fifty years ago—stepping out of their houses on Willow Street, carrying lunch buckets and thermoses of coffee all at the same time. And then, by the time the factory whistle blew, the street was empty again.

Colin looked around. The cars parked along the street were all definitely from the twenty-first century. A woman sitting on the front porch swing of the next house over was tapping away on a laptop. A teenaged boy walking toward them was peering at his phone screen and bopping his head up and down, undoubtedly in time with music he was listening to through earbuds so tiny that they were barely specks in his ears. Colin knew what year it was. But after spending the morning talking to old people, Colin felt like he could see layers of history in the neighborhood. The house on the corner had been the last one built, and back in the 1950s, all the kids in the neighborhood had had a clubhouse on that vacant lot. During the Iranian hostage crisis in 1979, every tree on the block had a yellow ribbon tied around it. (Colin resolved to look up what the Iranian hostage crisis actually was. And why the ribbons were yellow.) After September 11, 2001, every house on the block flew an American flag.

Nevaeh was right. This was like cleaning out an attic. And Colin felt just as overwhelmed as he always did staring at an attic packed to its eaves with ancient, dusty boxes. What he and Nevaeh wanted to know about Toby and Rosemary was buried in the past. The two kids had apparently both disappeared from Groveview in 1977, and it seemed like the only traces they'd left behind besides the letters were buried in old people's memories—underneath all those other memories about everything from arthritis to zebras.

He and Nevaeh could talk to everyone in town and never find out what they wanted to know.

"Have we done the whole list yet?" he asked Nevaeh, peering over her shoulder at the pages of addresses they'd both looked up online.

"Everybody who was home this morning," Nevaeh said glumly. She braced the papers against her knee and crossed off Mr. Robinson's name. "Maybe we should swing back around to the three houses where people didn't answer their doors, and try again?"

"I guess," Colin said, without much enthusiasm.

They turned around—and there was Mr. Robinson again, struggling toward them on his walker.

"I . . . remembered." He huffed and puffed, trying to catch his breath.

Colin and Nevaeh rushed back toward him, closing the distance in three giant steps.

"Thank . . . you," he panted. "It would have taken me ten minutes to get to you."

It'd just been a distance of four sidewalk squares.

Mr. Robinson brushed sweat off his bushy gray eyebrows.

"I remembered as soon as you left. . . ." He stopped to catch his breath. "I know where the Carters moved after they left Groveview. Ridge Hollow. Down toward Athens. A bunch of . . . the factory workers went there. Word was, the boot factory was hiring. You know about the famous boot factory in Ridge Hollow?"

"No, sorry," Nevaeh said politely, even as she waggled her eyebrows at Colin.

"Oh, then let me tell you. . . ." Mr. Robinson began a long, rambling account that didn't contain a single other mention of Toby's family.

Colin let Nevaeh fill in with lots of "uh-huhs" and "Oh reallys?" while Colin himself stepped to the side and whipped out his phone. He typed in "Toby Carter" with "Ridge Hollow, Ohio."

His phone told him nothing. Unless he counted the words "Your search didn't match any documents."

Nevaeh was gazing so hopefully at Colin that Colin felt bad having to shake his head.

"Okay, thank you," Nevaeh told Mr. Robinson. "It was really nice of you to come all this way to tell us that." They were only about fifty yards away from Mr. Robinson's house, but Colin understood what Nevaeh meant—Mr. Robinson had worked really hard to get to them. "I'm sure that'll help us. Somehow. Can we, um, help you get back to your house?"

"No, no." Mr. Robinson waved them off. "The doctors say I'm supposed to be getting exercise every day. This counts."

He turned and began hobbling back toward his house. Each step looked painful.

Nevaeh and Colin started walking in the other direction.

"What if we find Rosemary and Toby and they're like

that?" Colin muttered. "Old and miserable?"

That would ruin the letters, too.

"Who says Mr. Robinson is miserable?" Nevaeh asked. "Didn't you hear how many times he told us he's lucky to be alive?" She got a mischievous gleam in her eye. "And lucky every morning when he sits down on the toilet, and—"

"Stop!" Colin protested.

"Anyhow, Mr. Robinson has got to be, like, at least ninety," Nevaeh said. "Rosemary and Toby aren't anywhere near that. And Rosemary would be the type who'd retire in order to run marathons. Toby would—"

"Have eaten so many Lucky Charms marshmallows and Captain Crunch Crunchberries he exploded?" Colin asked. "Remember his list?"

One of Toby's letters was devoted almost entirely to his vow to never eat a vegetable again once he turned eighteen. He'd also included a list of what he thought the only food groups should be: Cakes, Cookies, Candy, and Sugary breakfast cereals—but only the sugary parts, not the healthy stuff grown-ups tried to sneak in along with the marshmallows.

"He probably didn't actually eat like that once he grew up," Nevaeh said.

"Isn't it funny that we feel like we know Rosemary and Toby so well, but we don't have a clue what either one of them looked like?" Colin asked. He couldn't decide whether to imagine Toby as hugely overweight or as one of those kids who ate constantly but still stayed super-skinny.

Nevaeh groaned and began typing on her phone.

"That's another question we should be asking," she muttered.

"That one lady did tell us that Rosemary was a 'pretty little girl,'" Colin said. "But that could mean anything. Any hair color, any eye color, any skin color . . ."

"No, we know the skin color," Nevaeh said, wincing. "Because, remember? There's that one letter where Rosemary was so mad at her grandmother for how she talked about anyone who wasn't white."

"Oh, yeah," Colin said. "How could she have been so prejudiced?" He struggled to remember details from social studies class. "Wasn't that after Martin Luther King and the civil rights movement and—"

"And *we're* living after the 1970s and some people are still racist," Nevaeh countered. "Or, remember, Rosemary went on and on about women's lib in her letters, and even now women still make less money than men do for the same jobs. Things don't change overnight. Or, sometimes, not even in forty or fifty years."

She looked so outraged. Colin realized he'd started picturing Rosemary looking exactly like Nevaeh. Rosemary's nostrils would have flared just as indignantly. Her eyes would squint together and glare just as intensely.

The way Colin imagined Rosemary, details like hair, eye, and skin color didn't even matter.

Colin peered off past Nevaeh as though he was trying to peer back through the past, seeing each historical era unfurling down the street.

Instead, he saw a green car pull up in front of Mr. Robinson's house. The man inside the car rolled down his window and started talking to Mr. Robinson. Colin saw Mr. Robinson point back over his shoulder toward Colin and Nevaeh.

And then the man got out of the car and started walking toward them.

"Uh, Nevaeh?" Colin muttered.

This man had a graying beard, but looked a lot younger than Mr. Robinson.

He walked a lot faster, too.

"You the kids asking about Toby Carter?" the man said. He almost sounded accusing. Even Nevaeh barely managed a nod. But the man went on anyway. "You're asking the wrong generation. Dad wasn't paying attention to all the kids running around this neighborhood in the 1970s."

"But you were?" Colin dared to ask.

"Heck, I was one of them," the man said, and now he grinned. "Though if anyone asks who hit the ball that went through the MacAllisters' front window, I still plead the Fifth. And I still blame Toby Carter for his bad pitch. . . ."

"You knew Toby?" Nevaeh breathed.

The man shrugged.

"Yeah, sure," he said. "I even know why you can't find him."

"Why?" Colin asked.

"Because," the man said, practically smirking. "That isn't his name anymore."

28

Nevaeh, Names, and the Wrong Side of the Tracks

"What?" Nevaeh asked. All the reasons someone might change their name flooded into her mind.

No, not just "someone," she thought, feeling as though Rosemary would be ashamed of her for not seeing the difference. *A man.*

Just about every married woman she knew had changed her name, and Nevaeh had wondered if Rosemary had done that, and that was why they couldn't find her.

But she'd never thought about Toby Carter not staying Toby Carter his entire life.

"Why?" Colin asked, reacting only a second behind her. "And when did Toby change his name?"

"After he moved away," the man said. "I got a letter from him—and I remember this, because what twelve-year-old kid writes letters?—and he told me that he started going by Robbie Carter in his new school."

Nevaeh saw Colin waggle his eyebrows at her, and she

knew exactly what he was thinking: *This man didn't know Toby wrote letters all the time to Rosemary.*

At least, he'd done that when he still called himself "Toby."

"I guess he'd always gone by his middle name here, and he was making a new start and using his first name instead," the man went on. "And I remember thinking that was funny, because he was still 'Robbie,' not Robert, still in his dad's shadow. . . ."

"So you guys must have been good friends, if you wrote each other letters," Nevaeh said.

The man with the gray beard winced.

"I don't actually think I ever answered Toby's letter," he said. "I mean, I wasn't all that great at writing things for school, so to write a letter that wasn't *required*? Naw, wasn't going to happen."

Nevaeh imagined how that must have felt to Toby—er, Robbie—who'd lost his friendship with Rosemary, and then moved to a new town where he probably didn't know anyone, and then written a letter to an old friend (or, *not* a friend) who didn't even bother writing back.

She had to bite her lip to keep from yelling at the man standing in front of her now: *How could you have been so mean?*

Maybe some of that showed on her face. Because the man with the gray beard said defensively, "Look, I was thirteen, okay? All I cared about was football and getting Becky Appleton to be my girlfriend. It felt kind of . . . weird that Toby was writing to me. Because we weren't good friends. We just lived in the same neighborhood for a while. And Toby was telling me he was stealing my *name*."

"*Your* name?" Colin asked, his voice sharp.

"Oh, sorry, didn't introduce myself," the man said. "Everyone called me Robbie Robinson back then. Because of my last name. You kids in high school yet? There's still a picture of me hanging in the hallway that leads out to the football field at Groveview High. Because I held the state record for rushing my senior year."

"We're not even in middle school yet," Nevaeh said. Robbie Robinson looked so disappointed that she added, "But it sounds like the football thing worked out for you. Did you ever convince Becky Appleton to be your girlfriend?"

Now Robbie Robinson gave her a sincere grin.

"Been married almost forty years," he said.

"Do you or your wife know anything else about Toby-who-became-Robbie Carter?" Colin asked. "Or do you know what happened to Rosemary Buvon after she left Groveview?"

"Rosemary Buvon?" Robbie Robinson shook his head. "Man, that's a name from the past. You're on the wrong side of the tracks for that one."

"Tracks?" Nevaeh repeated doubtfully. "You mean . . . train tracks?"

Robbie Robinson flashed her a look as if she'd asked if the sky was blue.

"Are you two even from Groveview?" he asked. Then he looked around, and his expression softened. "Oh, I guess you wouldn't know it from what houses in this neighborhood are selling for now. And how rundown other parts of town have become . . ." He gestured toward a railroad crossing sign three blocks away. "Back in the day, those tracks were the dividing line between rich and poor, between people who ate, I don't know, caviar, and people who ate fried bologna. Toby and me, we were fried bologna types. Rosemary Buvon, I bet she didn't even know what bologna was."

"You're saying she was rich," Colin said. He looked like he was trying to remember which side of the tracks his own house was on.

"Not just rich, but . . . like, classy," Robbie Robinson corrected. "The type who'd be on a float in the Christmas parade every year. Who took shopping trips out of town to buy her clothes. I remember because girls like my Becky, they wanted to *be* her. And boys like me, we knew she was out of our league. So if you're asking if Rosemary wrote a letter to Becky or me after she moved—no, sir, *that* didn't happen. People like Rosemary and people like us, we didn't mix."

"But—" Nevaeh began. Colin caught her eye and shook his head, and that stopped her from launching into, *But Toby and Rosemary were friends! They wrote letters to each other*

• 209 •

all the time! And from what you're saying, Toby lived on the wrong side of the tracks, so Rosemary would have been "out of his league," too!

It almost felt like she'd been on the verge of betraying Rosemary and Toby. If those two hadn't wanted Robbie Robinson to know they were friends fifty years ago, she shouldn't tell now.

"But what you were asking about Toby?" Robbie Robinson said. "I do know more about him. He became a college professor. Wrote one of those books that normal people make fun of, acting like what's on TV should be studied like Shakespeare plays. I know because my cousin's stepkid went to Ohio State and took his class. Three hundred kids sitting in a lecture hall listening to Toby . . . it made me remember all those times we'd yell at Toby, 'Unless Farrah Fawcett-Majors herself is on the sidelines cheering for us, shut up about *Charlie's Angels*, and catch the football like you're supposed to!' I almost asked the stepkid to tell Toby, 'Robbie Robinson says hello.' But I guess by then Toby was out of my league, too."

Now Nevaeh felt kind of sorry for Robbie Robinson. How had that happened? A moment ago, she'd almost wanted to punch him in the nose for bragging about his picture at the high school.

"Does Toby still call himself Robbie Carter?" Colin asked. "Is he still a professor at Ohio State?"

Nevaeh was glad he'd stayed focused. They would need to look up Toby/Robbie Carter's book. They could look up Ohio State professors.

Robbie Robinson snorted.

"That was the other thing that stopped me from having my cousin's stepkid say anything," he said. "I don't know what Toby goes by in normal life now, but the name on his book? It's 'Robb Tobias Carter.' 'Robb' with two *b*'s. Can you imagine? Some kid I used to tackle, with such a snobby name? I don't know how people don't just laugh in his face every time they see him."

And . . . now Nevaeh was back to wanting to punch Robbie Robinson.

"You just made it possible for us to find Toby," Colin said, his eyes wide, his face gone soft with astonishment. "Thank you."

Colin is nicer than me, Nevaeh thought.

"Yes, thank you," she repeated. "We really are grateful. And you know what? We're going to get in touch with Toby. And *we'll* tell him you said hello."

"You do that," Robbie Robinson said, as if that had been what he wanted all along. "Tell him I said sorry for never answering his letter, too."

Robbie Robinson could have done that himself, any time over the past fifty years. He'd known where Toby Carter was. He'd known Toby's new name all along.

I don't understand people who aren't Greeveys at all, Nevaeh thought. *No one in my family would wait like that!*

Would she understand Rosemary and Toby when she met them?

At least now it seemed like that really could happen.

29

Colin and the Email

By the time Robbie Robinson turned around to go back to his dad's house, Colin already had the name "Robb Tobias Carter" typed into his phone. He'd found the title of Toby's book—*Stay Tuned: How Television Reshaped American Culture in the Last Half of the Twentieth Century*—by the time Nevaeh glanced his way. Colin was halfway into searching for a list of professors at Ohio State by the time she opened her mouth.

Maybe sometimes he could be as quick at doing things as his mom. When he really wanted to.

"It'd be kind of cool if we sent Toby a letter," Nevaeh said, watching Colin's phone screen over his shoulder. "A letter about his letters—that'd be, I don't know, poetic justice or something. But I don't want to wait. Let's call him, if we can find a phone number."

"It'll have to be email," Colin said, holding the phone up higher to show off the web page he'd found.

"Ohhh," Nevaeh breathed. "There's a picture. He looks . . ."

"Grown up?" Colin asked.

Without even trying, he had started to form an image in his mind of Toby Carter. Toby would have had a mischievous smirk on his face. Toby would have had his mouth open, constantly talking about TV shows like *Charlie's Angels* or *Welcome Back, Kotter*, or *Happy Days*. Toby would be in constant motion, scrambling not to be tackled by Robbie Robinson.

Toby would look like a kid.

Robb Tobias Carter—*Professor* Robb Tobias Carter— was starting to lose his hair. He wore scholarly glasses. He looked like someone who ate kale and tofu all the time, not someone who lived on Captain Crunch Crunchberries and Lucky Charms marshmallows.

"I was going to say 'nice,'" Nevaeh said. "I don't know any professors, but he looks like one of those teachers who listen when you ask a question, instead of saying, 'That's not what we're supposed to be working on today.' The kind who would laugh when you told a joke in class, as long as it didn't hurt anyone's feelings."

Colin didn't tell jokes in class, and he tried to avoid asking teachers questions. But he could see what Nevaeh meant. Even as an adult, Professor Robb Tobias Carter had a twinkle in his eye. A twinkle that maybe said, *I remember being a kid*.

"But he must have hurt Rosemary's feelings fifty years ago, right?" Colin said uncertainly. "Because of how their last letters ended? If those were their last letters, I mean. If they didn't stay in touch after that. If—"

"It's time to find out," Nevaeh said, slipping Colin's phone out of his grasp. She clicked on the link for Robb Tobias Carter's email address and began typing.

Colin thought about objecting, *Why are you sending that from my phone? From my email address?*

What if Mom finds out? he thought nervously.

But he knew Nevaeh didn't want her family to find out, either.

She turned the phone around so Colin could see what she'd written:

> Dear Professor Carter,
> We are two kids who live in Groveview, Ohio. We found some letters you and your friend Rosemary Buvon wrote to each other a long time ago. We wondered if you and Rosemary would want them back. We also wondered if you know where Rosemary is now, so we can ask her the same question. You can email us back or call us at (740) 555-6308.
> Colin and Nevaeh

"You're giving him my phone number but not yours?" Colin objected.

Nevaeh pointed to herself.

"Twelve-year-old girl," she said. She clicked back to the picture of Professor Robb Tobias Carter. "Fiftysomething man I don't even know. You and me, we know this is all innocent, but . . . let's make sure no one thinks it's something creepy, okay?"

Colin hadn't even thought of that. He was still stuck on thinking of Toby as another kid. And as someone they knew really well.

"I should send it, right?" Nevaeh said, and now even she sounded a little unsure.

"Right," Colin said.

Nevaeh clicked back to the email and touched the screen once more, and then the message was gone.

Colin took a deep breath.

"I can't believe we did that," he said. "I kind of didn't even believe that Toby and Rosemary were real. But now . . . but now . . ."

Nevaeh slid the phone back into his hand. Colin kept staring at it as though it might ring any minute.

Or, maybe, explode.

Nevaeh laughed.

"He might not get that email for weeks," she said. "He might not even check his work email over the summer." She tugged on Colin's elbow, pulling him forward. They probably did look weird, standing in the middle of the sidewalk staring at a phone for so long. "We shouldn't just *wait*. Let's go back to the library while we figure out what to do next. We should see about looking up a home address and phone number. An Ohio State professor would probably live in Columbus, wouldn't he?"

"I guess," Colin said. "I—"

His phone started to vibrate in his hand. Colin glanced at the screen. An unfamiliar number scrolled across the top, with the words "Columbus, Ohio" right below.

Colin froze. The phone kept ringing. Finally Nevaeh snatched it from his hand.

"Hello?" she said. "Professor Carter?"

30

The Meeting

Nevaeh squirmed on the hard plastic of the picnic table bench at Morningside Park. It was only an hour later—only an hour since she'd sent the email to Professor Carter, only about fifty-five minutes since he'd called Colin's number . . . and only about ten minutes before she and Colin were going to meet Professor Carter.

To meet Toby.

It already felt like they'd been waiting forever. And that next ten minutes would probably feel even more endless.

But, really, it was amazing how quickly Professor Carter was getting here.

He'd said he was just getting into his car to leave a conference and, as luck would have it, he'd been about to drive down to see friends in Cincinnati, anyhow. He said it wouldn't be a big deal to detour through Groveview.

Not a big deal? Nevaeh thought. *What if he's not taking these letters seriously? What if he doesn't even care?*

He'd cared enough to call the very minute he saw Nevaeh and Colin's email. Groveview was not exactly on the direct route from Columbus to Cincinnati—Professor Carter cared enough to drive probably an hour out of his way.

Beside Nevaeh, Colin kept fussing with the boxes of letters, first putting one on the table and hiding the other one in his lap, then putting them both on the table and sliding them together and then apart, lining them up straight, then knocking them crooked. . . .

"What if he's an ax murderer?" Colin said suddenly.

"You mean Toby?" Nevaeh asked. "Professor Carter? Why would he be an ax murderer? *We* invited *him* to meet us." She rolled her eyes at Colin. "It's not like it'd be an effective ax murderer technique, luring kids to their death by hiding shoeboxes in attics. Especially not *underneath* floorboards in attics."

"You were the one worried about this seeming creepy," Colin said. "I mean, we are meeting a stranger, and no one besides him even knows we're here. . . ."

Nevaeh looked around. Morningside Park was barely big enough to be called a park. It held one forlorn, rusty swing set and a climbing structure that probably hadn't even been new when Colin and Nevaeh were little. They'd chosen this as a meeting spot specifically *because* it always seemed to be empty. And it was only a half block from the house on

Willow Street where Toby had lived as a kid. But now, even with the bright midday sun beating down on them, the empty park felt a little eerie.

"I don't want my family to know what I'm up to," Nevaeh said. "Because it's connected to you and, well, your mom. Do you want to call your mom so at least she'll know?"

"I don't want my mom to know I'm hanging out with you, either," Colin muttered.

Nevaeh slapped her hand against the table.

"Mrs. Torres," she said.

She pulled out her phone and texted Mrs. Torres: **Are you home this afternoon? Colin and I found the guy who used to live in your house, who left the letters. We're meeting him in Morningside Park. Do you want to meet him if he wants to see what your house looks like now?**

She waited a second, then added, **You can ask about the wallpaper put on with Elmer's glue.**

Mrs. Torres's reply was quick: **Sure. Just knock instead of ringing the doorbell, because the twins are sleeping.**

"There," Nevaeh said. "So if we just vanish, Mrs. Torres will be able to help the police solve the mystery." She stopped herself from rolling her eyes at Colin again. "That was a good idea. Mrs. Torres probably would want to meet Toby. *I'd* want to meet all the people who used to live in my house if, you know, it wasn't just one long line of Greeveys."

Colin was quiet for a moment, then he said, "Why is it ax murderers that people worry about all the time, anyway? The ax part, I mean. Is that something that happens a lot?"

"You're right," Nevaeh said. "Nobody ever says, 'What if you run into a gun murderer?' Or 'knife murderer' or . . . what are all the weapons in the Clue game? 'Rope murderer'? 'Lead pipe murderer'?"

"'Candlestick murderer'?" Colin suggested.

"Those are exactly the kind of questions Rosemary and I would have asked," a voice said behind them.

Nevaeh and Colin both jumped. Then they whirled around. Toby—Professor Carter—had come through the back of the park, instead of the front like they'd expected. He looked a little older and had even less hair than in his website picture, but he had the same kind smile. Now he also had a scratch on his arm, a curled-up maple leaf on the shoulder of his polo shirt, and some sort of prickly-bush vine stuck to the bottom of his khaki pants.

"Oh, sorry," he said. "You're talking about ax murderers, and here I am sneaking up on you. . . . Didn't mean to scare you. I just took my usual route through the park, and I didn't think about how the 'usual route' from fifty years ago would be so overgrown now. . . ." He brushed the maple leaf from his shoulder.

Nevaeh could tell the exact moment when Professor Carter

saw the shoeboxes sitting on the picnic table. He jerked back, and muttered, "Oh. Oh my . . ."

And then he just stood there.

And stood there.

"You can sit down," Nevaeh offered, because somebody had to say *something*.

Professor Carter kind of shook himself off.

"Oh, right," he said. "I just . . . I'm not sure I actually believed you when you said you'd found those. I . . . The letters are all there, too?"

Colin lifted the shoebox lids, first one and then the other. Nevaeh and Colin had been so careful about putting the letters back in the same order as when they'd found them. But that meant that the two cruelest letters were on top: Toby's begging, "Please please PLEASE don't hate me anymore!" and Rosemary's informing him, "I am never speaking to you again."

Professor Carter had leaned in, like someone following an amazing aroma. But now his shoulders slumped. He stumbled toward the bench on the other side of the picnic table and sagged down onto the seat.

"Are you okay?" Nevaeh asked.

Professor Carter waved his hand as if to say, *Just give me a moment. . . .*

"You think you've gotten over something, and then . . . ,"

he muttered. "How can that still hurt? It was decades ago! I was *twelve*!"

"Didn't you and Rosemary ever work things out?" Colin asked.

Professor Carter stared across the table at Colin and Nevaeh. His face had turned a little gray; he was still a balding, middle-aged man. But his dark eyes looked so forlorn behind his smudged glasses. It made Nevaeh think she could imagine him exactly as a twelve-year-old kid receiving a *Leave me alone!* letter from his best friend.

Or—former best friend.

"Rosemary . . . didn't lie," Professor Carter said, pointing a shaky finger at her letter. "I never saw or spoke to her again."

Toby's Story

"Why not?" Colin asked. His voice cracked. He had to remind himself, *This guy is a stranger! You don't even know Toby or Rosemary! Not really! Whatever they fought about was decades ago!*

Deeper down, there was another voice whispering in his head: *It's not like these are your parents you're trying to figure out. . . .*

Colin cleared his throat.

"I mean, how could that be?" Colin tried again. "It sounded like you went to the same school. You were in the same class! You lived in the same town!"

Professor Carter carefully placed the lids back on the shoeboxes, one after the other. It made Colin think of someone trying to put a genie back into a magic lamp.

"Not after those letters," Professor Carter said ruefully.

"*Because* of those letters?" Nevaeh asked. She shoved both hands into her hair, making it stick up wildly. "Or because of whatever made you mad at each other? Like, are we talking . . . *restraining orders*?"

"Oh—*no*," Professor Carter said, as if he'd just now realized how he'd made things sound. "It was just a case of bad luck, bad timing, everything bad happening at once. . . . Maybe I should tell the story from the beginning?"

"Please," Colin said.

Professor Carter did nothing but stare at the shoeboxes for a moment.

"Rosemary and I met in second grade," he finally began. "That's when the Groveview school district set up its first gifted program." He made mocking air quotes, as if he didn't want to sound like he was bragging. "I didn't understand until later that the real reason for that program was integration— the school district trying for more racial balance. I think it did help some Black kids. But it also *really* helped poor white kids. Like me."

"Because you were growing up on the wrong side of the tracks," Nevaeh said.

Colin elbowed her.

"She's not trying to insult you," he said quickly. "That's just what we heard someone else say. The guy we told you about on the phone. Robbie Robinson."

"Oh, it's true," Professor Carter said, shrugging. He brushed his fingers against the red shoebox sitting in front of him.

"*My* family couldn't have afforded Nikes. I got my shoes at Buckeye Mart, where they came rubber-banded together. So Rosemary even had to give me this *shoebox*."

"But you were friends?" Nevaeh said, as if even that was in question now.

How could that be a question when we've seen all those letters? Colin wondered.

"Yes," Professor Carter said, and now he was smiling. "We clicked. She was this feminist women's libber eight-year-old who didn't hesitate to tell anyone who'd listen that the world was going to be a better place in the future. I was this weird, scrawny kid who didn't fit in at all in my own neighborhood. Everybody said we both talked too much. Especially me."

"People say I talk too much, too," Nevaeh offered, as if trying to make up for her last question.

Professor Carter's grin broadened.

"That's not a crime," he said. "But . . . it kind of seemed like one in *my* neighborhood. You'd think I was growing up with Neanderthals—we were just supposed to grunt and give yes-or-no answers. We were supposed to care about fixing cars and scoring touchdowns, and we were *not* supposed to be good at school. Boys weren't, anyway."

"But the girls—" Colin began.

"Oh, they faced other societal limitations," Professor Carter said. "As Rosemary never hesitated to tell me, because she wanted to change it all!" He waved his hands as if wiping away everything unfair. "But for me, being bused to Sunnymeadow School—it was like being sprung from jail. The teachers there liked it when kids asked questions. We were *encouraged* to. And, yeah, when other kids invited me over to their houses to play, I saw that they had nicer toys than I did. But my attitude then was just 'This is fun!' The economic differences didn't matter as much as they did later."

"So Rosemary got mad at you because you were *poor*?" Nevaeh asked, as if she would find Rosemary just to beat her up if that were true.

"Oh no," Professor Carter said. "She wasn't like that." He looked a little lost for a moment. "At least, I never thought she was like that. . . ." He put his hand on the Nike shoebox, then seemed to decide against picking up any letters. "Anyhow, she and I meshed from the get-go. I think most of the other kids in our class that first year were chosen for their math skills. But Rosemary and I were word people. We could talk and talk and talk . . . and then that summer when my parents sent me to stay with my grandparents, it made sense for us to start writing letters instead."

"Because calling long-distance cost money," Colin said, as if he'd known that all along. "Because this was before cell phones."

"Yeah, going to Michigan always felt like moving to the

moon," Professor Carter said. "And coming back and seeing Rosemary every fall felt like . . . being able to breathe again. No one in my family was happy. If I hadn't had those years growing up with Rosemary, I wouldn't have seen any way out."

"But then you and Rosemary stopped being friends," Nevaeh said. "What happened? What changed?"

Professor Carter blinked. Colin had started feeling like he could see second-grade Toby before him—the weird, scrawny little kid with the big mouth. But now somehow Professor Carter looked older than ever—as old as Mr. Robinson, maybe, capable of nothing but looking back.

"We grew up," Professor Carter said. "We started listening to the people around us more, hearing what *they* expected of us. And . . . I asked Rosemary to be my girlfriend."

32

What Professor Carter Could and Couldn't Find

"So it was romance that did you in," Nevaeh said. She had to struggle not to sound disappointed. "A bad breakup. My sister says middle school relationships are just hot messes no matter what."

She avoided looking at Colin. What if he thought she'd been trying to become his girlfriend?

What if they messed things up, too?

"Your sister's probably right," Professor Carter said with a harsh laugh. "Maybe not so much now, because kids aren't as clueless as they used to be. You have the internet. We had locker room lies and . . . let's just say even our parents believed a lot of things that just weren't true."

A fly landed on the box of Rosemary letters in front of Nevaeh. It crawled along the zigzag of ancient rubber band remnants, as if, even after all these years, there was still something rotten there for the fly to feed on.

Professor Carter waved his hand to shoo it away.

"So all you did was ask Rosemary to be your girlfriend and she got mad and never spoke to you again?" Colin asked. His voice trembled, and Nevaeh remembered, *He doesn't know why his parents broke up, and I told him finding out about Rosemary and Toby would be a test case for seeing if he's brave enough to ask questions about them. . . .*

Right now, he didn't seem brave enough.

And maybe Nevaeh had been cruel to suggest it.

"Oh no," Professor Carter said. "Rosemary said yes to being my girlfriend, and I was over the moon. We were like some gender-flipped stereotype—I was the one planning the wedding and the white picket fence and, of course, the household responsibilities divided exactly in half."

"You were planning your wedding when you were twelve?" Nevaeh said, wrinkling up her nose.

"I'm kidding," Professor Carter said quickly. "Just . . . avoiding the next part of the story. I was so happy, but . . . Rosemary wasn't. And I couldn't understand why."

Maybe Colin was braver than Nevaeh thought. He nudged the lids off the two shoeboxes again and pointed to each of the top letters.

"Rosemary wrote, 'You're wrong!' and you wrote, 'I'm sorry! I didn't mean it!'" Colin asked. "What was that about? What did you do?"

Professor Carter recoiled.

What right do we have to ask him questions like that? Nevaeh wondered.

The answer was: none. Finding the shoeboxes in the attic, trying to solve the mystery of who they belonged to—that had just been one big adventure to Nevaeh and Colin. It'd been *fun*.

But the past wasn't just a story or an adventure to Professor Carter. It'd been his real life. And it still had the power to hurt him.

Professor Carter answered Colin's question anyhow.

"What did I do?" he repeated. "I . . . told Rosemary her future didn't matter as much as mine."

The fly came buzzing back. Nevaeh grabbed one of the shoebox lids and smashed the fly flat against the table.

"Are you nuts?" she asked. She forgot that she'd just decided she and Colin didn't have any right to ask Professor Carter questions. She forgot that he was a grown-up; she forgot that she didn't even know him. She grabbed the stack of Rosemary letters and shook them at Professor Carter. "Didn't you read her letters? She wanted to be the first female professional baseball player! She wanted to be the first female astronaut! She was going to be important! Her future mattered!"

Maybe Nevaeh wasn't just talking about Rosemary. Maybe she was thinking about how Prilla sounded when she said,

"Roddy will get all the scholarships he needs, but I'll have to get grants and loans." Maybe she was thinking about how her brother Dalton acted like Colin's mom deserved to be called "Fleas," but not anything as grand as "Felicia."

Maybe she was thinking about how Nevaeh herself had never even dared to tell anyone how much she admired Mrs. Creedmont.

Professor Carter's face flushed.

"I know," he said. "It's been decades, and I'm still ashamed. I've wanted to apologize to Rosemary—for real, not just on torn-out notebook paper—ever since. But you have to understand . . . it was the seventies. My mom might as well have been my dad's servant. She cooked for him, she cleaned up after him . . . she even wound his alarm clock for him every night, and if she forgot, he yelled about how maybe he should just divorce her, right there. Over an alarm clock! Or maybe the gravy was too salty, or the sheets felt too scratchy, or . . . He was always threatening to kick her out. The way I understood male-female relationships, based on what I saw around me . . . it made all Rosemary's talk about equal rights seem radical. Crazy." He looked down at his hands. He was almost whispering now. "Like just a little kid's fantasy that she'd have to outgrow."

"No," Nevaeh moaned.

She hated Professor Carter. He didn't deserve to get these

letters back. She hugged them to her chest, as if it was her job to protect them.

"But you did try to tell Rosemary you were sorry," Colin said, pointing at the box of Toby letters. "You did a lot of daydreaming with her. You wanted her to be the next Billie Jean King!"

Nevaeh had almost forgotten Colin was still there.

"But the last thing I ever said to her . . . it was awful," Professor Carter said. "We were both our school's representatives to the county spelling bee. It was a big deal. They still do the national bee, right? In Washington, D.C.? Rosemary and I were both dreaming of going there, of winning everything. I thought it might be my only chance to see anyplace new—or maybe my first step toward, I don't know, Harvard? Rosemary had already been to D.C. twice, on family vacations. I thought she wanted to win just to win. For fun. She'd just agreed to be my girlfriend, so I thought it was logical to tell her to let me win instead. It was like I saw that county spelling bee as a job interview. I didn't want to say, 'I should win because I'm poor.' Or, God forbid, because I was studying harder. I said I should win because I'm the boy and she was . . . just a girl. Because if I won, it would set up my future. And if she won, it would be . . . stealing the victory from me."

"'Just a girl,'" Nevaeh whispered. "'Stealing.'"

She felt numb, like she couldn't get the words to mean what they were supposed to mean.

How could *anybody* talk like that? Ever?

Professor Carter nodded miserably and dropped his head into his hands.

"So, um, who did win?" Colin asked.

"Neither of us," Professor Carter said. "I didn't even compete. Rosemary and I had our fight on a Friday morning, the day before the bee. By lunchtime, that note was crammed into my social studies textbook. I was so distraught, I didn't even see who passed it to me. Rosemary and I didn't have morning classes together, but I thought I would see her at lunch. But she wasn't there, and she wasn't in our afternoon classes, either. I missed the bus after school because I was looking everywhere for her. I saw one of her friends who was staying after school for dance lessons or something, and I gave her that note and asked her to give it to Rosemary." He pointed to the one on top of the box of Toby letters. "Honestly, I didn't know for sure until today that Rosemary ever got that letter. But she must have, right? For it to be in that box with the others?"

"You just wrote a *note*?" Nevaeh said. "That's all you did? Instead of texting or calling or—" She'd forgotten for a moment that this was ancient history, and Toby and Rosemary hadn't had cell phones. "Oh, sorry. Go on."

"I *did* try to call," Professor Carter said. "I walked home in the pouring rain—is Sunnymeadow School still there? Do you know how far away it is? That was a *long* walk. It was like my systems were shutting down by the time I got home. I was . . . robotic. I got home and I stuffed that note in the box in the attic and I went downstairs to use the phone in the kitchen. But there wasn't even a dial tone. Wait—you probably don't even know what that is, do you? The phone was dead. And I was shouting, 'Mom, Mom, why doesn't the phone work?' And it was only then that I realized our house was empty—I mean, literally empty. All the furniture was sitting out on the front yard in the rain. We'd been evicted that very day. Or I should say, we were in the process of being evicted. The bank was taking back our house because my dad had stopped paying the mortgage. He'd lost his job when the glass factory shut down. He *couldn't* pay the mortgage. There were men carrying furniture out—that was the only reason the doors were still open, the only reason the locks hadn't already been changed. And I hadn't even noticed."

"That's how it works?" Colin asked. "They could just . . . break into your house and leave your things outside?"

Professor Carter frowned and shook his head.

"Sadly, yes," he said. "Want to know what's worse? While I'm standing there yelling, 'Mom! Mom! What's wrong with the phone?' she shows up and yells at me because 'The neighbors might hear, and they'll know we didn't pay our phone bill!' As if the neighbors couldn't see all our possessions out in the yard . . . She was probably in shock, too. And then my dad was there, and he screamed at me, too. And then he stuck Mom and me in the car and sent us off to my grandparents."

"And then?" Nevaeh whispered.

"And then I never stepped foot in that house again," Professor Carter said. "It was years before I ever returned to Groveview."

Nevaeh and Colin could do nothing but stare at him, open-mouthed.

Professor Carter looked around, as if to remind himself they were sitting in sunny Morningside Park in the twenty-first century, not standing in the rain or listening to his parents yell in 1977.

"It's okay," he said. "Really. I survived. I had a few awful years—my *family* had some awful years. We bounced around, so many different places. But I was always good at school, and that became a way to prove I wouldn't be like my parents. And then I got a scholarship to college, and that opened up the world for me. All the pain was decades ago. I assure you, I'm fine now. I've been lucky, and I owe a lot of it to the teachers at Sunnymeadow, and to Rosemary. I wish I could find her again, not just to apologize, but to thank her. Because she really did change my life."

"But wasn't she right here in Groveview?" Colin asked. "I get it that *you* left town that day, but wasn't she still here? You had her address! You were used to writing to her!"

Professor Carter tapped a finger against the box lid.

"I don't think you understand the shame I felt," he said. "When we were driving away, not even sure my own grandparents would take us in, I could see neighbors' faces in their windows, watching us go. It felt like the whole town knew what happened. And my shame over what I'd said to Rosemary mixed with my shame over being evicted. . . . Lots of workers lost their jobs when the factory closed. But it felt like my dad was the only one who lost his house, too. Probably he was just the first, but—that's not how it felt then. For months after that—years, even!—I was sure that Rosemary found out what happened, and she didn't want anything to do with me."

"Wouldn't she have just felt sorry for you?" Nevaeh asked. "She had your grandparents' address, too. She could have written you, once she got over being mad. She was your friend! Your girlfriend!"

"My grandparents had to sell their house and move with us to Ridge Hollow when my dad got a new job," Professor Carter said. "By the time I was, shall we say, emotionally stable enough to try to reach out to Rosemary, she'd left Groveview, too. I found out her father died, and she and her mother moved, and . . . it wasn't like nowadays, when you can always keep track of people on social media. She might as well have vanished without a trace."

"But there *is* social media now, and—" Colin began.

"I have looked for Rosemary, all right?" Professor Carter said. "When it became possible to look up old newspaper clippings online—that's how I found out about her father. And about who won the 1977 spelling bee. I looked up marriage records, in case I just couldn't find her because of a name change. But there was nothing. And eventually, I started thinking, if I couldn't find her, that meant . . . maybe I didn't want to know what happened to her?"

"But she was going to be famous!" Nevaeh retorted, swinging her arms wildly. "There were, like, a thousand things she wanted to do that would have made everybody know about her!"

Professor Carter's eyes were so sad. Nevaeh could imagine him giving that look to some college kid in one of his classes who'd just given a spectacularly wrong answer. And Professor Carter was just going to wait until the kid figured things out on his or her own.

To Nevaeh, it felt like Professor Carter was waiting for her to grow up. To understand that not all stories had happy endings.

He's wrong about Rosemary, though, Nevaeh thought. *I know* her! *She would have triumphed no matter what!*

Professor Carter started to stand up.

"I am very grateful to you two for finding those letters and contacting me," he said. "It was a good reminder to me. I'm sorry if what I've told you was upsetting. Remembering the past . . . can be hard. But there are ways to make peace with it."

Nevaeh reached for the box of Toby letters on the table in front of her. Colin reached for the box of Rosemary letters.

"Oh!" Colin said, peering toward Nevaeh. "Which box are we giving him? The ones he wrote, or the ones Rosemary wrote to him? Or . . . both?"

Nevaeh could tell: Colin didn't want to give the letters back now either. Not either set. The two of them had made digital copies—that was how they'd been able to compare notes when they'd traded back and forth. So they wouldn't lose the letters completely even if they handed over both boxes right now.

But it wasn't the same as actually keeping the letters.

It wasn't the same as holding the originals in their hands, as they were right now.

Just as Colin and Nevaeh were staring at each other in confusion, Nevaeh's phone buzzed. Nevaeh glanced at the screen—it was a text from Mrs. Torres saying, **If you're going to stop by, it'll have to be in the next half hour. I need to run errands after that.**

Nevaeh had totally forgotten about Mrs. Torres.

"You don't want to go meet the people who live in your

old house now, do you?" Nevaeh asked Professor Carter. She explained, and it all came out sounding apologetic. She hadn't thought about Professor Carter having so many unhappy memories of his childhood home.

"Actually, I would," Professor Carter said, as if he were surprised by his answer, too. "I drove in on Willow, and it was nice to see how everyone is sprucing up the neighborhood. It'd be great to meet them, especially if they have questions."

Nevaeh and Colin, still clutching the shoeboxes, led Professor Carter to Mrs. Torres's house. Mr. Torres was there, too, and the grown-ups seemed to hit it off from the very first. The Torreses bragged about how their twins had started sleeping through the night that week. Professor Carter talked about how his job had changed over the years, from analyzing decades' worth of TV shows to studying fifteen-second TikTok videos. He admired all the Torreses' home improvements, and listened to them describe the other changes they'd planned.

Nevaeh sneaked glances at Colin, hoping he could read her mind: *Do you feel as invisible as I do now? Like we might as well not be here? Like they don't even care about what we care about?*

This was true even when Mrs. Torres draped her arm around Nevaeh's shoulders and announced, "These two kids were so much help with the twins when I was at my wit's end. Anybody who showed up and could get the babies to stop crying for three seconds, I was like, 'Sure, take anything you want out of that attic!'"

Everyone laughed.

"Is there anything else you left hidden in this house that we should know about?" Mr. Torres asked.

"No— er . . . , actually, maybe there is," Professor Carter said. "If it's still there." He looked toward the Torreses' stairs. "Unless your babies are sleeping in my old bedroom . . ."

"You're assuming our babies sleep in their cribs, not their stroller—as it turns out, they're easy to move!" Mrs. Torres said.

Everyone tiptoed up to the stairs and waited while Mr. Torres pushed the stroller down the hall.

Professor Carter stepped into the babies' room, then immediately spun around, frowning.

"Oh, sorry," he said. "Never mind. When I was a kid, this room had a wood floor, not wall-to-wall carpet. I'm not going to mess up your carpet looking for something that's probably not even there anymore."

Mr. and Mrs. Torres grabbed each other's arms.

"You're saying this hideous carpet might be hiding actual hardwood floors underneath?" Mrs. Torres asked, as if that was her dearest dream.

Nevaeh looked down, noticing for the first time that the carpet was a pretty awful shade of mustardy yellow.

"Ever since the twins were born, we've been calling this the baby-poop carpet, because it looks *exactly* like what's in their diapers. And it's been driving us crazy, trying to figure out how soon we could afford to replace it," Mr. Torres said, sounding just as excited as his wife. "If we've had the flooring we want down there all along . . . let's see!"

He bent down, like he was ready to rip up the whole carpet right away.

"I can't make any promises," Professor Carter said. "But what I'm looking for would be in that corner." He pointed toward a nook by the window. "So . . ."

Mr. and Mrs. Torres both grabbed the carpet by the window and began pulling.

"It *is* hardwood!" Mrs. Torres crowed. "It's beautiful!"

A thin cry sounded from out in the hall, immediately matched by a second. Mr. and Mrs. Torres only laughed. Then they both jumped up and ran out into the hall, calling out, "Nathan! Mateo! You have to see what we just discovered!" "Mommy and Daddy are so happy!"

"I don't think those babies are going to care," Nevaeh muttered, but she couldn't help grinning a little. The Torreses' joy was contagious.

"Now let's see if this floorboard slides out like it used to," Professor Carter said, crouching down by the bent-back carpet.

Colin and Nevaeh hovered nearby. Professor Carter lifted a piece of wood.

"I guess no one's moved this since 1977," Professor Carter whispered. "Look."

The space below this missing floorboard wasn't as deep as the hiding place Nevaeh and Colin had found in the Torreses' attic. There was only room here for a thin stack of what looked like four or five cardboard folders, all with a weird gray-and-white plaid pattern on the front.

Then Nevaeh noticed the fancy black script on the top folder: "My Classmates."

"My dad thought it was a waste of money to get school photos, but my mom lied to him about what our groceries cost and set money aside to buy these for me anyhow," Professor Carter said. "So I kept them hidden, just in case." He reached down for the top folder and lifted it out. He flipped open the cover, revealing a picture of four rows of kids standing with a woman holding a sign that said:

Sunnymeadow School

Grade 6

Mrs. Rundell

1976—77

He pointed to a girl standing exactly in the middle. A boy beside her seemed to be standing on tiptoes, trying to look just as tall as her, just as much the center of attention.

"That's Rosemary," he said in a choked-up voice. "And me."

33

A New Secret

Colin *itched* to take pictures.

The roll of ugly carpet reminded him of ocean waves pulling back, unearthing treasures on the beach. The small section of floorboard Professor Carter pulled up had a darker grain of wood running through it that looked like a sobbing face.

And then there was the class photo of Rosemary and Toby. Colin longed to have that picture on his phone so he could fade out the background and focus only on those two kids. He could draw hearts around Toby's head to draw attention to the way Toby's eyes darted toward Rosemary, even though the photographer had probably said, "Look here, everyone." Or he could adjust the color saturation to make Toby's brown shirt look drearier and cheaper, and Rosemary's purple wool dress look brighter and classier; he could draw spikes emphasizing the unevenness of Toby's haircut (done at home by his mom, maybe?) and spirals emphasizing Rosemary's perfectly curled long hair.

Maybe Colin wasn't really much of a photographer, after all. Maybe he just wanted to be a picture-fixer. Or whatever you called someone who enhanced photos, trying to make the hidden meaning apparent to everyone.

Though it already seemed as though anyone could look at this picture and see "That boy believes that girl hung the moon and the stars." And "That girl's the star of *everything*."

Mr. and Mrs. Torres came back into the room, each carrying a baby.

"Did you find what you were looking for?" Mrs. Torres asked.

"I did," Professor Carter said, fanning out all five of the "My Classmates" folders he'd found, as if they were cards he'd been dealt. "My family left . . . kind of in a hurry . . . so I didn't get a chance to take these with me."

Colin noticed that Professor Carter didn't tell the Torreses the whole story, as he had with Nevaeh and Colin. But maybe he didn't need to. Mr. Torres clapped Professor Carter on the shoulder and said sympathetically, "Lots of memories, huh?"

Only then did Colin see that Professor Carter had tears in his eyes. But he seemed to pull himself together immediately.

"You all have been so gracious, letting me reminisce," he said, standing up. "I hope you will enjoy your hardwood floors and your new babies and many, many years of good times in this house. Even if I couldn't help explain the dining room wallpaper, I can't tell you how glad I am to see a happy family in this house, taking such good care of it."

The grown-ups all started moving out of the room and toward the stairs, as if they understood some code Colin had missed. Nevaeh elbowed him, and Colin reluctantly followed her out of the room, too.

Down the stairs, out the front door . . .

Colin kept wanting to protest, *No, we can't go yet! We haven't figured everything out. What if there's some other hiding place Professor Carter forgot about? Or another letter Rosemary sent after Toby left that* . . .

Colin realized he was being ridiculous.

The Torreses thanked Professor Carter profusely and then he thanked them profusely and they all promised to stay in touch.

And then Colin and Nevaeh were walking Professor Carter back toward the park.

Colin and Nevaeh each still clutched a shoebox full of letters.

"That's mine," Professor Carter said. But he was pointing at a gray Honda parked by the curb, not at the shoeboxes.

He had to have seen the way Nevaeh and Colin darted glances at each other; the way Colin grimaced and Nevaeh wrinkled up her nose.

"Look," Professor Carter said, stopping by the car door.

"I can tell those letters mean something to you. You did a lot of work to find me. I wasn't lying to the Torreses when I said it was great to meet them, and to see how that whole street is thriving now. That really does make me happy. And it was good to meet the two of you. But those letters . . . they're like ticking time bombs. To be honest, if I took either of those boxes, I think they'd end up stashed away in my attic. I'd *intend* to read them again someday, but . . . I'd put it off."

"You don't even want the letters?" Nevaeh asked, her voice rising in disbelief. And maybe hope, too.

"I didn't say that," Professor Carter said. "I just think they're more important to you than they are to me right now. You said you made digital versions, right? Email me a copy of those. For now, that'll be enough. And . . ."

He began shuffling through the cardboard folders of class pictures. He flipped open the picture they'd seen before, of Rosemary and Toby's sixth-grade class. He laid it on the hood of his car, pulled his phone from his pocket, and snapped a photo.

Then he slid the sixth-grade picture into Nevaeh's hands.

"You can keep this picture, too," he said. "And I'll send you scans of the others, with each kid identified. Hearing about all the legwork you two did, I see now that I could have tried harder to find Rosemary. My friends in the psychology department would probably say I had a mental block. I *could* have contacted other classmates to ask about Rosemary. But I guess I was ashamed to talk to them, too."

"Oh, I see," Colin said, peering over Nevaeh's shoulder. "All the names are over on the side."

Some adult—Professor Carter's mom? A teacher?—had neatly printed the names of every kid in order. Colin's heart sank at the thought of contacting all those strangers.

But it'd be worth it to find Rosemary.

Colin waited for Nevaeh to thank Professor Carter. It felt like this was the same as back at the Torreses'—like everything was moving toward goodbyes. Colin figured Nevaeh would handle that. She'd be better at it.

But she just kept standing there with her head down, staring at the sixth-grade class picture. Or, no—she was staring at the names.

"You and Rosemary," she began in a funny voice. "You went to school with a girl named Maribel?"

"Uh . . . yeah," Professor Carter said. His voice sounded a little off, too. "Maribel Mason? She's right there." He pointed to a girl in the class picture with blond hair, intense eyes, and a striped shirt.

"Did she grow up to marry a man named Arthur Mongold?" Nevaeh asked. "And then they moved to Florida in 1989? And—"

"I don't know," Professor Carter said, as if he wasn't sure

he wanted to hear anything else about his former classmate. "I probably should have looked her up in particular, because she and Rosemary were friends. In fact . . ." He gulped. "Maribel was the one I gave that last letter to, to pass on to Rosemary. When I tried to apologize."

Nevaeh's jaw dropped, and she gaped at Professor Carter. She didn't say anything else.

"Do you know Maribel Mason?" Colin asked Nevaeh. "Or whatever her name is now—Maribel Mongold?"

Nevaeh slowly turned her head to peer at Colin.

"No, but . . ." Nevaeh stopped to clear her throat. Her voice dropped almost to a whisper. "But there's something I have to tell you."

34

The Mongold Story

Professor Carter left.

And Nevaeh talked.

She couldn't get the story of the Mongold storage unit to come out properly. Why did she start with the fact that she'd eaten her yogurt out of a plastic container that first morning? Or that her family had hoped to buy a lot of new stuff with the money they thought they'd earn from selling all the valuable antiques in the Mongold unit?

"*Why* did your dad think all that belonged to him?" Colin asked.

"Because he won the contract to do the clean-out and . . . I don't know, that's just how it works," Nevaeh said. "I think he was going to split the profits with Steve, the guy who owns the storage unit place."

What bothered her more: The fact that she didn't understand her own father's business?

Or that Colin was looking at her like her dad and Steve might be thieves?

"Nobody was paying for the storage unit anymore—what was Steve supposed to do?" Nevaeh asked. "Just leave the stuff there forever and give up on making money?"

"I guess this is why my mom says people get trapped by their stuff," Colin muttered. And even though Nevaeh agreed—even though Nevaeh wanted to be just like Felicia Creedmont—this made her a little mad at Colin.

Oh, right, I forgot. Your mom has all the answers. While my dad got tricked by an empty storage unit . . .

They'd been just standing at the edge of Morningside Park, but now, to cover her weird little burst of anger, Nevaeh went over to sit on one of the swings. She kept her feet on the ground but bent her knees, making the swing sway back and forth. Unfortunately, she'd ended up on a swing with torn canvas, and the broken place pinched her rear.

Of course I get the old, broken swing, Nevaeh thought. *Of course.*

Colin sat down on the next swing over.

"Can we get back to Maribel Mongold and how this connects to Rosemary and Toby?" he asked.

"I don't actually know how much it connects," Nevaeh admitted. "But Maribel died, and there wasn't anything in that storage unit except a letter that *said* it was from Maribel, making it look like she'd been the one who took everything. So there's a mystery about her, too."

"That doesn't sound like a mystery to me," Colin countered,

kicking the ground hard enough to launch his swing higher than Nevaeh's. But then he stomped hard against the mulch as he swung back down. This stopped his swing entirely. "It sounds like Maribel really did hate her husband, and she sold the antiques and hid the money because she was planning to divorce him. People do stuff like that when they're getting divorced. They cheat and they lie and . . ."

Nevaeh remembered that Colin's parents were divorced.

"Oh, sorry—does this bring back bad memories of how your parents treated each other when they were getting divorced?" she asked.

"I don't have any memories from when my parents were getting divorced," Colin said in a voice that was too careful, too stiff. "I was just a baby, remember?"

"Oh, right," Nevaeh said. "We'll just get back to the Mongolds . . . Anyhow, Steve, the storage unit guy, he couldn't believe Mrs. Mongold would have hated her husband. He said they were all lovey-dovey when they made arrangements for the storage unit. So that's why he and my dad—and Axel and Dalton, too—they all believe the letter was fake. And, Colin? I don't like this part of the story, and I don't even think it's true, but . . . Axel and Dalton and Dad and Steve even wondered if *your* mother was involved somehow. Because she'd been really interested in the story of the Mongolds, back when she worked for my dad."

Immediately, Nevaeh clapped her hand over her mouth. She hadn't intended to tell that part of the story. It just slipped out.

Nevaeh tasted metal and started coughing. She pulled her hand back—it was covered with specks of rust from the chains of the swing. She wiped her face on her sleeve and her hands on the bottom of her T-shirt, leaving streaks of orange both places.

Greevey manners, she thought, suddenly embarrassed. *The kind of manners people have when they spend their lives around junk.*

She dared to look over at Colin, and of course *he'd* ended up on a swing with brand-new chains.

But he was sitting there so stiffly, completely motionless.

"They thought my mother was 'involved'?" he repeated. "You mean, they think she *stole* something?"

"*I* don't think that," Nevaeh scrambled to explain. "I know it couldn't be true. And my mom was sticking up for your mom when I heard her and my dad talking about it. And my dad . . ." How could she make Colin understand that her dad wasn't a bad person, either? "He wouldn't normally make wild accusations like that. He's just . . . stressed. Because of the bad economy, and how not as many people are paying for junk removal right now. He even said . . . I heard him tell my mom that Groveview's not big enough for your mom and him to both stay in business."

Colin could have been a statue now: *Boy Not Moving on a Swing*.

"If only one of them can stay in business, who says it's your dad who deserves to win?" he asked, enunciating each word as though he was talking to a stranger.

Automatically, Nevaeh said, "Because my dad's business was here first. And there are seven people in my family, not just two. And—"

Colin suddenly stood up.

"You know what?" he said. "I need to go home. I didn't know how late it was."

The flurry of movement was surprising after he'd been sitting motionless for so long. For a moment, Nevaeh's brain couldn't even process what she was seeing.

"But . . . ," she began.

Colin was already stalking away. He unchained his bike from the rack. He put on his bike helmet. He hopped on the bike and began pedaling. He did everything so smoothly and gracefully that Nevaeh could only watch.

And then she was stunned to find herself alone in the park.

Is he mad? she wondered.

She was used to Greevey anger. When Greeveys got mad, they screamed and yelled and stomped around, and everyone knew it.

She didn't know what to make of someone who got mad and just went all stiff and formal and motionless.

Or . . . smooth and graceful.

He was mad, she thought. *I messed up.*

She yanked out her phone and texted Colin, I'm sorry about what my dad said. I DON'T agree! I wanted to clear your mom's name from the start! So call me when you get this!

She kept sitting in the swing with the broken canvas and the rusty chains. She sat and sat and sat.

Colin didn't call.

35

Colin and His Mom

Am I mad? Colin thought.

It was weird that he couldn't even tell. He felt . . . frozen. Numb. Like his every emotion was walled off, hidden as completely as the shoeboxes of Rosemary's and Toby's letters before Colin found them.

But he was pedaling down Willow Street as briskly as if he were competing in the Tour de France.

No—he was pedaling *furiously*.

I am mad, Colin thought, reaching the corner. He barely watched for traffic before whipping around to the right. *But who am I mad at? Nevaeh's dad? Nevaeh? Mom?*

Why would he be mad at Mom?

Maybe because she'd be the one going out of business, if it comes down to a contest between her and the Junk King.

But it wasn't her fault she hadn't inherited a junkyard from her father or her father's father or however far back it went for Nevaeh's family. It wasn't her fault everyone in Groveview knew and trusted the Greeveys, and not as many people knew Felicia Creedmont. It wasn't her fault there were only two Creedmonts and seven Greeveys.

Or was it?

Seriously? Colin thought. *Am I mad at Mom because she and Dad got divorced?*

Or was he mad at Dad?

Colin screeched to a halt, right in the middle of the street. A car horn honked behind him, and he caught a glimpse of a blue SUV swerving around him.

He'd almost been hit.

He stood in the street for a moment, panting hard, feet flat on the pavement. Adrenaline pumped through his veins in some kind of weird delayed reaction.

Then his knees went weak. Another reaction. He stumbled, pushing his bicycle up onto the sidewalk. Slowly, he began walking the bike home. He didn't trust himself to pedal anymore. He didn't trust himself to follow traffic laws.

Finally, after what felt like a million hours, he reached his own house—the house that had once belonged to Nevaeh's grandfather. Colin wasn't like Toby walking home in the rain from Sunnymeadow School. Colin couldn't have walked blindly past furniture strewn haphazardly across the lawn. Instead, Colin was hyperaware of every detail of his home— every detail of how it looked from the outside. He saw how small the house was, but how perfect. He saw the fresh paint job Mom had done herself, the steel blue accented with precise white trim. He saw the cheery red of the front door, the carefully braided mat on the doorstep, the begonias blooming by the porch.

He saw how perfect it all was, and still it skewed in his vision, all the right angles tilting out of whack. He couldn't get himself to see things properly. He dropped his bike and bike helmet on the front lawn—totally against Mom's rules—and burst in the front door.

"Colin?" Mom said from the kitchen table, where she was sitting behind her laptop. Working, as usual. "Is something wrong?"

He caught a glimpse of himself in the mirror over the fireplace. He was sweaty and red-faced, his hair molded into weird waves and spikes.

He didn't try to smooth it down. He didn't wipe away any sweat.

"My father—" Colin began. He gulped in air and tried again. "He knows where I am, right? We aren't one of those families where parents fight and one parent steals away with the kid or kids without the other one knowing. Are we? That isn't one of your secrets. Is it?"

He hadn't known he was going to say that. But that was what he'd come to, on the long walk home. He'd been thinking about the story Nevaeh told him, about the woman all those years ago who secretly hated her husband and took away all the furniture he loved more than he loved her.

In his mind, it had started feeling like that could be the story of his own family.

And that made him nothing more than a table or a chair or a couch.

Mom's eyes flooded with tears. But she kept her gaze steady on Colin's face.

She wasn't going to lie.

"Oh, Colin," she said. Sadness flowed across her face like a curtain falling. It was hard to watch. But Colin didn't look away, either. "No. That isn't what happened. That isn't what happened at all."

Colin felt his whole face start to quiver. He sagged down onto the couch.

"But that's worse!" he protested. "It means my father didn't want to see me. He didn't want to know me. He didn't—he *doesn't*—want me!"

Mom was by Colin's side in a flash. She hugged him. She smoothed down his hair. She wiped the sweat from his brow and the tears from his cheeks. But the tears kept coming— hers and his.

"That means your dad is a bad person, not that there's anything wrong with you," she said, holding Colin close.

Holding him together. "I'm sorry. So, so sorry. I made a big mistake in marrying him. I don't regret it, because it led to you. You are nothing like him, and I mean that in the very best way. Having you—it gave me the courage to leave your father, because I couldn't let you grow up around him. You saved us both, just by being born."

Colin buried his face in his mother's shoulder and sobbed. He could have been a baby again—like the Torres twins, capable of nothing but crying. He couldn't speak. He couldn't tell Mom about Nevaeh or Professor Carter or the shoebox letters or the empty Mongold storage unit. He couldn't tell her about the Junk King's crazy accusations or ask her how they were going to survive.

But he didn't need to. All he needed right now were his mother's arms around his shoulders.

He had that, and that was all that mattered.

36

Nevaeh, Still Searching

It was late, and the house was dark.

And Nevaeh was sneaking into her father's office.

She pulled the door shut behind her, and only then did she turn on the light. Then she waited a moment, listening. Mom and Dad were in the family room watching TV—she could hear some announcer excitedly saying, "But that's not all!" Nevaeh had seen all her older siblings rush out the door and drive away: Axel out with his fiancée; Dalton back with his on-again, off-again girlfriend; Roddy and Prilla headed to some high school party after Prilla had done a little arm-twisting: "Come on, Roddy, it won't be the theater crowd as much as a 'Nerds of the World Unite!' kind of thing. You're bound to find someone to discuss Einstein's theories with you!"

Nevaeh had never felt so much as though the rest of her family had grown up and left her behind.

Or, with even Roddy out at a party, she'd never felt so

much as though everyone else had friends and she . . . didn't.

It's just that I'm making new friends this summer, she told herself. *Er—one new friend, anyway. I'm friends now with Colin.*

But was that still true after this afternoon?

Colin still hadn't texted her back.

He's not someone who looks at his phone all the time, she told herself. *Maybe he's working with his mom again, and he's too busy to even glance at his phone.*

It was Saturday night. Colin and his mom wouldn't be cleaning out someone's house now.

Nevaeh slid her phone out of her pocket, ready to try again.

Maybe you didn't see my text before . . . she began. She stopped and looked at the six texts before that one, all variations of her first apology to Colin, and all unanswered. She remembered overhearing Prilla one time with a friend who was having boyfriend problems: "Show some pride. If he's not answering your texts, do *not* act like you have nothing better to do than sit around waiting."

Colin wasn't Nevaeh's boyfriend. She didn't even want him to be. Still, she erased her half-written text and put her phone back in her pocket.

Fine, she told herself. *I'll just solve the Toby-Rosemary-Maribel mystery on my own. That'll show him.*

Nevaeh did want to solve the Toby-Rosemary-Maribel

mystery, but she didn't want to do it alone. She wanted to do that with Colin, so they could bounce ideas back and forth, so they could analyze everything Professor Carter had told them, so they could laugh about stupid TV shows from the 1970s, which had become their own private language.

So it would have been fun.

Together.

Nevaeh sighed and squared her shoulders and walked over to the row of filing cabinets along the far wall. They bulged with folders; some of the drawers were so overstuffed they wouldn't even close completely. And, because this was Dad's office, the filing cabinets were all secondhand and a range of heights and colors, everything from a Victorian-era wood to a 1970s-era avocado green to, strangely, one that was fire-engine red.

"Some people just use computer files, Dad," Nevaeh muttered, though she knew how he always answered suggestions like that: *What? And risk losing an entire Junk Kingdom worth of knowledge because some troll in Russia decides to send me malware? No, thanks!*

At least, in spite of the messy look of his files, she knew they were actually very well organized. She went straight for the drawer labeled "MC–MU." But when she pulled it out, there was nothing between "Monastery Architecture" and "Moravian Furniture."

"Where's all your Mongold information, Dad?" she mumbled. Apparently, she was going to become one of those people who talked to themselves because they didn't have any friends.

Maybe she should sit in Dad's chair for a moment and pull herself together.

She sat down—and there was the Mongold file right in the center of Dad's messy desk.

Nevaeh flipped it open, and everything spilled out.

Here was the wedding announcement from the *Groveview Chronicle*. Maribel Mason had been only twenty when she married Arthur Mongold, and he'd been forty.

That made him . . . old enough to be her father? Nevaeh thought, looking doubtfully at the blurry photo of a young, smiling blond woman in a lacy dress alongside a man with a bushy mustache.

Nevaeh put that aside. Entire newspaper sections lay below, with breathless society page coverage of parties at the Mongolds' house, as well as magazine articles about Arthur Mongold's growing reputation in the antiques world. One article after another described the amazing finds he'd made, the number of treasures he'd bought for almost nothing that turned out to be worth hundreds or thousands of dollars.

Then Nevaeh came across an article that began:

Arthur Mongold brags about what an eye he has for collecting beautiful things.

"Just look at my wife," he says proudly.

Ugh, Nevaeh thought. *Did people really talk like that back in the 1980s? Acting like a woman—an actual person!—was just another "thing" someone could collect?*

She wanted to go back in time and ask Rosemary, "How could you let your friend marry a man like that?"

But for all Nevaeh knew, maybe Rosemary and Maribel had stopped being friends, just like Rosemary and Toby had stopped being friends. Maybe Rosemary and Maribel hadn't talked to or seen each other after 1977 either.

Nevaeh didn't like to think about friendships ending. She skimmed ahead, through descriptions of priceless discoveries the Mongolds had made in out-of-the-way locations. The magazine writer seemed in awe of Arthur Mongold's "business acumen," his "crafty bargaining skills," even his "ability to calculate profit margins in his head, down to the penny."

Finally Nevaeh reached a sentence where Arthur Mongold called his wife "my secret weapon."

But the rest of the sentence was "because the people I'm dealing with are so busy looking at her, they forget how much money they're losing, selling their one-of-a-kind antique that's been in the family since the Revolutionary War!"

And the two paragraphs after that said:

Asked if she agreed with her husband's description of her value to the business, Mrs. Mongold temporarily deprived this reporter of a view of her lovely blue eyes to modestly gaze down and whisper to her husband, "Yes, dear. If you say so, dear."

But she winked at this reporter afterward.

Nevaeh nearly gagged. How could Rosemary ever have been friends with a woman like that?

She remembered what Steve at the storage unit had said about Maribel Mongold, how she'd been all, "Yes, dear," "No, dear," "Whatever you think is best, dear . . ." when she and her husband had come in to rent the unit.

Had Maribel Mongold even had a brain of her own?

That woman needed one of Prilla's lectures: "Show some pride!" Nevaeh thought.

Then Nevaeh felt guilty, because the next article down was Maribel Mongold's obituary.

She'd been only twenty-five when she died.

She'd been buried in Florida, which, according to Steve, was a place she hated.

And, if you believe the note we found in the Mongold

storage unit, she went to her grave also hating her husband, Nevaeh thought.

Nevaeh wasn't sure what to believe.

She put the obituary aside, too.

The other papers in the "Mongold storage unit" file were Dad's notes—speculation about which pieces of furniture might have been there, scribbled numbers about what that furniture would be worth now. Then there was a list of all the antique stores Dad had checked with, trying to trace the furniture to find out who had sold it when.

Nevaeh had almost reached the bottom of the folder when the whole pile of papers on Dad's desk began to vibrate. Then it began to blare out a rap song about junk—the ringtone for Dad's phone. Frantically, Nevaeh shuffled papers out of the way. There the phone was, under an invoice. Nevaeh snatched it up and stabbed blindly at the screen to silence it.

Then she sat still for a minute, her heart pounding.

If Dad heard that and comes in, I can say . . . I can say I heard his phone ring as I was walking by, and I was going to bring it to him, but whoever was calling just hung up, and . . .

Nevaeh listened hard. She could still hear the TV noise from the family room, some loud laugh track.

She did not hear Dad's footsteps coming her way.

The phone beeped, and Nevaeh jumped. But it was just the sound indicating a new voice mail.

What if that's Axel or Dalton or Prilla and Roddy needing help? Nevaeh wondered. *What if a car broke down or they ran out of gas or something?*

She clicked into Dad's voice mail to check. But the message wasn't from any of Nevaeh's siblings.

It was from Holden Antiques—one of the stores on the list Nevaeh had just seen.

Nevaeh hit the arrow to listen. A man's voice poured out of the phone, so loudly Nevaeh had to turn down the volume:

"Hey, Lloyd, sorry to take so long getting back to you, but looking for our records from before we got computers, it's basically like that scene at the end of *Raiders of the Lost Ark*—we *have* all the documentation, and it's all in order, but that doesn't mean it's easy to find. Anyhow, I do have an answer for you now. We bought those tables, chairs, and sideboards back in 1989, but Maribel and Arthur Mongold didn't make the sale directly. They worked through a representative—which is weird, because I don't see any evidence that they'd ever used a representative before. It's some woman named Rosemary?"

Rosemary? Nevaeh thought. *ROSEMARY?*

How many Rosemarys could Maribel Mongold have possibly known?

The Holden Antiques guy was still talking on the voice mail:

"I'd tell you Rosemary's last name if we could make it out,

but it looks like someone put a coffee cup down on that page, and it's kind of smudged. I'm visiting my dad in the nursing home tomorrow afternoon—he was running the business then, and I'm pretty sure he can tell me where to find the whole list of who we bought things from back in 1989—he's still sharp as a tack. Sharper than me, I'll admit. My dad will have all the answers about this Rosemary person. I'll call again after I've seen him. . . ."

It sank in, what this message meant.

This is proof! Nevaeh thought. *Colin's mom isn't guilty of anything connected to the Mongold unit! The valuable furniture that was supposed to be there really was sold way back in 1989!*

But how could Nevaeh rejoice? Sure, Felicia Creedmont's name could be cleared.

But was Dad going to find out tomorrow that *Rosemary* was a thief?

37

Lots of News for Colin

The doorbell woke Colin Sunday morning.

He could tell by the slant of light across his pillow that it was later than he usually got up. But he still felt groggy and disoriented, as if he were waking up in a different place.

Because of last night . . .

He and Mom had talked. Really talked. She'd shown him the actual divorce decree, proving Colin's dad had given up all his rights to custody—all his rights even to *visit* Colin.

Colin's parents hadn't been like the Mongolds. They hadn't fought over Colin the way the Mongolds might have fought over a table or chair.

Mom had wanted only the best for Colin, and that meant getting him away from Dad.

The doorbell pealed again, out at the front of the house.

"Coming!" Mom called.

Colin rolled over, because Mom would handle it, and he could just go back to sleep.

He heard the click of the front door being unlocked, and then a familiar voice asking, "Is Colin home?"

Nevaeh?!? No, no, no, no, no . . .

Colin jumped out of bed, stuffed his feet into his shower flip-flops, and ran for the door.

"He is, but he's still asleep," Mom was saying. "Want me to tell him you stopped by? You look familiar, but I'm sorry, I don't think I know your name. And . . ."

Colin scrambled down the hallway in three steps, and flew across the living room in four. He skidded toward the front door, the flip-flops sliding back and forth on his feet.

"No, Mom, I'm awake. My friend and I are going to take a little walk. Don't wait breakfast on me. Okay, bye," Colin said quickly, tripping out the front door.

He caught a glimpse of Mom's puzzled face—maybe his words had mushed together so much she couldn't understand them. But Colin pretended she'd given permission. He grabbed Nevaeh's elbow, mainly to keep from falling over. Somehow that was enough. Nevaeh turned with him, and the two of them together made it down the porch steps and out to the sidewalk.

Did Mom say, "Okay, see you later" behind him?

Did she sound slightly amused?

When Colin dared to look back, she was no longer standing in the doorway, and the door was shut.

"Are you *crazy?*" he asked Nevaeh. He stopped holding on to her elbow. "Coming to my *door?* Talking to *Mom?*"

"Maybe?" Nevaeh said, and it didn't sound like her at all. He'd never heard her sound so unsure.

She stopped beside him, facing him directly.

For the first time, Colin noticed that she was wearing a dress. It was a casual-looking one: sleeveless, blue and white striped, with a ribbon belt tied loosely at the back. But Colin had never seen her in a dress before, only T-shirts and jeans or shorts.

Nevaeh's hair was pulled back more tidily than usual, too, held firmly in place by barrettes or rubber bands or whatever girls used. There was no fuzzy cloud of escaping strands or any tendrils snaking out of some loose braid.

Nevaeh seemed to notice Colin noticing.

"Oh!" she said, turning red. She gestured toward the dress. "This doesn't mean anything. It's kind of camouflage—I don't look so much like a Greevey when I'm all neat and tidy. Also, I was supposed to be at church this morning, helping in the toddler room. I mean, I *was* there, until . . ."

"Until what?" Colin asked. He glanced back over his shoulder toward his own house. "Um, maybe we really should walk?"

Nevaeh nodded and strode out ahead of him.

"Until I found out there were already enough helpers."

Nevaeh's step faltered. She bit her lip. "Okay, that's true, but not the whole truth. There's this thing in the Bible, I don't remember where exactly, but it's basically about how if you're going to worship or make an offering or whatever, and you remember you've been fighting with someone, you should go make peace with that person before you do anything else, and . . . Colin, were we fighting yesterday?"

Colin wasn't actually sure, either. He didn't answer. But he started walking alongside Nevaeh.

Nevaeh pointed at him. No—she was pointing at his clothes.

"Are *you* all right?" she asked. "That's the same shirt you were wearing yesterday. I mean, *I* do that kind of thing all the time, but you're Colin Creedmont, and—"

"It is surprising my mom let me out of the house like this," Colin said with a laugh. He'd slept in his clothes—probably the first time in his life that *that* had ever happened. He patted his hair, because he suddenly felt like it might be sticking up all over the place.

It was.

Somehow the laugh and the patting-down-the-hair made Colin feel better.

"I'm not mad at you now," he said.

"Are you sure?" Nevaeh said. "What I told you yesterday—I thought about it, and it was almost like what Toby said to Rosemary. That his future was more important than hers. But it's like, with what my dad was saying, maybe you thought it meant he believes his business is more important than your mom's just because he's a man, and she's a woman and . . . does this make any sense at all?"

"It's not our fault our parents don't make sense," Colin said, stomping his foot as hard as possible, given that he was wearing flip-flops. "Their mess is theirs, not ours."

That was almost exactly a quote of what Mom had told him yesterday about Colin's dad. It was her explanation for why Colin didn't need to know everything his father had done wrong.

Nevaeh let out a deep sigh.

"Good," she said. "Because I found out so much last night. Your mom is innocent. She didn't steal anything from the Mongold storage unit."

"Of course she didn't," Colin retorted. "Didn't I tell you that yesterday?"

"No, actually you didn't," Nevaeh said slowly. She winced. "You left before we could talk about it."

That's what Mom and I do, Colin thought. *We run away. We get rid of things we don't want to deal with. And . . . we leave people behind, too.*

But Nevaeh had come after him.

"I'm breaking the Greevey Girl Code," Nevaeh said. "Prilla would be so mad at me. She says if a friend dumps you, and they ignore you when you text or call to apologize, then you do *not* go and beg to be friends again."

Colin patted his shorts pockets. They were empty.

"Did you text or call?" he asked. "I haven't looked at my phone since . . . maybe the park yesterday? Mom and I . . . talked about Dad when I got home."

"Oh," Nevaeh said, as if she understood what a big deal that was. "Do you . . . do you want to talk about it? With me, I mean?"

"No," Colin said.

They walked on in silence, except for Colin's flip-flops slapping his heels. It felt like he and Nevaeh were doing some kind of dance, but they hadn't figured out the steps.

Nevaeh will say something to make everything right again, Colin thought. *And then we'll be back to finishing each other's sentences and talking about* Happy Days *or* Laverne and Shirley. *We'll be like Toby and Rosemary again. . . .*

Except, Toby and Rosemary had had a fight in 1977, and never seen or spoken to each other again.

Nevaeh didn't say anything.

They crossed the street and walked an entire other block, and Nevaeh didn't say anything there, either.

Finally, on the last square of the sidewalk, Nevaeh turned to him and said, "Well, I need to make sure I get back before church is over and someone figures out I'm not in the toddler room or the worship service either. I just wanted to . . . make sure you were okay."

And then she was walking away from him.

Colin reached for her arm again.

"Wait!" he said. How could he say what he was thinking? *No! Don't go! I don't want to lose you as a friend! I want us to be like Toby and Rosemary before 1977, not after!* "If . . ."

He swallowed hard, unable to go on.

"Yes?" Nevaeh asked, turning back.

"If—no, I mean *when*—I'm ready to talk to someone about what my mom said last night, you're the one I want to talk to," Colin said. "You're the one I'd trust to listen and not . . . not make things worse. But for now . . . can't we just talk about Toby and Rosemary? Can't we still have that? Together?"

The smile that burst across Nevaeh's face was like sunlight breaking through clouds.

"I thought you'd never ask!" she said. "I felt like I was going to explode, with everything I found out last night, and I didn't have anyone I could tell except you, and . . . that sounds really pitiful, doesn't it?"

"Pitiful" was about the last word Colin would ever have used to describe Nevaeh. She took charge. She always seemed to know what to do, whether it was dealing with the screaming Torres twins or knocking on strangers' doors. She oozed confidence, just like Colin's mom.

But Colin had seen his mother crying last night.

And Nevaeh was biting her lip again, and grimacing as if she were completely serious.

"You and I are the only ones who know about Toby and Rosemary besides Toby and Rosemary themselves," Colin said. "It's like, they're ours and nobody else's."

"Are they still 'ours'?" Nevaeh asked quietly. "You took off yesterday without even looking back. You left the shoeboxes behind."

Colin gasped. Then he turned sharply to the left, as if he was going to run back to Morningside Park immediately.

"No!" he moaned. "They're not still there, are they?"

"Don't worry—I picked them up," Nevaeh said. "They're hidden in my closet at home right now."

Colin relaxed.

"I trusted you," he said. "But . . . sorry I forgot."

"And sorry about what I said," Nevaeh said, as if she were agreeing.

And just like that, the little dance they'd been doing seemed to be over.

"If you really have to go back now, let's set a time to call each other and you can catch me up on everything," Colin said.

"Yeah, no . . . the 'I have to go back now' was only if it was going to take me half an hour to walk five blocks," Nevaeh said, with another grin. "Kind of a little white lie because . . .

man, that was awkward, wasn't it? Walking that last block?"

Colin laughed, because he could do that now.

They were friends again. Completely.

"What if Toby and Rosemary would have made up, too, if they'd only had another day together?" he asked Nevaeh. "If they'd only had one more chance to see each other in person?"

Nevaeh's smile dimmed.

"What if they wouldn't have?" she asked. "Maybe there was something . . . wrong . . . with Rosemary that Toby just never saw? I don't think that's true, but . . . we're doing this no matter what, right? Even if there isn't a happy ending for us to find?"

"We still want to know what happened to Rosemary," Colin said firmly. "We want to know the truth."

He thought about what he'd found out last night from Mom. It hurt. And it hurt that there were still details out there about Dad that she thought were too terrible to tell him.

Someday he would want to know the truth about all that, too.

But not yet.

"I'm not Rosemary," Nevaeh said. "You're not Toby. No matter what we find out about them, you and me, we're going to stay friends."

"I know," Colin said.

He'd never felt so sure of anything before in his life.

38

Things Changing for Nevaeh's Family

All Sunday afternoon and evening, Nevaeh stayed close enough to Dad to hear his phone if it rang.

She kept remembering the voice of the man from Holden Antiques in her head: *My dad will have all the answers about this Rosemary person. I'll call again after I've seen him. . . .*

If someone said they were visiting a nursing home Sunday afternoon, wouldn't they have done it by four or five o'clock? Or six at the latest?

Dad's phone didn't ring.

Monday morning, Axel, Dalton, Prilla, Roddy, and Nevaeh had all assembled in the kitchen before Dad even got up. Nevaeh was chewing her way through some awful high-fiber cereal—it must have been on sale last week. She was wondering how much of it she could sneak into the garbage without someone yelling at her about wasting food, when Dad stumbled into the room. He blinked, bleary-eyed and surprised.

"Oh," he said. "Maybe I trained you all too well, if you're getting up earlier than your old man now. I guess I forgot to tell you . . . the clean-out job for today canceled on us. I couldn't reschedule anything from later in the week so . . . we don't have any work today."

"You mean, it's a free day?" Nevaeh asked. "A vacation?"

"That's not a good thing, Nevaeh," Dalton practically snarled at her. "When you run your own business, if you don't work—"

Nevaeh knew there were two endings to that saying. One was *you don't get paid*. The other was *you don't eat*.

She took another bite of her awful cereal.

"Don't be too hard on your sister, Dalton," Dad said. "She's still learning."

He sank into one of the kitchen chairs. It was weird to see him just sitting.

"Don't worry, Dad," Axel said gently. "I can pick up some electrician work today instead. Dalton, it's for that new housing complex out on Strewsbury Road. I heard they need more plumbing help, too."

Prilla tugged on Roddy's arm.

"We've got our own project to work on, don't we, Roddy?" she asked. She leaned just close enough to Nevaeh's ear to whisper, "I'm making him write practice college application essays with me. Mega-scholarships, here we come!"

It was a jolt to glance from Prilla's face, glowing with hope, to Dad's, sagging with defeat.

"Dad, you say there's always paperwork to catch up on, right?" Nevaeh asked. "I can help you with that, if you want. *I'm* not going anywhere today."

Behind Dad's back, Axel gave her a thumbs-up. Roddy ruffled her hair fondly. Prilla hugged her shoulders. Even Dalton bobbed his head up and down in a curt, approving nod. Nevaeh had never noticed this kind of thing happening before. But the Greevey "One for all and all for one" instincts applied to protecting Dad, too.

And that was when his phone rang.

39

Things Changing for Colin and His Mom

"What are you looking at?" Mom asked.

Colin almost fell off the porch.

It was early morning, and while Mom was in the shower, he'd sneaked the photo of Toby and Rosemary's sixth-grade class outside. When Nevaeh had come to see him on Sunday—and after they'd had their talk—she'd handed him the old photo and asked if he'd take a picture of it so they both could have a digital copy. This morning had been his first chance to do it with good lighting.

(Actually, the lighting yesterday or indoors would probably have been fine for what Nevaeh wanted. But Colin wanted the best copy possible, so he could enhance it and zoom in and play around with changing the photo the way he'd imagined ever since he first saw it.)

But Colin had lost track of time, trying again and again to take the perfect picture. He sent Nevaeh one version, then decided he could still do better. Was the lighting best on the porch railing? On the top step? On the porch swing?

And now Mom was out of the shower and fully dressed and ready for the day—and staring at Colin holding Toby and Rosemary's class picture in his hand.

"Uh . . . it's just an old picture," Colin said.

Mom looked puzzled. "Old" anything did not belong in the Creedmont house. Or even on its porch.

"Where'd that come from?" she asked. Her voice was not exactly accusing, but . . .

Yeah, Colin thought. *It's accusing.*

"My friend—the one who was here yesterday—it's hers," he said, which was about half true. Professor Carter had given the picture to Nevaeh *and* Colin. "She's, um, kind of trying to solve a mystery, and I told her I'd take a picture of this so she could have a digital copy. Then I'm giving it back."

"Oh, so you're a photographer now?" Mom teased.

Colin felt like his face was rearranging itself. If he'd glanced in a mirror just then and discovered his eyes, nose, and mouth were as misplaced as in a Picasso painting, he wouldn't have been surprised.

He couldn't answer. Just as he'd wanted to hide the picture a moment ago, now he wanted to hide his own face.

But Mom saw. And the way she was looking at him now wasn't teasing anymore.

"Oh, Colin," she said. "I just made a big mistake, didn't

I? This is important to you. It's okay if you want to be a photographer. Lord knows, plenty of people belittled me for what I wanted to do with my life—I always vowed I would never ever do that to you about anything."

"I'm twelve," Colin said. "I'm not making any big pronouncements about what I do or don't want to do with my life."

"And . . . that's fine, too," Mom said gently. She looked down at the picture in Colin's hand. He had the folder wide open, as if he'd been trying to show off Toby and Rosemary to the whole world. Mom did a double take. "Oh my goodness— those fashions! I'm glad I missed the 1970s. All that polyester, those garish colors and patterns . . . And those collars! You complain about wearing a collared shirt at all—just think if you'd lived back when shirt collars could double as kites!"

"Yeah, it's hard to believe anyone wore those clothes, and it wasn't even Halloween," Colin agreed weakly.

Everything was going to be okay. He just had to put the photo away and ask Mom how soon they needed to leave to clean out the next attic or basement.

But Mom was still gazing at Rosemary and Toby's class picture. She even touched a corner of the paper frame, holding it open.

"Sunnymeadow School, huh?" she said. "I've worked in a lot of houses over near there. Wonder if any of my clients were sixth graders back in 1977?"

Now she was peering at the names of all the kids.

Suddenly Mom jerked back. She put one finger on the column of names. Her lips moved; she seemed to be silently counting over to the center of the picture. She pointed straight at Rosemary and Toby. No—at Rosemary and the girl standing on Rosemary's other side.

"Your friend's mystery," Mom said, her voice coming out faintly. "Is it about these two girls, by any chance? Rosemary and Maribel?" She squinted at Colin, and it was her "You better tell me the whole truth" squint. She tilted her head suspiciously. "And your friend who was here yesterday, whose name you said 'didn't matter' . . . was that Nevaeh *Greevey*?"

40

A New Clue about Rosemary

Rosemary Desjardins.

Nevaeh heard the Holden Antiques guy say that name through the phone that Dad was holding up to his ear. She brought Dad paper and a pen when he gestured for it, and she watched him write down each letter of the name when he asked Mr. Holden Antiques to spell it for him.

Nevaeh kept sitting right beside Dad, listening secondhand to the whole conversation, though she pretended she was only taking a long time to work through her now-mushy cereal. Even when her phone pinged with a text from Colin, with an attached picture, she didn't bother answering it.

"Sounds made-up, don't you think?" Dad was saying into the phone. "Wouldn't 'Desjardins' be French, meaning something about gardens? If someone's first name is the name of a plant, isn't it a little too much to have the last name be 'gardens'?"

Across the kitchen, Axel and Dalton gave Dad and Nevaeh a silent wave and headed out the door. Prilla and Roddy finished rinsing their breakfast dishes and piled them in the drainer. Then Prilla tugged Roddy away, too.

Dad didn't shout after any of them, *No, wait! I'm solving the Mongold storage unit mystery! You have to hear this, too!*

And none of them stopped in their tracks to ask, *Do you have the answer to the Mongold mystery now? Tell us everything!*

Only Nevaeh understood that he was talking about an important name.

But is *Rosemary Desjardins the same person as Rosemary Buvon*—our *Rosemary? Is that her married name, or . . . or . . .*

Dad said, "Thanks so much for your help. Tell your dad I said hello." And then he put his phone down on the table.

"Hmm," he muttered. "Fishier and fishier."

Nevaeh paused in the middle of googling "Rosemary Desjardins" on her phone. She kept her phone angled away from Dad.

"What was that about?" she asked, trying to sound like she didn't know.

"It's . . . oh, never mind," he said. "Long story. Let me get you started typing up some mailing labels for me before I make a few more calls."

Later, Nevaeh wouldn't be able to say what set her off. Maybe it was the slump of Dad's shoulders, the way he just kept looking more and more defeated the whole time he was talking to Mr. Holden Antiques. Maybe it was his instructions, the way he was acting like she was just a little kid who could barely be trusted to type mailing labels.

Maybe it was just because she truly was a Greevey, and not at all good at keeping secrets.

Or . . . at holding back questions.

"What if I told you *I* know who that Rosemary is?" she erupted. "What if I told you I'm pretty sure that Rosemary and Maribel Mongold went to elementary school together? And . . . maybe I even have proof?"

41

Colin's Mistake

"Let's go inside to have this conversation," Colin's mom said sternly, gazing around as though she feared every single one of their neighbors was a spy.

It didn't even look like any of their neighbors were awake this early.

Colin gulped, which probably made him look guiltier. But it was a little too late for him to hide the class picture from Toby and Rosemary's sixth-grade year behind his back. It was too late for him to pretend he didn't know Nevaeh.

Mom held the front door open, and he meekly stepped inside. Mom started to follow him, then she seemed to change her mind.

"You know what? Give me a minute," she said. "I need to make a phone call first."

She eased the door shut between her and Colin. She stayed out on the porch; he felt trapped in the house. But Colin didn't move past the entryway rug. He typed in a quick text to warn Nevaeh: **I just made a big mistake.** But he hesitated before hitting Send. What if Nevaeh saw his text and called him back immediately? What if she came over again?

That would probably make Mom even angrier.

But is *Mom actually angry?* he wondered. *Or . . . afraid?*

He gazed out at her standing on the porch. He noticed the furrow in her brow, the way she kept tugging on one of her curls. Mom didn't have nervous tics like that.

At least, she didn't unless she was really, really worried.

Colin leaned back against the door. Faintly, he could hear Mom talking into the phone: "Yes, it's important. I wouldn't try to reach her at work if it weren't. But if she's in the middle of dealing with an emergency case, then, yes, of course, I could just leave a message. . . ."

Who was she talking to?

Colin's own phone pinged so loudly it made him jump. He squinted down at it, and the text he hadn't sent yet seemed to have repeated itself:

I just made a big mistake.

I just made a big mistake.

Oh, wait—that second message is from *Nevaeh, not to her,* he thought.

Were he and Nevaeh so much in sync now that they were making giant mistakes at the same time?

Before he could text back, he heard Mom again out on the

porch: "Yes, please. Tell her it's about her daughter Nevaeh. And Rosemary."

Her daughter, Colin thought. *Her.*

Why was Mom calling Nevaeh's mom?

What would she know about Rosemary?

42

Finding Rosemary

"Here's a Rosemary Desjardins in Yellow Springs, Ohio," Nevaeh said, peering at the computer screen in Dad's office.

"Bingo," Dad said, throwing his arms out wide. "That makes total sense!"

Nevaeh's stomach churned. She wanted to be doing this research with Colin, not Dad. With Colin, it would feel like they were looking for an old friend.

With Dad, it felt like they were tracking a criminal.

But maybe Rosemary needs me here during Dad's research, Nevaeh thought. *So I can defend her. Be on her side.*

"What do you mean?" Nevaeh asked Dad. "What makes sense?"

Her voice came out sounding as though Dad had accused Nevaeh herself of a crime.

"Haven't I ever told you about Yellow Springs?" Dad asked. "Interesting place. It's kind of where all the hippies in Ohio went to live after the 1970s. They also have a lot of antique shops there . . . er, anyhow, a lot for such a small town. This has to be the right Rosemary Desjardins. But if she's so big into antiques, why have I never heard of her?"

"Maybe she's retired?" Nevaeh suggested weakly.

"Or maybe she lost her supply of antiques after she emptied out that storage unit back in 1989," Dad said, glowering at the computer screen as if even Rosemary's name offended him.

Dad snatched up his phone. Nevaeh tried to look over his shoulder without him noticing.

"Hey, Steve, want to go on a road trip with me this morning?" Dad said into the phone.

Steve, Nevaeh thought. *The guy who owns the self-storage place.*

She gazed longingly toward her own phone, which she'd accidentally left behind on the kitchen table. She needed to tell Colin what was going on. Maybe she even wanted his advice about what she should *do.* But she couldn't walk away while Dad was still talking.

Dad was explaining how he'd tracked down the person who'd taken the valuable antiques.

"Yeah, I'm a regular Sherlock Holmes," he bragged.

Hello? Nevaeh wanted to interrupt. *Don't you remember who actually did the computer search for Rosemary's name?*

Steve seemed to be agreeing to go for a drive.

"Are you sure that's safe?" Nevaeh interrupted. "I mean, if you think she's some horrible criminal, wouldn't it be better to go to the cops and let them handle it?"

She just wanted to slow them down. Wouldn't the cops make Dad and Steve fill out paperwork—and give Colin and Nevaeh time to contact Rosemary and warn her?

Why was Nevaeh so certain Dad was wrong about Rosemary being a criminal?

Because of the letters, Nevaeh thought. *Because I don't believe she could have changed so much from wanting to do great things at twelve to stealing antiques at twenty-five....*

Dad put his hand over the phone.

"Nevaeh, the information we have so far—I don't think that would really count as enough proof," he said. "And remember, we don't want negative publicity for Steve's business. But if we go and confront this Rosemary person, and we surprise her into confessing . . . then we'll have proof, and can go to the cops then. And we'll be heroes! Everyone will know the lengths Steve will go to, to protect the items put in his care! It could be good publicity for my business, too!"

Nevaeh remembered what she'd overheard Mom saying to Dad in the barn: *You've gotten Axel and Dalton so fired up about this, I'm worried they're going to go all vigilante on her, and do something really stupid. Remember what a hothead you could be when you were their ages?*

It felt like Dad was still being a hothead. Like he hadn't changed from when he was Axel's or Dalton's age.

"Okay, pick you up in fifteen minutes," Dad told Steve.

"Where *is* Yellow Springs?" Nevaeh asked.

"An hour away," Dad said. "It's about halfway between Columbus and Dayton. So I should be back by lunchtime. You'll have time to get all the mailing labels done by then."

Nevaeh scraped back the chair she was sitting in.

"Oh no," she said. "I'm going with you."

For a moment, it felt like she and Dad were dueling with just a look. She set her jaw stubbornly, but he did, too. She pursed her lips. He furrowed his brow.

But then Dad shrugged.

"Okay, sure," he said. "Guess you want to see your dad being a hero, huh?"

Nevaeh had to bite her tongue to keep from yelling back at him, *This isn't about you! It's about Rosemary!*

She grabbed her phone from the kitchen on the way out the door. Once she'd scrambled into the back seat of the truck, she texted Colin, explaining everything. He texted back, I've got a lot to tell you, too!

But then, oddly, he didn't send another text.

Hello? Hello? Nevaeh wrote.

Nothing.

When Dad stopped to pick up Steve, Nevaeh used that as

a cover to try to call Colin instead, but the call went straight to voice mail.

Settling into the front seat beside Dad, Steve began unleashing conspiracy theories.

"The way I see it, this Rosemary was probably in love with Arthur Mongold herself, and maybe she stole everything out of the storage unit and left that note about Maribel secretly hating Arthur as a way to try to turn him against his own wife," Steve said as they drove toward the highway. "The joke's on her that both Maribel and Arthur were dead before anyone found her note."

"That's far-fetched," Dad scoffed. "What if . . . what if the note was true? And what if Maribel staged her own death and just stole the identity of some girl she'd known in elementary school to hide out—so nobody knew she'd stolen all her husband's antiques?"

"And you think *my* idea's far-fetched?" Steve challenged.

Nevaeh leaned up over the front seat, her seat belt cutting into her waist.

"What if this Rosemary person isn't even home when we get there?" she asked. "Or what if she orders you off her property and threatens to call the cops on *you*? Or . . . threatens you with a gun?"

"You're no fun," Steve objected.

Dad caught Nevaeh's eye in the rearview mirror.

"Nevaeh, *we're* not doing anything illegal," Dad assured her. "If she asks us to leave, we'll leave. This is just a fact-finding mission. Nobody's going to get hurt. I'm not putting anyone in danger."

"You're no fun, either," Steve said, but he had to be joking. Wasn't he?

They were on I-70 now, and out in the countryside. The scenery whipped by quickly. Cornfields. Soybean fields. Trees.

Steve turned around in his seat to address Nevaeh.

"Your dad says you were the one who figured out Maribel Mongold went to school with some girl named Rosemary," he said. "How did *you* know that?"

"I . . . kind of started collecting old school pictures this summer," Nevaeh said, not entirely lying. She did have digital copies now of all the pictures Professor Carter had found in the Torres house. "I thought they might be . . . valuable . . . to somebody."

"Chip off the old block, huh, Lloyd?" Steve asked Dad. "She only started working with you this summer, and she's already trying to hustle people with old school pictures. Playing on their nostalgia . . . or is she just taking things from houses *you're* getting paid to clean out?"

Was Steve accusing her of stealing from her own father? Or from his customers?

"The pictures I have didn't come from any of the houses

I cleaned with Dad," Nevaeh said stiffly.

But what if he asks where the pictures actually came from?

Steve shrugged instead.

"It's lucky you had that particular picture," Steve said.

"Oh, you know, it's the Groveview effect," Dad said, before Nevaeh had a chance to answer. "In Groveview, everybody's connected to everyone."

"Yeah, did I ever tell you about the time someone tried to fix me up on a blind date with my own sister?" Steve said. "She was divorced by then, so different last name, and it was someone new to town who got us together, so he didn't know the connection. . . ."

Steve was off on some convoluted story that involved bowling leagues, people who met in Little League thirty years ago, and eventually, his sister slapping him for saying no one would ever want to date *her*.

Nevaeh sat back, relieved to be out of the conversation.

She texted Colin once more, but he still didn't answer.

While Steve droned on in the front seat, Nevaeh tried looking up Rosemary Desjardins on her phone again. Someone with that name definitely lived in Yellow Springs, and according to a people-finder site, she was approximately the right age to have been in sixth grade in 1976–77.

But that was the *only* information Nevaeh could find online. There was nothing about Rosemary Desjardins being the first woman to do anything. She wasn't the first woman to play on the Cincinnati Reds. She wasn't the first female astronaut to go to the moon.

Well, there's not any woman who's gotten to do either of those things, Nevaeh thought sadly.

Rosemary Desjardins hadn't been the first female Supreme Court justice, either. She hadn't become a world-famous surgeon or an Olympic champion or a movie mogul.

As far as Nevaeh could tell, Rosemary Desjardins hadn't ever done anything that would bring her to anyone's attention. Not even something as dull as playing in a bowling league, like Steve.

"New theory," Steve said. "What if this Rosemary woman both stole the antiques from my storage unit *and* arranged to have the Mongolds killed in Florida? Except, her hired assassin only managed to kill Maribel?"

"Are you *crazy*?" Nevaeh asked.

"Nevaeh," Dad said, catching her eye in the rearview mirror again and giving her a little head shake. It was partly a "Don't be disrespectful toward an adult" look, but there was more to it. Maybe he was also trying to say, *Steve's just talking. That's all. Let him have his fun.*

"Great detectives consider every theory," Steve told Nevaeh loftily, and Nevaeh let it go.

But how would Steve and Dad treat Rosemary if they

thought she was both a thief and a murderer?

Nevaeh looked at her phone again. Still no text back from Colin. She clicked over into email and began writing to Professor Carter: **Professor Carter: I think we found Rosemary. . . .** It took a long time to write out everything. She finished with, **And now I'm in a truck with my dad and this Steve guy, on our way to see Rosemary Desjardins. They're so sure she's a criminal. I'm worried.**

"Yep, this is the Yellow Springs I remember," Dad said so loudly from the front seat that it made Nevaeh jump. "Nevaeh, stop playing with your phone and look out your window."

Nevaeh sent the email and lowered her phone.

They were off the highway now, in a town that looked even smaller than Groveview. Dad pulled up to a stoplight. Outside Nevaeh's window, she did indeed see an antique store. It had a large peace sign in the window, the symbol shaded in purple paisley. Across the street was a little restaurant labeled "Haha Pizza."

"Right turn up here," Steve said, squinting at the GPS on his phone. "Looks like she's outside the main part of the village, out in the country. . . ."

They quickly left the quaint little village behind. After passing a cornfield and two cow pastures, they reached a tidy little house down a long lane, with a woods beyond.

"That's it," Steve said. "Fifteen-oh-eight Hyde Road. Yeah, lady, you can't hide from us!"

Dad steered the truck down the long lane. When he parked and shut off the engine, the sudden silence seemed a little frightening.

"Nevaeh, maybe you should stay in the truck," he said. "Just in case."

Nevaeh obeyed, but after Steve and Dad got out, she opened the truck door again so she could hear better. She watched Dad and Steve stride up to the front door and knock.

"Hello? Rosemary?" Dad called.

Nobody came to the door.

"Looks like nobody's home," Nevaeh called. "We drove all the way out here for nothing."

"The windows are open," Steve pointed out. "Who goes out for the day and leaves all their windows open? Especially when it looks like rain?"

Maybe he was a better detective than Nevaeh gave him credit for.

Nevaeh heard a rustling sound from the backyard. Then a brown dog came bounding around the corner of the house.

"Dad! Watch out!" Nevaeh cried.

"Don't worry—he's friendly," a woman's voice called from farther away.

Nevaeh looked toward the woods. The woman was just stepping out from the trees. She waved.

Does she look like twelve-year-old Rosemary Buvon? Nevaeh wondered. *Or . . . to consider Dad's theory . . .*

twelve-year-old Maribel Mason?

The woman was too far away. Nevaeh could tell only that she was wearing olive-green hiking pants and a pale T-shirt. Her hair was either gray or brownish-turning-gray; it was long and pulled into a single braid that hung down her back.

The woman was getting closer, crossing her backyard in long, athletic strides.

People change too much between the ages of twelve and fifty-whatever, Nevaeh thought, her heart sinking. *This woman could be anyone.*

The woman reached the front corner of her house. Now Nevaeh could tell that she had brown eyes. Brown like Rosemary, not blue like Maribel. And they were intelligent brown eyes. Friendly brown eyes. Curious brown eyes.

That part *was* familiar.

Nevaeh slipped out of the truck.

"Did you used to be known as Rosemary Buvon?" she called. "Were you friends with Toby Carter when you were a kid?"

The woman stopped in her tracks and put her hand over her mouth, as if she was too stunned to speak or even nod.

That means yes, doesn't it? Nevaeh thought.

But before she or Rosemary could say another word, Dad and Steve rushed over to the woman.

"What did you do with the money from selling Arthur and

Maribel Mongold's possessions?" Steve demanded.

The woman froze. But then she dropped her hand from her mouth. She straightened her shoulders.

"You know," she said, "I've been waiting more than thirty years for someone to show up and ask me that question."

43

Surprises for Colin, Almost an Hour Earlier

Colin's mom took off running for the SUV.

"Mom, Mom, hold on! What are you doing?" Colin cried as he scrambled after her.

"Trying to prevent a giant misunderstanding," Mom said grimly. "Helping someone who helped me. Either get in, if you're coming with me, or—"

Colin didn't wait to hear the second choice. He jumped into the car, barely managing to shut the door before Mom pulled away from the curb.

"You're acting like someone's house is on fire," Colin protested. "Why are you so upset that Nevaeh and her dad are going to . . . what's it called? Green Springs? Yellow Springs?"

That was all he'd had time to tell her before she'd jumped into action.

But Mom wasn't even listening. She had her phone to her ear as she drove, and was yelling, "Answer! Please, please, please answer!"

Mom *never* violated the rule about holding a phone while driving.

Colin bent over his own phone and texted Nevaeh: I've got a lot to tell you, too!

Then his phone screen went dark.

Oh no! Did I forget to plug it in last night?

There'd just been too much to think about last night.

"Mom, my phone battery died," he complained. "Can we go back for my charger? Or can I borrow your phone?"

"No time for that," Mom said, turning a corner recklessly fast. "And, no, you can't borrow my phone. I need it."

Mom seemed to be dialing a new number now. Someone must have answered this time, because Mom cried out, "I'm on my way. Be there in five minutes."

The SUV's Bluetooth kicked in just then, so Colin heard a woman's voice from the SUV's speakers: "I'll be ready."

Where were they going?

And who was that woman?

44

Rosemary and Nevaeh. And Dad and Steve.

Nevaeh ran over in between Rosemary and Dad and Steve. Rosemary's dog did, too—as if the dog sensed that Rosemary needed protection.

"Stop!" Nevaeh cried, flailing her hands at Dad and Steve. She turned around to face Rosemary. "Be careful—they're trying to trap you! If you confess anything, they're going to record you without you knowing. That's got to be illegal, too, right? They should at least say that thing from TV about how you have a right to an attorney, and—"

"Nevaeh," Dad said warningly.

Rosemary looked . . . amused.

"Actually, I am an attorney," she said. "I went to law school, anyway. And it would be legal for someone to record me secretly. Ohio is a state with one-party consent for that. But I appreciate you looking out for my legal rights." She smiled at Nevaeh, and maybe it was a little bit like the smile in Rosemary's sixth-grade class picture. "Now, who *are* the three of you? And what do *you* know about Maribel and Arthur Mongold?"

"Oh no, you don't get to ask the questions," Steve said. He turned to Dad. "Don't let her trap us with any lawyer tricks!"

Rosemary seemed to be sizing up Steve, Dad, and Nevaeh. Nevaeh suddenly wished she'd known that morning when she was getting dressed that she'd be finding Rosemary, instead of cleaning out yet another filthy attic or basement. Her ideal meeting-Rosemary clothes *wouldn't* have been battered jeans and a T-shirt that advertised the Groveview Drive-In (even though the drive-in had closed down before Nevaeh was born).

But Dad and Steve didn't look any better. Dad's Junk King T-shirt had a hole in it. The cap Steve wore advertising his own business could very well have dated back to the day in 1989 when Maribel and Arthur Mongold rented their storage unit from him.

All three of us look like junk, Nevaeh thought. *We look like that name Steve called us as a joke. Trash pickers.*

She could almost see Rosemary deciding she could just send them away. She could order them off her property—and maybe even threaten to call the police to get them to leave.

"You went to elementary school with Maribel," Nevaeh blurted out. "You were friends in sixth grade. Did you stay friends after that?"

Rosemary's eyes widened, then glistened. Was she holding back tears?

"Yes," she whispered. "After sixth grade, I considered her my best friend. From then until she died."

She means, after Toby, Nevaeh thought. *After they had their big fight and he left town.*

"You weren't even in the Mongolds' wedding party," Dad scoffed. "Maribel didn't even ask you to be a bridesmaid, let alone maid of honor."

Nevaeh shot a glance at Dad in surprise—how would he know that?

Oh, right, the wedding announcement from the newspaper, Nevaeh realized. It had listed bridesmaids and groomsmen. Nevaeh had read right past the names, because she hadn't recognized any of them. But evidently Dad had paid attention.

He might have even called every single one of the people listed, trying to track down information about the Mongolds' antiques.

"Maribel *did* ask me to be a bridesmaid," Rosemary said, lifting her head defiantly. "But I refused. Because I begged her not to marry Arthur. I couldn't have lived with myself even attending that wedding."

"Because you wanted to marry him yourself?" Steve challenged. "Because you were in love with Arthur? Or, at least, you wanted to be the one living in that big house, collecting all that expensive furniture, being a lady of leisure?"

Steve would make a terrible detective, after all, Nevaeh thought. *He can't keep his mouth shut.*

Rosemary really was going to demand that they all leave.

"Rosemary didn't need Arthur Mongold's money," Nevaeh announced. "She grew up rich herself. She was the first person in their class to get a home video game system. So she could play Pong."

Rosemary went from glaring at Steve to gaping at Nevaeh.

"How in the world would you know that?" Rosemary gasped. "That stupid game . . . Even *I'd* forgotten about Pong."

Nevaeh ran over to the truck and pulled out a shoebox: the Nike one that contained all of Rosemary's letters. She held it out to Rosemary like a gift.

"Because of this," Nevaeh said.

Rosemary's face went white.

"You know Toby," she whispered. "He kept those, even though he never . . . he never . . ."

Nevaeh shook her head.

"I only met Toby last week," Nevaeh said. "I tried to give him back the letters that belonged to him, but—"

"Nevaeh, what is all this?" Dad asked.

"Um, it's a long story?" Nevaeh said, suddenly remembering she needed to protect Colin. And she couldn't tell the true story of the Toby and Rosemary letters without mentioning Colin.

"Looks like your daughter's as big a scammer as you are, Lloyd," Steve told Dad with a harsh laugh. "But she needs a little guidance." He turned to face Nevaeh and said in a pretend-whisper, "Kiddo, you forgot to set a selling price."

He meant money. He thought Nevaeh was trying to sell Rosemary's own letters back to her.

"I'm *not* trying to make money off this," Nevaeh told Rosemary. Her voice went high and screechy with distress. She could feel her eyes going wide, too, and filming over with tears. Rosemary had to believe her. "This doesn't have anything to do with money."

"Fool," Steve muttered. "Everything's about money."

Rosemary grasped the box and opened it. She riffled through the letters, half smiling, half frowning. Then she looked up, blinking as if the shoebox of letters had completely thrown her off.

"Maybe we should sit down," she said, gesturing toward a small round table and four chairs on a little brick terrace beside her front door. The whole set was what Dad would call "frilly"; it was painted lilac, and Nevaeh could imagine it in some Paris café.

Not that she'd ever seen Paris.

"Thanks for the offer, but I don't think you want me and Steve sitting there," Dad said apologetically, gesturing at his own belly, at Steve's height. "We don't want to break your furniture."

"Oh, it's sturdier than it looks," Rosemary said.

Everyone sat down. The dog settled in at Rosemary's feet. He still looked to be on alert.

"Can we get back to the missing antiques?" Steve said. "What I'm hearing is, you were jealous and didn't want Maribel to marry Arthur, so you stole everything they owned?"

"You're not listening right," Rosemary snapped. "What you should be hearing is . . . is . . ."

"Tell us," Dad said quietly.

Nevaeh wanted to shout, *Be careful!* again. She wanted to remind Rosemary that she'd seen Steve hit the Record button on his phone screen. But she couldn't seem to get the words out.

She'd never seen a grown-up look like Rosemary did right now. She'd never seen anyone look like that. It was almost as though Rosemary was shedding layers, letting emotions she'd held inside for more than thirty years show on her face for the first time.

It was like seeing someone naked.

"I didn't care a thing about antiques," Rosemary said. "I didn't want Maribel to marry Arthur because I was afraid he'd kill her. And he did."

45

Colin, Still Confused

"Please," Colin said. "Let me call Nevaeh now. She can stop things. She can make her dad turn around and just go home."

"You don't know Lloyd Greevey," Mom retorted.

They were turning into the driveway for Groveview's hospital. Mom zipped past all the parked cars and sped right up to the main entrance. Mom hadn't even hit the brakes yet when the giant plate-glass doors of the hospital slid open, and a woman in pink scrubs stepped out.

For a moment, Colin thought he might be seeing some vision from the future. This woman looked like a middle-aged version of Nevaeh. She had the same thick, dark blond hair, though this woman's was cut short and practical, and had streaks of gray. She moved briskly, as if she, like Nevaeh, was always sure of where she was going. And her eyes—though tired and surrounded by lines Nevaeh didn't have—held the same directness, the same steadiness.

"That's Mrs. Greevey, isn't it?" Colin asked. "Nevaeh's mom?"

"My friend Pam," Mom said with a nod.

Friend, Colin thought. *Interesting.*

He was certain he'd never heard his mom mention a friend named Pam. He was certain that in all of Mom's grumbling about the Junk King, she'd never once said, *But I like his wife. She's a friend of mine.*

"Want to climb into the back seat to make room?" Mom asked.

"Uh, sure," Colin said, awkwardly banging his knee on the console between the seats as he scrambled out of the way. He seat-belted himself into the middle of the back seat so he could still see out the front window. But it felt symbolic: he wasn't taking sides.

He couldn't. He didn't understand anything right now.

Mrs. Greevey was quickly climbing into the seat Colin had vacated and shutting the door firmly behind her.

"You remember Colin," Mom said.

"Oh yeah," Mrs. Greevey said, flashing him a friendly smile that reminded him even more of Nevaeh. "Though it's been about twelve years."

Colin knew he was supposed to say something polite like *Nice to meet you.* Or maybe *Nice to see you again* would be more appropriate. What he wanted to do was shout, *If you two are such great friends, how come you haven't seen me in twelve years? What is going on?*

But Mrs. Greevey had already turned back to Mom.

"We're really doing this, right?" she asked. "This rescue mission?"

Mom wasn't slamming the gearshift into Drive. She wasn't hitting the gas. She just gazed sadly back at Mrs. Greevey.

"The thing is," Mom said, "when you've kept a secret for so long, how can you be sure that it's time to reveal it?"

46

Rosemary's Story. And Maribel's.

"You're accusing a dead man of murder?" Steve asked Rosemary, leaning forward across the frilly table. "That's convenient, now that he can't defend himself. If you believed Arthur Mongold killed his wife, why didn't you go to the police back in 1989?"

"Maribel Mongold died in a car crash," Dad said. "It was random. Arthur Mongold wasn't even at fault. Someone else hit *them*."

"There are different ways to kill a woman," Rosemary said. "Arthur Mongold killed Maribel's spirit years before she died."

Nevaeh clutched the lacy edge of the table. Rosemary's voice was so heavy, Nevaeh had to hold on to *something*. Even if it was only a flimsy table painted lilac, with cutouts of a heart and stars in the middle.

"Oh, this is just some feminist garbage," Steve said disgustedly. He grabbed the bill of his ball cap and hit it against the table. "Arthur didn't let his wife get new flooring for their kitchen, or they had some stupid lovers' spat about moving to Florida, and you're making it out to be like 'Oh, she was so oppressed.'"

"Steve," Dad said quietly. "Stop."

Nevaeh was not sure she'd ever felt as proud of her father as she did right then.

But why did it have to take Dad—a man—saying that, to get Steve to actually shut up?

"You're saying he hit her," Dad said to Rosemary, still in a hushed tone. "Or . . . he was cruel in other ways. You're saying the Mongolds had an abusive marriage."

Rosemary ran her hand across her face. She smoothed back stray hairs that had escaped her braid.

"I don't know why it's any of your business," she retorted. She glared at Steve. "You don't want me to speak ill of a dead man? I don't want to speak ill of a dead woman, either. Especially a dead *friend*. I wouldn't be sitting here talking to you at all if it weren't for this girl bringing me this box of letters." She swept the Nike shoebox from the table down onto her lap, as if to protect it. "I don't even know who you people are or why you're here."

Behind Rosemary's house, the cicadas out in the woods were building toward a crescendo of sound. Dad and Steve acted like they were just waiting for that roar to die down.

Or maybe, for once, Dad and Steve didn't know what to say?

"I'm Nevaeh," Nevaeh said, reaching out to shake Rosemary's hand. She did have manners, after all. And then, though she normally avoided telling anyone this, she added, "That's 'Heaven' spelled backward. My parents like strange names." She rolled her eyes, as if that explained everything. "That's my dad, Lloyd Greevey."

Rosemary raised an eyebrow.

"I remember Greeveys in Groveview when I was a kid," she said. "Greevey's Junkyard and Car Parts?"

"That was my dad and granddad," Dad said. "I took the family business in a different direction. We're more into . . . upcycling . . . now."

Nevaeh remembered Dad and Axel and Dalton cracking up over the term "upcycle." But now Dad was using it seriously.

Had *Dad* actually been ashamed of his junkyard family when he was a kid?

She'd never really thought about how much Dad had changed the family business. Even he hadn't just continued doing everything the same way as his father and grandfather.

"Steve Owens," Steve said, pointing to himself. "I own Steve's Self-Storage in Groveview. So when you stole from the Mongolds, you were also trespassing on my property. . . ."

Rosemary turned to Nevaeh as if she hadn't even heard

Steve speak. Or, as if she wanted to make it perfectly clear she wasn't listening.

"All through elementary school, I had two best friends," Rosemary said. "Toby Carter and Maribel Mason. I played baseball with Toby and took dance lessons alongside Maribel."

"So what were you, really?" Steve asked, as if this was a question to trap her, too. He had a look on his face like, *Look how patient I'm being, letting you answer this before you get to what I really want to know.* "Tomboy or girly girl?"

"I was a *kid*," Rosemary said. "Growing up in the 1970s, I totally bought into the whole Marlo Thomas 'Free to Be You and Me' idea. I really did think society would view women as one hundred percent equal to men by the time I was in high school. I thought every door was open to me. To all of us. I could be anything I wanted. Toby could be anything he wanted. Maribel could be anything . . ."

She snapped her mouth shut.

"But you and Toby had a fight in sixth grade," Nevaeh said. "And never made up."

Talking to Professor Carter, Nevaeh had been so mad at *him* over what he said to Rosemary. But he'd apologized. He'd tried to make up.

Now Nevaeh was kind of angry at Rosemary, too.

Rosemary darted her gaze toward Dad and Steve, as if she didn't want them there at all to hear any of this conversation. But she locked eyes with Nevaeh.

"Toby said horrible things to me," Rosemary said. "I was *so* mad. In homeroom, I sent him a note telling him I'd never speak to him again. By first-period history, I was thinking about what I'd say when he admitted he was wrong—I was so sure he'd admit he was wrong! But then, five minutes into first period, I got called down to the school office."

"Why?" Nevaeh asked, recoiling a little. "Were you in trouble for fighting? The school punished you but not the boy who—"

"Oh, no—you don't know this part of the story?" Rosemary looked down at the box of letters in her lap. "I guess it *wouldn't* have been in these letters. . . ." She swallowed hard. "My dad had a stroke that same morning. It looked like he wasn't going to make it, so my mom wanted me at the hospital right away to . . . to say goodbye."

Nevaeh could just see it. She didn't know this woman sitting before her, but she knew twelve-year-old Rosemary, with all her hopes and dreams and lofty goals. And her faith that her life would be good, that she'd get to do great things. Nevaeh wanted to fly back in time and throw herself between twelve-year-old Rosemary and the fight with Toby, the horrible news about her dad. To protect her from *anything* that would hurt the young Rosemary.

"I don't see what this has to do with anything," Steve complained.

Nevaeh ignored him.

"Did your dad die the same day as your fight with Toby?" she asked Rosemary.

Nevaeh sneaked a glance at Dad. What would it be like to lose your father when you were only twelve?

"You don't have to . . . ," Dad began, and this was Dad being quiet, Dad being restrained. He was giving Rosemary permission to avoid reliving her pain.

Rosemary ignored him just as completely as she and Nevaeh had ignored Steve.

"My dad surprised everyone and hung on for three weeks," she said. "Three really, really awful weeks . . . Mom and I didn't leave his side. I didn't go to school, I didn't talk to anyone outside the hospital. . . . I was supposed to be in a spelling bee that I'd thought was the most important thing ever—I'd studied so hard, and it was going to be my big moment of glory. But I didn't even go. And you know who was there for me the day my dad died? The day of the funeral? And the day after, when my mom got up and said, 'We can't stay in this house. It's too sad. Pack a bag—we're leaving'? Do you know who actually packed that bag for me? Maribel. Maribel Mason. Again and again and again, she was by my side. . . ."

"Toby didn't know about your dad," Nevaeh said, as if she'd suddenly decided to be a defense attorney for *him*. "His family was . . . having problems, too, and they'd left town."

"Yeah, I found that out later," Rosemary said. "When I wrote him a letter and it came back, 'Forwarding address unknown.' But by then I was in a new town and at a new school, and Mom was getting remarried, and my new stepdad wanted to adopt me, and . . . and I wanted Toby to know that I was going to be Rosemary Desjardins. But I couldn't find him. So Maribel became the only person from Groveview I stayed in touch with. The two of us, we were like *this*"—she held up two fingers, pressed together so tightly they might have been glued—"in a way we wouldn't have been if we'd stayed in school together." She glanced over at Steve and Dad, as if she was ready to include them in the conversation again. "I owed her."

"So you paid her back by stealing her stuff?" Steve asked mockingly.

Rosemary darted her gaze back to Nevaeh's face, as if she was refusing to even look at Steve.

"There was a TV show on when I was a teenager called *The Paper Chase*," Rosemary said. "It was all about how hard law school was. And I wanted that—I wanted to lose myself in all that work. It seemed like a way to escape the grief of losing my dad, the loneliness of moving to new places and never having anyone think I was as special as people had thought in Groveview. . . . By the time I was in law school, Maribel wasn't just the only person I'd stayed in touch with from Groveview. She was the only friend I kept from the past at all. But that was hard, because I'd visit, and she'd just become this . . . puppet . . . for her husband. She was so afraid she might do something wrong—say 'yes, dear' with the wrong tone of voice, or curl her hair wrong, or, or . . . have a better eye for antiques than he did. . . ."

"You're saying she was the antiques expert," Dad said. "It was her, not him, who built up the collection. But he took credit."

Rosemary nodded.

"And then my only *female* law school professor mentioned a situation she'd heard of," Rosemary said. "How a woman in an abusive marriage hid assets so she could escape. She'd done it by borrowing a friend's identity, setting up a secret bank account in the friend's name."

"So you told Maribel about that," Nevaeh said, catching on. "Right?"

"Not only that, I left my social security card and driver's license out where she could see them," Rosemary said. "I made it *easy* for her to steal my identity." A near-smile teased at her lips, but it quickly turned sad. "That was about the time Arthur insisted they should move to Florida. Where she wouldn't have any friends, any family . . . anyone to turn to. I also told Maribel—just theoretically—how someone could show up at an airport in Florida and arrange for a flight back to Ohio the same day. Even just a few hours before takeoff. So she wouldn't have to buy her plane ticket ahead of time and risk Arthur seeing it. She could be hundreds of miles away before he found out she was gone."

"Then you totally knew what she was doing," Dad began. "You knew she sold the furniture Arthur thought she put into storage. You knew she had it shipped directly to the buyers, using your name on all the invoices. You knew *nothing* ever went into that storage unit. And—"

Rosemary silenced him with only a look. Then, slowly, she shook her head. No. She hadn't known any of it.

"Not while Maribel was still alive," she whispered.

For a while, Rosemary just stared down at the cutout heart and stars in the middle of her table. When she spoke again, her voice was choked and hollow.

"Later that year—a few days before their move—Maribel sent me a birthday card that said, 'There's a surprise gift coming for you soon!'" she murmured. "And then I started getting bank account statements from an account I knew nothing about. An account with hundreds of thousands of dollars, all in my name."

Her gaze was intense when she looked back up.

"The first statement arrived the day I heard Maribel was dead."

For a moment nobody said anything. Then Steve began clapping in a slow, sarcastic way.

"What a story," he said. "Did they teach you how to lie like that in law school? You made yourself out to be the hero—after all, you were just trying to save your poor, tortured friend. But you still ended up with all the money." He glanced back at her house, at the woods beyond. "Bought yourself a nice little house and a nice little plot of land, didn't you?"

"No! That's not where the money went," Rosemary protested. "What would *you* have done? Given the money back to Arthur Mongold?"

"Yes," Dad said.

Nevaeh jerked her head in his direction in surprise.

"But, Dad—" she began.

"I'm sorry about your friend dying," Dad said. "And I'm sorry if her husband treated her badly. But the money from the sale of all that furniture belonged to Arthur Mongold, not you."

"'If'?" Nevaeh repeated. "*If* he treated her badly? Rosemary just told you—"

"Yeah, *Rosemary* told us a story," Steve said. "I knew some of the same people the Mongolds knew. All of them thought the Mongolds were this happy, fairy-tale couple living in a beautiful house with all this fancy antique furniture. If Maribel had such a bad marriage, why didn't she tell any of them?"

Rosemary's jaw dropped.

"It was the 1980s," she said. "Do you know how many secrets women had to keep back then? Do you know what domestic violence laws were like? Do you even know what they're like now?"

Dad scraped his chair back from the table.

"I think we're done here," he said. He put his hand on Nevaeh's shoulder and peered directly at Rosemary. "You were right. This isn't our business."

Dad's a terrible actor, Nevaeh thought. It felt like he was really saying, "This is our business, because we still believe you stole something from us. And now we have you on tape confessing, and we're going to do something about it."

"You mean, you're going to the cops," Rosemary said flatly. Dad hadn't fooled her, either. "Please don't. It's not me you'd hurt. I have that birthday card saying Maribel was sending me a gift—that would hold up in court. I have proof from the IRS that I paid gift tax on the money. I . . . Please don't drag Maribel's name through the mud. Please don't hurt anyone else."

"You're only worried about your own name, your own money," Steve taunted.

Nevaeh's phone buzzed just then—Colin had picked a great time to finally get back to her.

But when she glanced down at her phone, the text wasn't from Colin. It was from Nevaeh's mom: **Do you need help? Does Rosemary need help?**

How would *Mom* know anything about Rosemary? How did she even know the name?

Nevaeh looked at the three grown-ups around her, facing off. Dad and Steve were both on their feet now, both glaring down at Rosemary.

Nevaeh typed a one-word answer back to Mom:

Yes.

A moment later, she saw an unfamiliar SUV turn down Rosemary's lane.

47

The Two Moms and Colin

"We have to do this," Nevaeh's mom said, holding her cell phone in the air.

Colin's mom swerved the car onto a gravel lane. They were so far out in the country now, Colin could see more cows than houses. In fact, he could see only one house: a small, light blue one at the end of the lane, nestled against a backdrop of giant trees.

Then he noticed the Junk King truck parked in front of the house. And the people clustered around a small metal table: Nevaeh's dad standing alongside another man, Nevaeh and a woman sitting down.

"Is that Rosemary?" he asked.

Neither his mom nor Nevaeh's bothered answering him. Mom was slamming the car into Park, shutting off the engine. Practically as soon as the car stopped moving, both women threw their doors open and hopped out. Colin followed only an instant later.

"Pam?" Nevaeh's dad asked, looking completely puzzled. *"Felicia?"*

"And Colin," Colin muttered, but none of the adults were listening.

At least Nevaeh gave him a tiny, hopeful smile.

"Whatever you're accusing Rosemary of, *stop*," Nevaeh's mom said. "She's done nothing wrong."

"She took money that didn't rightfully belong to her." This came from the man standing with Nevaeh's dad. "According to every law I ever heard of, that's called theft."

Nevaeh made a face, gestured at the man, and mouthed the name *Steve*. Her frown told Colin everything he needed to know about Steve. Steve was the one making trouble. Steve was the one they had to worry about.

"Did Rosemary tell you what she did with the money?" Colin's mom asked.

"She donated it!" Nevaeh's mom added.

"Again, a convenient story," Steve muttered. He flicked his gaze from Nevaeh's mom to Colin's mom to Rosemary. "Why didn't you say that from the start? Or show us receipts from United Way or the cancer society or wherever you sent the money?"

Colin's mom took a deep breath.

"Rosemary started her own charity with the money," she said. "She helped other women. Women like me."

"What?" Nevaeh cried, almost toppling from her chair. "How—?"

Colin noticed that Mom didn't even blink. Her voice was steady and strong as she went on.

"She helped me start my own business and buy my own house when no bank I went to would loan me a dime. They said I was too much of a risk. But Rosemary said . . . Rosemary said my business plan was brilliant. Rosemary said I deserved the chance that her friend Maribel never got. The chance to start over."

Mom reached out and put her arm around Colin's shoulders, hugging him close.

"Rosemary changed my life," Mom said. "She changed *our* lives."

Colin felt dizzy. What would have become of him and Mom if it hadn't been for Rosemary's money (which was really Maribel's money)? Would they have had to go back to live with Dad, even though Mom thought he was a terrible person?

When he'd found the letters between Rosemary and Toby, he'd never dreamed that either of them could have had a connection to him and Mom.

But he thought about how looking for Rosemary and Toby had led to him and Nevaeh becoming friends. It'd led to them helping Mrs. Torres and babysitting the Torres twins.

It'd led to them finding out about the history of Groveview. It'd even led to him finding out that Deepak had a crush on Nevaeh's sister.

Colin wasn't surprised anymore to find out how many ways people were connected.

Nevaeh's dad snorted.

"So when I started suspecting that *you* might have stolen the Mongolds' antiques—I was almost right," he said bitterly to Colin's mom. "I just missed seeing the middleman." He darted his gaze toward Rosemary. "Or—middle*woman*."

"Yeah, it's like we've uncovered a girl gang," Steve crowed. "Or is it a girl *mafia*?"

Now Colin understood the disgust on Nevaeh's face when she'd pointed to Steve.

"It's not right to talk about adult women and call them girls," Colin said. "Or to make it sound like a crime just to—"

"Yeah, that's how little boys talk when they don't have any male role models," Steve mocked.

Colin had never been so angry before in his life.

He peered at Mom, waiting for her to tell off Steve. But Mom looked frozen.

Because she wonders about that, too, Colin thought. *She worries that she has hurt me by not exposing me to more male role models. But she knew Dad wasn't the right male role model.*

The Greeveys and Rosemary looked frozen, too.

Or maybe they were just letting Colin fight his own battles.

"My mom is a *great* role model," Colin said. "Not that it's any of your business. But she has exposed me to good male role models, too." He thought of Deepak, Derek, and Daryl, with all their jokes and the easy way they'd tried to befriend him. *They* wouldn't talk about women and call them "girls." He narrowed his eyes at Steve. "And this isn't just about women. I'm a boy, and *I* benefited from the money Rosemary gave my mom."

"You did, too, Lloyd Greevey," Mom burst out. She looked over at Nevaeh's mom, as if to get permission to keep talking. Mrs. Greevey nodded. "You . . . and your sons . . . and your daughters . . . and your wife . . . Your whole family. Every single one of you benefited from Rosemary's charity."

Nevaeh and her dad looked equally puzzled. But Nevaeh recovered first.

"Mom?" she cried. "Does she mean . . . did you get money from Rosemary that was supposed to help you leave Dad?"

"No!" Nevaeh's mom wailed. "Rosemary gave us money to help our family survive!"

48

Another Surprise

"I . . . I don't understand," Dad stammered.

Nevaeh wanted to loop her arms through Mom's and Dad's elbows and draw them both together. She wanted them to remember that they were Greeveys, and Greeveys stuck together. Always.

But Dad stayed on the other side of the table from Rosemary, and Mom stayed a few steps away, beside Colin and Mrs. Creedmont.

"Is it all right now to . . . ?" Mom asked Rosemary, and Rosemary nodded. Now Mom at least gazed at Dad, even though she didn't move any closer to him. "Lloyd, do you remember what it was like when we found out I was pregnant with Nevaeh? The economy was bad then, too, and your business was off. And I was barely making anything at all, the few hours I could pick up working at the grocery store. And you started talking about how maybe it was time to give up on your dream and get a regular job with benefits.

Remember? And I said maybe *I'm* the one who should get a different job, and maybe it would be possible for me to go back to school and do something in medicine like I'd always wanted . . . if only I could get some kind of scholarship or grant or loan. . . ."

"*Rosemary* gave you a scholarship?" Nevaeh exploded.

She felt like puzzle pieces were locking into place in her mind—puzzle pieces of her own life she'd never even realized were missing. It had never occurred to her to wonder how Mom had afforded to go to school. But there had always been hints. Whenever Prilla talked about how Mom was such a superwoman, getting her degree while pregnant with her fifth child, Mom would always add, "But I had help. I couldn't have managed it otherwise."

Nevaeh had just thought she meant Dad helped her, and other people helped with babysitting and carpooling.

"If all that's true, why did it have to be so secret?" Steve asked. "Is this like . . . Lloyd, even you and your wife received stolen property?"

"I guess . . . I guess nothing was stolen," Dad said. He squinted at Mom. "But, Pam, we weren't that desperate. I never . . . never hurt you, and you getting that money makes it sound like . . . like I did."

"I used Maribel's money to help women in all sorts of circumstances," Rosemary said gently. "Not just women whose partners hurt them. I knew there were other ways for women to be defeated. For *humans* to feel defeated." She held up the box of letters Nevaeh had handed her. "If I remember anything about what's in these letters, it's all the times I told Toby what great things I was going to achieve as a female. He encouraged those dreams, because he had dreams, too."

"You were going to be the first female astronaut to walk on the moon," Nevaeh whispered. "The first female to play for the Reds. The first female Supreme Court justice."

"I was," Rosemary said, sounding a little dazed. "I was going to do all of that." She blinked, and her face hardened. "But after I grew up, my dreams changed."

"There was nothing wrong with your dreams," Colin blurted out. "If you'd really wanted to, you could have—"

Rosemary held up her hand.

"No, there wasn't anything wrong with those dreams," she said. "But there's also nothing wrong with dreams changing. When I was ten, eleven, twelve, my life felt limitless. But then my dad died. And I lost other people in my grief. Like Toby. Then when Maribel died, too, I felt like . . . life is short. I wasn't the same person at twenty-four that I'd been at twelve. I lost interest in hunching over law books, spending years inching toward a goal. I wanted to make a difference as soon as I could, in case that was all the time I got."

Nevaeh shivered. Who knew when anyone might die? But Rosemary was talking about how she'd felt at twenty-four, and that was more than thirty years ago. Rosemary had had decades to make a difference. She probably had decades more ahead of her, too.

Even Steve was quiet, listening to Rosemary.

"And after Maribel died," she said, "I was less interested in achieving something for myself, and more interested in helping as many other women as possible. *That* was my new goal. If I'd done everything publicly, I'm sure there would have been lawsuits. It would have tied up the money for years, even though I believed I would ultimately win. I kept expecting Arthur to find out the antiques were missing—the antiques that Maribel herself sold, pretending to be me. I thought he'd track me down and challenge everything I was doing. So each time I helped a woman, and she succeeded, I'd think, *There. That's a change he can't reverse. That's something he can't stop. A woman he can't stifle or destroy.* Then the secrecy became a habit."

"And none of us who got help wanted to be the one who ruined it for others," Colin's mom said. "So we all . . . went to extremes with the secrecy, too."

"I didn't even know you two were friends!" Colin said, gesturing at his mom, and Nevaeh's, too.

Mom and Felicia Creedmont are friends? Nevaeh marveled.

Not just acquaintances who knew each other twelve years ago, but . . . friends?

She had so many questions she needed to ask her mom. But that would have to come later.

"Well, now Arthur Mongold is dead," Steve said flatly. "The empty storage unit's been opened. So what are you going to do now?"

"I . . . don't know," Rosemary said. "It feels like I've been living under a cloud for more than thirty years. I've gotten used to hiding. I felt so strongly that it was right then, but . . . maybe it stopped being right."

"No one has to hide anymore!" Nevaeh announced. But her words were swallowed up by the sound of a car driving by on the road. She started to repeat herself, but just then the car turned around and came back.

And then it turned down Rosemary's lane.

"Steve?" Dad said quietly. "Did you call the cops, after all?"

"No," Steve protested. "I wouldn't have done that once I heard you and your family were involved!"

Nevaeh squinted at the car, which was partially obscured by the cloud of dust rising from the gravel lane. Whoever it was, they were driving too fast.

And then the car veered off into the grass, stopping behind Dad's truck. A man sprang out.

"Rosemary!" he cried. "Am I too late? Can I do anything to help?"

"Oh," Nevaeh said sheepishly. "Maybe I should explain that I emailed—"

"Professor Carter?" Colin gasped. "You emailed *him*?"

Comprehension seemed to dawn on Rosemary's face like a sunrise. She didn't ask any questions. She seemed to have forgotten about Nevaeh. And Dad, Steve, Mom, Colin, and Colin's mom as well. Rosemary rose from her chair and stumbled toward Professor Carter. She held out the box of letters as if she needed to give them away now, too.

"Toby?" she whispered. "Is it really you? It is!"

She ran over and hugged him.

Nevaeh caught Colin's eye. And it felt for a moment as though she could read his mind. Because he had to be thinking exactly the same thing as her:

It wasn't too late.

The Ending—or Is It?

LOCAL KIDS REUNITE OLD FRIENDS
AFTER MORE THAN 40 YEARS

A shoebox stuffed full of letters and hidden in an attic more than 40 years ago sparked the curiosity of two Groveview 12-year-olds earlier this summer. By the time they were done investigating, these two young Sherlock Holmeses had found a second hidden shoebox of letters, become experts on 1970s pop culture—and reunited two childhood friends who'd been searching for each other since 1977.

"We owe everything to Nevaeh [Greevey] and Colin [Creedmont]," said Robb Tobias Carter, an Ohio State University professor who was born in Groveview, but moved away when he was 12, shortly after a fight with his then–best friend, Rosemary Buvon (now Rosemary Desjardins). "It's been so much fun catching up with Rosemary. Just getting these boxes of letters back . . . You never lose the person you were at 12."

"It was such unfortunate timing that Toby and I never got the chance to repair our friendship back in 1977," Desjardin said. "We're making up for lost time now."

Nevaeh lowered her cell phone, which she had been using to read aloud to Colin.

"So far it's not too bad," she said.

"Yeah, because you stopped before you got to any of our quotes," Colin retorted.

They'd agreed to read this story from the local newspaper together, as soon as it was posted on the website. They were sitting in the library's courtyard again, which had become their meeting place when they were trying to find Rosemary and Toby.

But before, it had felt like no one was paying attention to them. Now it felt to Colin as though the people walking by might know everything about them. That woman holding a toddler's hand—was she staring? The cluster of teenagers laughing in the parking lot—were they laughing at Colin and Nevaeh?

"Colin! They used your picture!" Nevaeh squealed, holding out the phone so he could see. There on the screen was a photo Colin had taken of Rosemary and Toby hugging in Rosemary's front yard, that moment when they'd seen each other for the first time since 1977. Colin had only meant to take the picture for himself, and maybe Nevaeh, too—how could he have resisted preserving a memory of the joy and relief and surprise on Rosemary's and Toby's faces? He was just lucky the sky was so blue that day, and the green of the trees and cornfields framed Rosemary and Toby so perfectly. But Nevaeh had insisted he get actual printouts of the photo, so Rosemary and Toby could have copies. She'd even come up with some cool old (upcycled!) frames to put them in. Then when Nevaeh's dad had mentioned Rosemary and Toby to his friend who worked at the local paper, he'd shown his friend the picture, and . . .

And now Colin was staring at the result.

"'Photo credit: Colin Creedmont,'" Nevaeh read breathlessly. "Colin, you're famous!"

"*We're* famous," Colin corrected. He pointed to a line below the picture, where he was quoted as saying, "I may have found the first shoebox of letters, but Nevaeh was the one who figured out the most."

So what if people stared at them? Who cared if anyone laughed? They'd done something good.

And Toby and Rosemary had wanted to share their story with other people because, as Toby was quoted saying, "We thought it might inspire others to reconnect with people from their past who'd made a difference to them."

Nevaeh finished reading the story and sat back in satisfaction.

"It tells everything Rosemary and Toby wanted to make public, and nothing more," she said. "But I'm glad *we* know the full story."

Rosemary was still trying to protect her friend Maribel's memory, as well as the privacy of all the women her charity had helped. So when the newspaper reporter had asked her about her job, she'd said she wanted to be identified only as "leading a private philanthropy for the empowerment of women."

But she'd also contacted Arthur Mongold's widow in Florida—his second wife—and offered to give all of Maribel's remaining money to *her*, to do with as she wished.

And the second Mrs. Mongold had written back: "Keep it. Keep helping women like Maribel. And like me."

Nevaeh thought that "And like me" were the saddest three words she'd ever seen in writing.

But now that Rosemary wasn't worried anymore about Arthur Mongold suing her, she'd thrown a big party for all the women and families she'd helped with Maribel's money over the years. Nevaeh and Colin had wandered through the crowd picking bizarre foods off trays offered by servers in tuxedos—why would anyone bother wrapping bacon around water chestnuts, instead of just eating the bacon straight? Why make so many tiny tarts that were mostly crust, instead of just making one big pie that everyone could share?

They'd also started keeping a running tally of how many times they heard people say, "Here, let me give you my business card" versus "Let's connect on LinkedIn. . . ." The party included women who were doctors and mechanics, daycare owners and marine biologists, a filmmaker and an Olympic hopeful and a county judge. . . . Nevaeh heard someone say about the judge, "You know, she's going to be on the Supreme Court someday. . . ." Rosemary might not have made her own childhood dreams come true. But she had planted the seeds for some of those dreams to come true for lots and lots of other women.

By the time they got back to their own families—where the two moms were chatting away happily, while Nevaeh's dad stood awkwardly to the side—Nevaeh had an idea.

"Dad, you know how you work with Steve all the time, even though he acts like it's still the twentieth century when it comes to how he thinks of women and girls?" she asked. "Or maybe . . . the sixteenth century? If you can work with him, you should be able to work with Colin's mom, who's way nicer. I think you should do that."

Nevaeh's dad looked even more awkward than ever.

"Felicia and me . . . we're competitors, remember?" he asked. "Or if you're saying one of us should buy the other one out, uh . . ." He looked apologetically over at Colin's mom. "I think each of us likes doing things our own way."

"Right—and that means you're *not* competitors," Nevaeh argued. "Colin's mom helps people get organized, and you take people's junk off their hands when they don't want it anymore. What if you got together and offered customers a package deal?"

"She's right," Colin said. "Mom, this would make it so you wouldn't have to hire another set of movers when Deepak, Daryl, and Derek go back to school in the fall. Or just when they're at band camp the next two weeks."

"Huh," Nevaeh's dad said.

"We'll . . . have to think about that," Colin's mom said.

But Prilla had a post up on social media about their partnership by the end of the party. And the two families had done their very first clean-out together the very next week. Soon, Colin was offering to take eBay pictures for Nevaeh's family. Nevaeh was working side by side with Colin's mom sorting jewelry.

It was like dreams had come true for both of them.

Now Nevaeh read through the news story one more time before putting the phone down on her lap. She paid special attention to a picture of her and Colin holding onto the Thom McAn and Nike shoeboxes while Rosemary and Toby hovered behind them. The photo was in black-and-white, which made it seem old-timey, as if it was already part of the distant past, too.

"Seeing this in print . . . that means it's over now," she said. "We solved the mystery, Rosemary and Toby found each other, Rosemary got to stop hiding. . . . Don't get me wrong, it's all great. But . . . I didn't want the fun to end."

"We'll still see each other," Colin promised. But his shoulders slumped, too.

They were thinking alike again. Finding Rosemary and Toby would always connect them. But their friendship had been a summer thing, and what if they didn't stay friends once the summer ended? When they went back to school in the fall, they'd be at different schools, and it would be other kids they'd text about homework assignments and "What clubs are you going to join?" and "Did you see what happened in the cafeteria today?"

Both of their phones buzzed at the same time. Both of them looked at their latest text messages.

"Mom says, 'Have you seen the big story yet? I am so proud of you for helping Rosemary and Toby (and for taking that great picture!),'" Colin reported. "And, get this, she says she's already gotten two calls from people who want to hire her because of that article!"

"Dad says he's getting Junk King calls because of the newspaper story, too," Nevaeh reported.

Her phone buzzed again, and Nevaeh let out a surprised "Oh!"

"What?" Colin asked.

"Now he says he's getting calls from people who want to hire you and me!" Nevaeh said, squinting at her phone screen in confusion.

"No way," Colin said. "Neither of us is going out on our own for cleaning out houses!"

It had turned out to be all right working for Mom. It was even better when he worked with Mom and the Three Brothers. Or with Mom and Nevaeh's family. But he was *not* going to be like Mom—or Nevaeh's dad—and start any sort of business dealing with junk.

"Unless," he said slowly, "are they asking for photographers?"

Nevaeh's phone buzzed again, and Nevaeh laughed.

"No—they want us to solve mysteries!" she announced. "Track down *their* long-lost friends! Figure out the weird things they found in their attics!"

"You're saying yes, right?" Colin asked.

Nevaeh was already sending the text.

So it wasn't over, after all. Nevaeh and Colin wouldn't be like Rosemary and Toby, who'd been such good friends for a while and then lost touch. They wouldn't become the type of grown-ups who looked back at old pictures and asked, "Wonder whatever became of *that* person I used to know?" Colin and Nevaeh both felt completely certain: they would stay friends—and business partners.

"When do you want to start?" Nevaeh asked. Colin saw that she had her finger hovering over a phone number and name her dad had just forwarded to her.

"Now," Colin said. "Let's start right now."

· AUTHOR'S NOTE ·

Like Rosemary and Toby, I was a kid during the 1970s. Writing this book, I focused more on details from that era that were important to Rosemary and Toby, rather than what mattered most to me. But one thing I shared in a big way with Rosemary was a sense of excitement about changing opportunities for women.

The horrifying facts that Nevaeh discovered during her quick internet search about women's liberation—for example, about women not being allowed to get credit cards without their husbands' or fathers' permission—were true in 1970 but were no longer common and/or legal by the end of that decade. The detail about a woman being fired for not making coffee also came from one of the many, many legal cases filed during the 1970s, changing the lives of women. (Fortunately, that was ruled an unfair reason for the woman to lose her job.)

As a kid, I wasn't aware of all the legal challenges going on in other places in the United States. I was more aware that by the mid-1970s, there were numerous female sports stars for me to look up to, along with the male sports stars my brothers admired. I was aware that my parents expected my sister and me to go to college, just like our brothers—in contrast to my mother's situation as a kid, when her parents decided they'd pay for her brother's college education, but not hers. (My mother found a way to go to college anyway, by working and saving money on her own. This is something I have always been very proud of her for.) However, like Rosemary, I also remember being taught that the proper way to address a letter to a married woman always involved more of her husband's name than her own—for example, "Mrs. John Smith" instead of, say, "Susan Smith." Like Rosemary, I didn't like thinking that if I got married, I could essentially lose my first name as well as my last. (You can see the solution I found on this book's cover: I ended up holding on to both my first and maiden names—Margaret Peterson—and made my married name, Haddix, an addition, not a replacement for my identity.)

I referred to many other details from the 1970s that you may not be familiar with, so here's other background, if you're curious:

bicentennial quarter—This is the type of quarter Colin and Nevaeh found in the box with the Rosemary letters. In 1976, the United States celebrated its two hundredth birthday (i.e., bicentennial) with lots of parties and commemorative items, such as these special coins marked *1776–1976*. Some kids collected these coins, expecting them to gain immensely in value. But except for bicentennial quarters that meet special criteria, the ones issued in 1976 are now worth all of . . . twenty-five cents.

Billie Jean King—This extremely talented female tennis star became a hero to lots of athletic girls like Rosemary in the 1970s (and not-so-athletic ones like me, too). In 1973, a male tennis player, **Bobby Riggs**, challenged her to what became known as the **Battle of the Sexes**. The game was enormously hyped in the media. It wasn't exactly a fair matchup, since King was decades younger than Riggs. But after she won decisively, she was quoted as saying that she'd worried about setting women's causes back by fifty years if she hadn't triumphed.

dial tone—*Maybe* you've had the experience of using a landline telephone, not just a cell phone? Or maybe not . . . A dial tone—a low buzzing—was the first thing anyone would listen for, picking up a telephone in the 1970s. If there was no sound at all, you'd know the phone wasn't working.

ERA (Equal Rights Amendment)—The idea of an amendment to the U.S. Constitution ensuring that women and men would have equal rights dated back to the 1920s, soon after women won the right to vote. (The original wording dealt only with men and women, not acknowledging any other gender definitions.) By the 1970s, the push for passage of the ERA was intense. The amendment passed in Congress in the early 1970s, and states were given a 1979 deadline for ratifying the amendment. That deadline passed without the necessary thirty-eight states ratifying the ERA; the thirty-eighth state—Virginia—added its ratification only as of January 2020. However, by then, five states—Nebraska, Tennessee, Idaho, Kentucky, and South Dakota—had taken back their ratification.

Free to Be You and Me—This was a joint book and record album released in 1972; a TV special with the same name followed two years later. Actress and author **Marlo Thomas** conceived the project, wanting to teach her niece that anyone could be anything, regardless of gender. Celebrities of the day joined the project. It included, for example, excerpts from a book about a boy caring for a doll, and a famous football player singing about how it's all right to cry.

integration—You probably already know names such as **Ruby Bridges** or the **Little Rock Nine**—a few of the brave kids or groups of kids who became the first African Americans to attend formerly all-white schools during the 1950s and 1960s. The efforts to give kids equal access to education continued in the 1970s, and school districts used a variety of methods to bring together kids of different races at the same schools—i.e., integrate. Sometimes this involved court-ordered busing. Another approach was to create magnet schools focused on gifted programs, the arts, sciences, etc. that would appeal to all students.

Iranian hostage crisis—On November 4, 1979, a group of

militant Iranian college students took over the American embassy in Tehran and captured fifty-two Americans as hostages. This became a huge news story in the United States, and the Americans were held captive for 444 days. During that time, Americans back home showed their support for the hostages with yellow ribbons. This was because of a popular song from 1973 called "Tie a Yellow Ribbon Round the Ole Oak Tree," which was about a man who's "done his time" in prison, but isn't sure he'll be welcomed home afterward. (Spoiler alert: He is. When he gets home, there are yellow ribbons everywhere.)

Jaws—The biggest movie of 1975, *Jaws* made people terrified of sharks and kicked off the notion of summer blockbuster movies. The plot revolved around a great white shark scaring away tourists from a town dependent on tourist dollars. The movie's special effects look pretty cheesy nowadays, but the movie was groundbreaking for its time.

mood rings—These rings contained a stone that would change colors, supposedly to show the wearer's mood, based on finger temperature. They were first sold in 1975. Expensive versions came with information about "biofeedback"—they were pitched as serious "scientific" items. The knockoff versions kids wore were definitely not scientific. (And they were very disappointing for kids like me whose hands were always cold—I remember being jealous of friends whose mood rings actually changed colors!)

Nike Swoosh—I bet you know this one already! You might be surprised to know, though, that the Nike shoe company first used the "Swoosh" logo in 1971.

Richard Nixon—U.S. president from 1969 to 1974, and the first (and so far, only) to resign from office.

pet rocks—Colin's guess about pet rocks is correct—they were rocks that people treated as pets. This was a fad in 1975 and early 1976; the rocks were sold and shipped in cardboard boxes with holes for air (as if the rocks needed that!). These were gag gifts more than anything else; I don't remember anyone taking them seriously. However, the advertising executive who thought of pet rocks became a millionaire, selling more than a million of them for $4 each.

Pong—Pong was one of the first arcade sports video games, released in 1972. A home version came out in 1975, as part of a setup that could be attached to TVs. I'm not sure it's possible to explain to kids now what a big deal this was, considering that you are probably used to being able to play video games anywhere, anytime (unless your parents or teachers tell you not to). But the game itself was . . . not that exciting.

Rolling Stones—This long-lasting English rock band was formed in 1962, and was hugely popular during both the 1960s and 1970s. They've continued to perform concerts into the twenty-first century, even touring in 2021. The band has become such a part of the culture that scientists have named types of actual rocks in honor of band members **Mick Jagger** and **Keith Richards**.

Skylab—This was the first U.S. space station, a predecessor of the International Space Station, which is operated jointly by multiple countries. American astronauts occupied Skylab for a total of twenty-four weeks in 1973 and 1974. After that, funding cuts and delays in the space shuttle program meant that Skylab was essentially abandoned. Its orbit became unstable, and it fell to Earth in 1979. At the time, people worried a lot about where the debris might land—and what damage it might do to populated areas. NASA ground controllers were able to adjust the orbit somewhat, aiming for a landing in the Indian Ocean. But some debris also landed in Western Australia.

Thom McAn—Colin's guess that this was an old shoe company was correct. The first Thom McAn shoe store opened in 1922. (The name apparently came from a Scottish golfer, Thomas McCann. I don't have a clue why the store's name was spelled differently.) In the 1970s, Thom McAn stores were commonly found in American shopping malls. I can remember buying back-to-school shoes there year after year.

Because of Toby's love of TV, I also mentioned lots of TV shows. Colin is right that TV played a bigger part of kids' lives in the 1970s than now. Because this was before streaming

TV—and before most people had access to more than three or four TV stations—kids usually all watched the same shows at the same time. So with a popular show, you'd know that it would be a topic of recess conversation the next day. I was a kid who liked reading books a lot more than watching TV. But . . . I did not have to do any extra research to give Toby and Rosemary TV shows to talk about. Here's a little more info about shows I mentioned:

Bionic Woman—After the success of a show called *The Six Million Dollar Man*, about a man who became a "bionic" cyborg, this show launched in early 1976. It revolved around a female tennis star horribly injured in a skydiving accident, who became bionic as well. Sometimes the bionic pair worked together in crossover episodes; sometimes they worked independently. A remake of the show was done in 2007.

Charlie's Angels—The original series ran from 1976 to 1981, and was later rebooted various times as movies and other TV shows. It involved three beautiful crime-fighting women who worked for Charlie, a mysterious boss who was never seen, only heard. (Apparently, TV writers couldn't stretch their imagination enough to visualize three beautiful crime-fighting women working for themselves.) One of the actresses, **Farrah Fawcett** (then called Farrah Fawcett-Majors), became known as a huge sex symbol. I remember watching the show and wondering how the women could possibly keep their hair always looking so perfect even as they ran, drove fast cars, and engaged in hand-to-hand combat.

Happy Days—This nostalgic show about life in the 1950s ran from 1974 to 1984. Its most memorable character was Arthur Fonzarelli, better known as **Fonzie** or sometimes just **the Fonz**. He always wore a black leather jacket, and was portrayed as the epitome of cool. The actor who played Fonzie, **Henry Winkler**, later became coauthor of a series of books for kids called Hank Zipzer.

Land of the Lost—Beginning in 1974, this Saturday-morning TV show may have been a lot of 1970s kids' first exposure to science fiction. A father and his son and daughter go over a waterfall during a camping trip and find themselves in an alternate universe where they coexist with dinosaurs and scary, human-sized lizard creatures known as the **Sleestak**.

Laverne and Shirley—This TV show was a spin-off of *Happy Days*. The two main characters (you can probably guess their names) worked in a fictional beer factory in Wisconsin.

The Secrets of Isis—Arriving in 1975, this show barely beat *Bionic Woman* and *Wonder Woman* to the air, making it the first weekly American live-action series with a female superhero as the main character. The plot revolved around a high school teacher on an archaeological dig to Egypt, who found an amulet giving her the power to turn into the Egyptian goddess Isis.

Welcome Back, Kotter—This 1975–79 show began with a teacher—Gabe Kotter—returning to the high school he had graduated from, in order to work with a group of supposedly unteachable students known as the Sweathogs. The students were ethnically and racially diverse, which was a change from many earlier TV shows. But the situations that arose were not exactly handled sensitively. One of the students, Arnold Horshack, would wave his hand in the air and scream, "Ooo! Ooo! Ooo! Mr. Kotter!" whenever he knew an answer. I remember my sixth-grade teacher being very strict about not wanting us to do that.

Wonder Woman—Airing from 1976 to 1979, this superhero action show depicted Wonder Woman during World War II in the first season, and then, in the second and third seasons, during the 1970s.

ACKNOWLEDGMENTS

I treasure the help I got from other people while writing this book. (It's all treasure, no trash, in this section!)

When I was still just vaguely thinking about writing a story with a connection to the 1970s—and libraries were shut down because of the Covid pandemic—my friend and fellow writer Edith Pattou loaned me several books about the era that gave my brain a jump start. Skylab! Pet rocks! Mood rings! How could I *not* want to write about that time period?

When I was struggling to figure out how Rosemary and Maribel might take actions that could be seen as questionable but not outright illegal, I appreciated getting information from two lawyer friends: Linda Schuster Richardson, who's a divorce attorney, and Mark Senff, who has expertise in dealing with wills and estates. (Here's where I need to add the usual caveat: any mistakes that show up in this book are my fault, not anyone else's.) Both Linda and Mark were also kind enough *not* to suspect that I was planning some illegal activity of my own when I laid out scenarios without much context, and then realized belatedly that it sounded like I was really asking, "How could I get away with this crime?"

When I wanted some extremely technical information about whether there'd be fingerprints on a piece of paper from more than thirty years ago, my cousin Karima Tahir, who is a sergeant II with the Los Angeles Police Department, gave me both scientific details and some true-life stories. (She also gave me reasons to think twice about discarding Starbucks cups in public trash cans, but alas, that belongs in a different story.)

When I needed help deciding what kids now would know or not know about life in the 1970s, I appreciated the assistance I got from my sister, Janet Terrell, who's a fourth-grade teacher, as well as from my nieces and nephew, Meg, Jenna, and Will Terrell.

When I was stuck figuring out a title for this book, I got help from a lot of family and friends, especially my two Columbus-area writers groups: Jody Casella, Julia DeVillers, Linda Gerber, Lisa Klein, Erin McCahan, Jenny Patton, Edith Pattou, Nancy Roe Pimm, Natalie D. Richards, and Linda Stanek. In the end, both my sister and Sara Schonfeld, associate editor at Katherine Tegen Books, deserve credit for suggesting different versions of what became the series title, Mysteries of Trash and Treasure.

And at every stage of the transition from this being just an idea in my head to an actual book for you to read, I'm very grateful for the help and encouragement I got from my agent, Tracey Adams, and editor, Katherine Tegen. I appreciate everyone at HarperCollins who worked on this book at every stage along the way: in addition to Katherine and Sara, also Kathryn Silsand, Mark Rifkin, Christina MacDonald, Allison Brown, Molly Fehr, Amy Ryan, Emily Mannon, Aubrey Churchward , Susan Bishansky, and Daniel Seidel. I am also very grateful to cover artist Yas Imamura.

Finally, to back up a bit, I also owe three people in particular from my own childhood. The whole time I was in second grade through sixth grade—the ages Rosemary and Toby were, writing letters to each other in this book—I had two particularly good friends, Bill Mark and Lori Roe. The circumstances of our lives were very different than the circumstances of Toby's, Rosemary's, and Maribel's lives, so this is definitely not one of those situations where a novel is just a fictionalized account of the author's real life. (For starters: Bill, Lori, and I all grew up on farms and/or in the country, and that alone made our lives very different. And our adult lives have been nothing like the characters' adult lives in this book.) But writing this book made me think with such gratitude about what good friends Lori and Bill were, and how lucky I was to have both a male and a female "best" friend as a kid.

The third person I wanted to thank from my childhood was my junior high band director, Ms. Jan Dekany—emphasis on the "Ms." It was an act of courage for her to move to rural/small-town Ohio in the late 1970s and insist to everyone, "No, no, do not call me 'Miss' or 'Mrs.' I'm a 'Ms.'" At the time, she was the only person I knew who claimed that title, and it made me think about the world around me a little differently. The flute-playing skills Ms. Dekany taught me are, sadly, very rusty now. But the example she set and the lessons she taught me about standing up for myself as a female—and about how much words matter—are deeply embedded, and I continue to be grateful.

Thank you as well to everyone reading this book! May you be blessed with good friends around you—and the ability to discover all sorts of treasures where others see only trash.

"A thought-provoking and thrilling exploration of what it means to be human."
—ALA *Booklist* (starred review)

Turn the page to start reading
THE SCHOOL FOR WHATNOTS

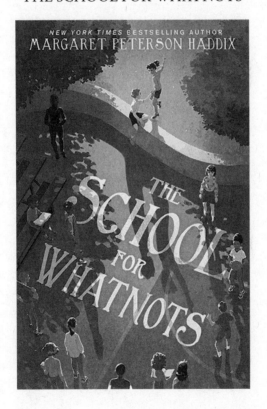

ONE

Eleven Years Ago

When Maximilian J. Sterling was born, his family celebrated by throwing a party for the whole city, complete with the biggest fireworks display anyone had ever seen.

Though his parents showed off the baby throughout the day from the terrace of their mansion, by nightfall they'd retreated indoors. The night air brought mosquitoes and unhealthy fogs, and everybody understood that newborn Maximilian must of course be kept safe from such threats. But his mother held him up to the terrace windows as the dark sky exploded into bright lights above him. And below, every person from the entire city seemed to be crowded onto the mansion grounds to ooh and aah and cheer.

"Look, little man," Mrs. Sterling murmured to her swaddled baby. "Everyone is so happy that you're here, so delighted to rejoice with us. . . . You will always be surrounded with love."

Behind her, the night nurse snorted. Up until that moment, Maximilian's mother had viewed the night nurse as a great friend and ally. Mrs. Sterling had learned the nurse's name—Beverly—and her favorite flavor of chocolate (dark, with orange peels). But now Mrs. Sterling felt a slight, nagging fear that Nurse Beverly was gifted at more than bottle prep and the proper positioning of a baby in need of a good, solid burp. What if she was like one of those evil fairy godmothers in a fairy tale, about to foretell an innocent baby's doom?

Mrs. Sterling wrapped her arms tighter around the bundle of soft blankets that surrounded baby Maximilian. She might have looked dainty and decorative, but she was a stalwart woman with a strong grip.

"Why do you make that noise?" Mrs. Sterling asked Nurse Beverly. "Do you . . . do you disagree?"

"Er—" Nurse Beverly gulped. She did not want to be fired. She had not intended to be heard. She was more accustomed to talking with babies than anyone else, and sometimes she forgot that humans over the age of one tended to expect more give and take in their conversations.

"Please," Mrs. Sterling pleaded. "Be honest. I need to know if there's ever going to be anyone around my son who's *not* kind and loving. I need to know, so I can protect him."

Nurse Beverly had the unpleasant sensation that she was about to let out a belch. This was one of the reasons she enjoyed being around babies more than anyone else: Babies didn't care about manners. Nurse Beverly liked it when the parents she worked for went to bed, and she could settle in with the tiny, sleepless babies and whisper all night long into their ears, *You. You are wonderful just the way you are. You are a miracle even now, even before you become anything else. Even before you grow a minute older. Don't let anyone tell you different. You be you, I'll be me. We'll get along great.*

She also liked to tell them the plots of her favorite mystery novels.

But with the belch coming on, Nurse Beverly rushed to answer Mrs. Sterling before she had time to think. Nurse Beverly had a tendency to do that.

"Begging your pardon, ma'am," Nurse Beverly said. "But this baby is the son of a billionaire. I'm guessing he himself became a millionaire just by being born. Of course he'll have *some* people around him who love him just for himself. You, of course. Your husband. Probably at least one or two of his friends. But he'll also be surrounded by people who just want invitations to the best birthday parties in town. People who want to water-ski on your family's private lake or fly on your family's private jet. People who want to ride in the Porsche he gets for his sixteenth birthday . . ."

Nurse Beverly wondered if she'd gone too far mentioning the private lake and the jet and the Porsche. Was she not supposed to know that the Sterlings owned a lake bigger than some countries? (Small countries, of course, but still.)

Was she not supposed to know that Mrs. Sterling's husband collected custom cars and antique planes, and had hundreds of them stashed in garages and hangars all over the city? Or that one of their family companies held mining rights to most of the moon (which probably made them trillionaires, not just billionaires)? Those weren't facts she'd *tried* to learn. They were just things everybody knew.

"You fear that my son will be surrounded more by greed than by love," Mrs. Sterling said, jutting her jaw defensively skyward. "And that he will never learn to tell the difference."

Behind her, the sky exploded with red and yellow and green lights, and a boom shook the windows a second later. But Mrs. Sterling seemed to have forgotten the fireworks.

"You're saying that my son will grow up as a spoiled brat," Mrs. Sterling continued. "You believe he will never know the difference between the beauty of his own soul and the appeal of all his money."

"Um, er," Nurse Beverly said, flustered. She forgot that she'd been about to belch. It was surprised out of her. Usually only babies seemed to understand her. But here was this woman who could still look beautiful mere hours after giving birth, who wore a silk robe that probably cost more than Nurse Beverly had earned in her entire life—and she seemed to be plucking thoughts straight from Nurse Beverly's brain. And then speaking them with fancier words.

Mrs. Sterling gazed down at her son's tiny face. He puckered his lips at her, which might have been his first ever attempt at a kiss.

Or it might have been his first practice for sucking.

"My son will *not* grow up spoiled," Mrs. Sterling pronounced, as grandly as if she were the one in a fairy tale who got to foretell the future. "He will not be surrounded by greedy people. He'll always know that his own soul is more valuable than money."

"Okay," Nurse Beverly said, because she'd learned at the very, very beginning of her career that it was unwise to make enemies of the women she worked for. Nurse Beverly generally did not think about what happened to the babies she tended past the advent of their first birthdays. But Mrs. Sterling was making her curious about Maximilian's future. It wasn't wise to linger on this dangerous topic, but Nurse Beverly asked another question anyway: "How do you think you're going to accomplish that?"

"I know how," Mrs. Sterling said. She'd lifted her chin so high into the air now that it seemed to be pointing straight for the sky. "Maximilian will not grow up around other children at all. He'll have whatnots."

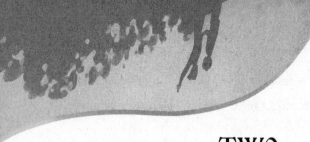

TWO

The Narrator's Aside

You know about whatnots, right?

No?

I guess they're mostly only whispered about. Mostly secret. Unless you travel in certain circles, you probably think they're only rumors.

But of course they're real. And of course, like most things discussed only in whispers, there are dozens of ways of explaining them.

Some say that the first rich parents who ordered the first set of whatnots remembered only two things from childhood: that kids can be mean.

And that sticks, stones, *and* words can all hurt you.

It's a little up in the air whether those parents meant to protect their kids, their kids' friends—or their own reputations.

Because, what if it was *their* kid who turned out to be a bully?

It's also a little up in the air whether the inventor of

whatnots, Frances Miranda Gonzagaga, wanted to help the rich people or just become rich herself.

But rich parents ordered whatnots in droves. More than the mansions, more than the humongous bank accounts, more than the private self-piloting helicopters, whatnots became the symbol of who was wealthy and who wasn't. Everybody who was anybody had whatnots for their kids. Soon the children of those rich parents were surrounded by nothing but whatnots in their schools, on their sports teams, in all their extracurriculars like plays and musicals (where the rich kid was always the star, of course).

You get the idea.

And that name? Whatnots?

Of course that's just a fancy rich-person name for something anybody else would describe with ordinary words. You know. Like how caviar is really just fish eggs. Take away the mysterious name, look past the elegant packaging, ignore the status-symbol maneuvering, and it's clear: whatnots are just . . .

Robots. Robots that look and act so much like humans that no one can tell the difference—androids. Automatons.

Machines.

And now don't you feel a little sorry for all the rich kids who have nothing but machines for friends?

And they don't even know it?

THREE

Six Years Ago—Maximilian's First Day of Kindergarten—
The Beginning

"I like jumping in mud puddles. Do you?"

Maximilian peered at the small person who'd plopped down onto the plush carpet square next to his just as class was about to start. The teacher was still standing in the doorway, greeting the last arrivals. All the other children in the circle were sitting quietly and tidily, their hands folded in their laps, their legs tucked together crisscross applesauce. But not this . . . girl? (Maximilian guessed she was a girl, though it didn't matter to him one way or another.) She stood out, not just because she was talking, but also because she had what must have been dried finger paint not quite scrubbed off the otherwise pale skin of her hands, and even dotted up onto her wrists. (It couldn't possibly be dirt, could it?) Her dark hair stood up in two tufts circled haphazardly with ponytail rubber bands on opposite sides of her head. She bounced up and down, her eyes positively dancing.

Because of . . . mud puddles? Maximilian wondered.

Wasn't that just rain that didn't go anywhere? And it got dirty sitting around on the ground?

"I don't know if I like to jump in mud puddles or not," Maximilian said politely. "I've never tried."

"Oh no!" the girl said, as if Maximilian were admitting to never having eaten cake before, or never having petted a dog. She patted his back as if he were sad or sick or desperately in need, like the poor people Maximilian had seen lined up along the street once when the limo driver took the wrong turn. (The old limo driver. Before he got fired.) "Well, I heard school has this thing called recess, when we can go outside and do whatever we want. I'll show you about jumping in puddles then."

"Okay," Maximilian said. He waited, trying so, so hard not to squirm. His teachers in preschool had always told him he had a problem with that. He couldn't understand how other kids could sit so still. Like statues.

Maximilian couldn't even play Flying Statues or Freeze Tag without squirming.

At least Bouncy Girl wasn't sitting still either.

"What's your name?" Bouncy Girl asked.

Maximilian flattened the folds of his new shirt and pointed to the neatly written name tag the teacher had put on his chest when he'd arrived at school.

"Max-i-mill-yun," he sounded out the name for her,

touching each syllable in turn.

"Oh no!" the girl said again, just as distressed as before.

"What?" Maximilian said, peering around in case a band of marauding monkeys had just entered the room. Or storybook pirates or fairy-tale witches—those were the worst disasters Maximilian could imagine.

But Bouncy Girl was only gazing at Maximilian's name tag.

"Your name has so many letters!" she said. "Don't you know we'll have to write our names again and again and again in school? Quick! Let's make it shorter."

She ran over and grabbed a fat green marker from the nearest table and came back to scribble out most of the letters on Maximilian's name tag.

"Leave the *x*!" Maximilian said anxiously. "That's my favorite!"

"Okay," the girl said. "I like the *s* best in my name. Because . . ." She made a jerky motion with her head, like a snake slithering side to side. "It *shimmies*."

"What *is* your name?" Max asked, because he couldn't make sense of the jumble of letters on her name tag.

"I'm Josie," the girl said. She put her marker down. "And now you're Max. Don't forget. Three letters. Not ten."

"Max," Max repeated.

He was enchanted by the girl's shimmying head and his own easier name and the promise of mud puddles. Maybe he was like a child in a fairy tale, falling under a magical creature's spell.

Because it didn't even occur to him to wonder how she was already so good at reading and counting.

Or how she was already in charge.

"Gripping, heartfelt, thoughtful, and fun."
—*School Library Journal* (starred review)

Turn the page to start reading REMARKABLES

ONE

Marin stared at the towering wall of cardboard boxes that ran down the middle of her family's new living room. It was like something out of a fairy tale—it seemed like every time she or Dad moved or unpacked one box, another one grew in its place.

Dad reached over to give her ponytail a playful tug.

"Here's the game plan, kiddo," he said. "We do two more boxes, then we take a break. A *well-deserved* break."

"But we told Mom—" Marin began.

A sudden, furious cry sounded from upstairs. Dad threw his arms up in the air as if someone had scored a touchdown.

"Yes!" Dad said. He did a little victory dance. Dad was a gym teacher—he was good at victory dances. "Baby Owen thinks it's break time *now*."

"I'll get him," Marin volunteered, scrambling up and jumping over a lampshade and a long sheet of Bubble Wrap that hung half in, half out of the box in front of her.

"You just want to leave me to deal with . . . more pillows? Why do we have all these pillows?" Dad asked, staring down in mock dismay at the box he'd just opened on the floor before him.

Marin giggled and took the stairs two at a time, almost smacking into the wall. She wasn't used to a staircase that bent in the middle yet. Their house back in Illinois had had stairs that just went straight up and down. Sometimes when Mom and Dad weren't looking, she and Kenner and Ashlyn used to sit on a blanket on the top step and shove off and then . . .

Stop thinking about Kenner and Ashlyn, Marin told herself.

She turned the corner into her baby brother's room. His cries were louder now; it was amazing that such a tiny creature could make so much noise.

"Shh, shh," Marin murmured, just like she'd heard Mom and Dad do. "I'm here, Owen. Did you think we'd left you all alone?"

That word, *alone*, stuck in her throat a little.

She took three steps to her brother's crib, which was the only furniture in the room so far. The pieces of the changing table lay on the floor, waiting for her and Dad to put it together. Owen's cries echoed off bare walls.

"Are you hungry?" Marin asked, peeking over the crib railing. "Or just mad? Or do you have a dirty diaper?"

Owen's cries turned into more of a snuffling sound as he

peered up at her. Tears trembled in his eyelashes.

Marin still wasn't used to having a baby brother. She'd had eleven years to get used to being an only child, and only eight weeks to get used to being a big sister.

And Owen was so tiny and helpless. His miniature hands swiped the air as if he hadn't figured out how they worked yet. His face was red with crying, and his lips quivered. But his dark eyes tracked Marin's movements as she reached down to slide her hand under the back of his *Play Ball!* T-shirt and lift him up.

Mom and Dad said Owen looked and acted almost exactly like Marin had when she'd been his age.

"Don't be like me," Marin whispered. "Be better. Make Mom and Dad proud."

TWO

"This is one of the greatest things about having a new baby in the family," Dad told Marin as he settled into the couch with Owen in his arms. "Baby on my lap, bottle in his mouth, ESPN on TV . . . When you were a baby, your mother and I used to fight over whose turn it was to feed you. Of course, she almost always won. Home court advantage, you could say. But now . . ." Dad winked. "Don't tell your mother, but I'm kind of glad she has to work so much right now."

Dad meant that when Mom was around, she didn't need a bottle to feed Owen. Even now, the milk Owen was drinking came from her. She'd pumped it just that morning before leaving for her new job.

Dad patted the couch cushion beside him.

"Join us," he told Marin. "We can have a three-fourths-of-the-Pluckett-family cuddle. It's just about time for the baseball bloopers reel from the weekend."

Dad loved blooper reels from any sport. He always looked

for the dumbest mistakes professional athletes made so he could show his gym classes whenever he introduced a new sport.

"Look at that!" he'd say. "That guy is making millions of dollars a year playing soccer, and he *still* kicked the ball into the wrong goal! So don't worry about doing this wrong, kids! You could *never* mess up as badly as the pros!"

Marin wasn't in the mood to watch people making mistakes.

"I think I'll go outside for a little bit," she said. "Explore the backyard, since it was too dark last night."

"Good choice!" Dad nodded enthusiastically. He clunked his forehead with the hand that wasn't supporting Owen's head. "What kind of a dad—or phys ed teacher—am I that I didn't suggest that? Of *course* you should go outside and play! Get some fresh air! Go! Just do it!"

Back in Illinois, Kenner had said to Marin once, "Is your dad ever anything but loud? Does he ever stop being a gym teacher?"

And Ashlyn had giggled in a way that somehow wasn't very friendly, even though Marin and Ashlyn had been friends practically their whole lives.

"It's like Marin's dad is just one big puppy dog," she said.

How was it possible to make a puppy dog sound like a problem? Like something to be ashamed of?

Kenner and Ashlyn aren't here, Marin told herself. *They're back in Illinois. I live in Pennsylvania now. I'll probably never see them again in my entire life.*

She slid open the glass door that separated the far end of the family room from the brick patio outside. The side of the patio was lined with three huge bushes, and all three were in different stages of blooming: one with the remains of dried-up yellow blossoms, one with purple flowers at their peak, and one with thick glossy leaves and just the start of dignified white flowers.

Forsythia, lilac, rhododendron, Marin said to herself. She liked knowing the names of things.

She stepped out and shut the door behind her, and that was enough to silence the cheering from Dad's TV.

Back in Illinois, their backyard had been small and flat and square. Every year at Easter, Dad always complained that there was no good place to hide eggs, because everything was out in the open. Mom always teased, "Don't you just mean, Marin's better at finding things than you are at hiding them? Come on, can't you admit that your daughter is smarter than you are?" It was kind of a little routine they had.

This backyard looked like it'd be a great place to hide *anything.* Maybe even another house. Only a small strip of grass lay beyond the patio, and then the yard sloped up and turned into an expanse of wildflowers and brambles and gently swaying trees. It was like their own private family woods. Marin couldn't even see through it to tell what lay on the other side.

If I have a bad day at school here, I'll be able to come home and step out into those woods and shut it all out, Marin thought. *Nobody will know if I'm crying.*

One of the sprigs of lilac blew against her arm, as if to remind her she wasn't in Illinois anymore. The lilac blooms had already withered back in Illinois.

I'm not going to have bad days at school here, Marin told herself firmly. *I won't have any reason to cry.*

Marin walked over to the edge of the woods. Up close, she found that the undergrowth had gaps she hadn't seen from the patio. And one of the gaps turned into a narrow, pebble-covered path that wound back through the trees.

"It's our yard. I belong here," Marin said out loud, as if someone might be watching in disapproval.

She stepped onto the path. Vines brushed against her bare legs, and when she looked down, she saw that little prickly bristles had already embedded themselves into the shoelaces of her sneakers.

No one was watching her. She bent down and split open one of the bristles to find the seed inside. Mr. Wu, her fifth-grade science teacher back in Illinois, had been right.

"Aren't plants brilliant?" he'd raved, waving his arms joyously in front of the Smartboard image of all sorts of bristles and burrs. "Plants can't walk around, so they pack up their seeds in little containers, and send them out on creatures that can walk. Like *us*."

Kenner had made fun of Mr. Wu the same way she made fun of Marin's dad. Kenner said Mr. Wu spiked his hair up too much. And Ms. Condi, their language arts teacher, didn't know how to put on makeup, and Mr. Stewart, the social studies teacher, had bad breath, and . . .

Marin took off running deeper into the woods. Even though it was a sunny June day, the light dimmed under the trees. This would definitely be a good place to hide, if Marin ever needed one.

I won't need that here, she told herself, in time with the sound of her feet hitting the ground. *I won't. I won't. I won't.*

And then Marin reached the end of the woods.

THREE

Marin *knew* that their new house was at the top of a hill. She knew that their new town was called Summitview, and that the road that led to their neighborhood circled up and up and up, higher and higher.

But knowing that was one thing. Looking down on an entire town was something else.

The roofs of some of her neighbors' houses were beneath her. The tops of church steeples were beneath her. The clock tower of the county courthouse was beneath her.

It wasn't exactly all easy to see, because the house directly behind the woods was in the way. And suddenly, Marin wanted to see everything. If only she was a little taller. Or—

Marin looked up. The tree beside her was a huge maple, with thick branches that started right above her head and went up like a ladder. The tree rose so far up into the sky that she couldn't see the top.

This was an excellent tree for climbing.

Marin reached for the lowest branch, and swung and flipped her body around until she could wrap a leg around the branch, too. It would have been good if she'd been wearing jeans instead of flimsy running shorts, because the bark scratched her legs. But she managed to hoist herself up, so in just a matter of minutes she was standing on the lowest branch. Then she stepped up to the next and the next and the next.

When she was about twenty feet above the ground—and hundreds of feet above the main part of her new town—Marin reached a gap in the branches. Now she had a clear view. The town in the valley below looked like a doll village, or maybe one of the scenes her grandfather built for his model railroads. But the sun was in her eyes when she gazed in that direction. It was easier to look down at the houses closest to the edge of the woods, where the glow was more subtle. The roof of the nearest house, right past Marin's toes, almost seemed to shimmer.

"Race you!" someone called below.

"It's too hot for that! I concede! You win!" someone else laughingly called back.

Marin tightened her grip on the thick center branch of the tree and ducked her head behind a clump of maple leaves. She didn't want anyone seeing her. It would be too hard to explain why she was in the tree, and that she really wasn't spying. It was hard enough to think of saying, "Hi, I'm Marin.

I'm your new neighbor." She could hear Kenner's voice in her head, the way Kenner complained when Marin didn't want to talk much: *Why do you always have to act so weird? What's wrong with you?*

But Marin *was* curious about who was down below. She inched her face ever so slightly to the side, peeking out again past the leaves.

A pack of kids had just turned the corner onto the street that stretched out before her, leading up the hill toward the woods. They all looked older than Marin—one of the boys actually had a curly beard shadowing his jawline.

Teenagers, Marin decided. She took note of the back-packs sagging from their shoulders, some decorated with rainbow-colored duct tape or leopard-print ribbons or cam-ouflage patches. She remembered Mom texting pictures of Summitview when she'd come out ahead of the rest of the family to house hunt, and how she'd narrated, "And this is the high school, which is actually walking distance from the house I like best. . . . Marin, for middle school, you'll have to take a bus, but after that, it would just be a short walk. . . ."

These teenagers were coming home from school. Even though Marin had had *her* last day of school two weeks ago back in Illinois, the school year went later here in Pennsylvania.

None of the teenagers tilted their heads up toward Marin's

tree. She dared to peek out a little more.

One of the girls had a hand resting on the shoulder of one of the guys; one of the other girls was braiding another girl's hair, even as they walked. One of the boys bounced a basketball back and forth with everyone else, with all the others taking turns. And they all looked . . .

Happy, Marin thought. *No, not just that. They're happy together.*

These kids might as well have been an alien species. Marin had never really known any teenagers well. Neither she nor Ashlyn nor Kenner had older brothers or sisters. And when Mom and Dad wanted to get a babysitter and go out somewhere without her on a Friday or Saturday night, they always made arrangements with friends.

Mom and Dad had a lot of friends. Marin was pretty sure they'd both had a lot of friends their entire lives. They weren't like she'd been in fifth grade, watching the other friend groups on the playground and wondering, *How is it that Amirah and Sadie are best friends, when Amirah sits and draws all the time, and Sadie is constantly in motion? What do Stana and Alex whisper about all the time? What happened, that Josie and Emma stopped being friends on a Monday and were friends again by Wednesday and then not friends ever again after Friday?*

Now Marin watched the teenagers, and Kenner wasn't

here to say, *What are you doing? Why are you staring like that? You look so weird!*

The squad of teenagers reached a portion of their street where the pavement turned sharply uphill. It was clear they were used to the dramatic incline, because none of them slowed down. One of them—a girl with tangled red curls and a yellow skirt that flowed around her knees like sunbeams—even turned around, so she climbed the hill backward while she kept up a conversation with the kids behind and below her.

When the group was about halfway up the hill, a battered old car spun around the corner at the bottom of the street. Even more teenagers leaned out the side windows, one of them jokingly taunting, "Oh, did you leave early so you could get the snacks ready for us?"

"No, we just didn't have to wait in the line of gas-guzzling cars!" the red-haired girl retorted. "We were more environmental and healthier and"—she raised her face to the sky—"we got to enjoy the nice weather!"

She spun completely around, her skirt flaring out. From above, with her bright hair and swirling skirt, she looked like a kindergartener's drawing of the sun.

"Yes, but we . . ." The boy in the car dropped his voice. Marin leaned closer, but she couldn't hear what he said.

The car putt-putted on up the street to the last house, the one closest to Marin's tree. Three boys and a girl climbed out. The girl and one of the boys began an old-fashioned dance—a waltz, maybe?—on the yard while they waited for the walkers to catch up.

Was this the beginning of a party? For all Marin knew, maybe high school kids had parties every day after school.

Or were they all brothers and sisters? Did every single one of those teenagers live in the same house?

Marin decided she had brothers and sisters on her mind just because of having a new brother herself. The nine teenagers would have had to include multiple sets of twins or triplets, to have that many siblings so close in age. And they didn't look anything alike—some were short and some were tall; some were bony-thin and some were comfortably padded. Also, their noses and eyes and mouth shapes were all different; they had a wide range of hair colors and skin tones. It made Marin think of first-grade art class, when the teacher had held up a fistful of different crayons and said, "Draw your self-portrait however you want! Show me how you see yourself!"

It had to be that these teenagers were just a bunch of friends. But Marin kept thinking they acted more like family.

Maybe some or all of them were adopted. Maybe they were foster brothers and sisters.

Marin blinked, trying to figure it out.

And in that one instant, every single one of the nine teenagers vanished.